THE CARSTAIRS CONSPIRACY

As sole heir to the late Duke of Penrith's estate, Abigail Carstairs suspects that someone is trying to kill her for her fortune. In desperation she turns to the notorious Lord Sebastian Denver. Unable to deny a lady in distress, Sebastian inveigles his way into Abby's hunting lodge where all the prime suspects are gathered. However, distracted by his growing attraction towards Abby, he is unprepared when a further attempt is made on her life. As Sebastian lays a daring trap for her aggressors, he's in a race against time to keep her safe . . .

Books by Wendy Soliman
Published by The House of Ulverscroft:

LADY HARTLEY'S INHERITANCE
DUTY'S DESTINY
THE SOCIAL OUTCAST

Wendy Soliman grew up on the Isle of Wight and started writing stories from a young age. Her published novels also include *Lady Hartley's Inheritance*, *Duty's Destiny* and *The Social Outcast*.

See her website: www.wendysoliman.com for further information.

WENDY SOLIMAN

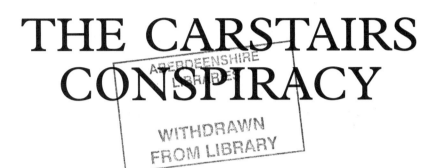

THE CARSTAIRS CONSPIRACY

Complete and Unabridged

ULVERSCROFT
Leicester

First published in Great Britain in 2008 by
Robert Hale Limited
London

First Large Print Edition
published 2009
by arrangement with
Robert Hale Limited
London

British Library CIP Data

Soliman, Wendy
    The Carstairs conspiracy.—Large print ed.—
    Ulverscroft large print series: historical romance
    1. Inheritance and succession—Fiction 2. Romantic
    suspense novels 3. Large type books
    I. Title
    823.9'2 [F]

    ISBN 978–1–84782–597–1

Soliman, Wendy

The Carstairs
conspiracy /
Wendy Soliman
                                      LP

1855355
Published by
F. A. Thorpe (Publishing)
Anstey, Leicestershire

Set by Words & Graphics Ltd.
Anstey, Leicestershire
Printed and bound in Great Britain by
T. J. International Ltd., Padstow, Cornwall

This book is printed on acid-free paper

For Penny,
a sister in a million

1

Abigail Carstairs feared for her life: a situation which negated much of the pleasure she might otherwise have taken from making her curtsey to the *ton*.

A series of misfortunes, at first easily explained away, had become more frequent in the months leading up to Abby's removal to London, causing her vague suspicion that persons unknown viewed her with murderous intent to develop into a firmly held conviction. Not unnaturally the prospect alarmed her; especially since she was quite unable to account for it. She had been forced by circumstances to lead a secluded existence during the course of eighteen summers which had not, to her precise knowledge, afforded her the opportunity to acquire any enemies.

As she stood at the head of the stairs which led to the ballroom in the Duchess of Albion's palatial mansion, nerves that had little to do with fears for her personal safety attacked her from all directions. It was the period before Christmas when half the families were still in residence at their country estates. Lord Bevan had thought to introduce his niece to the *ton* at this quiet time, allowing her to become accustomed to the ways of society, and the avid attention that was bound to be focused upon her, gradually.

But he had clearly miscalculated, since the ballroom was full to capacity at an unfashionably early hour. Such was the speculation surrounding Abby that not a single invitation had been declined and several families, not usually seen in Town at this time of year, had made a point of returning early. It would appear that no one intended to miss the opportunity to make an early impression upon the lovely young heiress.

'Relax, my dear!' expostulated Lord Bevan, patting the fingers that were drumming a nervous tattoo on his sleeve. 'You look perfectly lovely and have nothing to fear.'

'Do you really think so, Uncle Bertram?' asked Abby anxiously.

'There is not a gentleman in attendance, or lady either I am prepared to wager, who would argue otherwise.' Lord Bevan smiled his reassurance, his jovial face dimpling. 'Have courage, Abby! I just wish your dear mother and father could be here to see you tonight, since I am persuaded that they would be as proud of you as I am at this moment.'

Abby's smile faded abruptly and her brow

took possession of a delicate frown. 'I would give everything I own if I could but make it so,' she said quietly.

'Don't frown, m'dear,' cajoled her uncle. 'This is your first ball. Try to enjoy it.'

'Thank you, Uncle Bertram,' she said, squeezing his arm with genuine affection. 'I believe that I shall do precisely that.'

A hush descended upon the ballroom at the announcement of Abby's name and several hundred faces turned simultaneously in her direction; some displayed mild curiosity, the majority determination to be noticed by her. Abby put years of training to good use and greeted her hostess not only with serenity, but with a certain elegance of manner too, which belied her nervousness and made her appear, to the more spiteful of her observers, as being full of superior pride.

An endless procession of spectacularly attired aristocrats clamoured to make Abby's acquaintance. Her fingers were squeezed until they felt raw, suggestive winks were directed at her by some of the less scrupulous gentlemen, and requests for dances saw her card filling rapidly. Abby had been warned to expect that her appearance would create interest and speculation but nothing could have prepared her for the reality of her situation. Everyone seemed anxious to get close to her, their reasons for doing so ranging from optimistic aspirations of marriage, avaricious intent or straightforward curiosity. Curiosity about an heiress in such singular circumstances and about whom rumour and innuendo abounded with tenacious disregard for the facts. Even by the standards for gossip set within the *ton*, Abigail Carstairs, sole heir to the late Duke of Penrith's extensive fortune, vastly protected and seldom seen in public before tonight, was already established in the questionable annuls of folklore surrounding *The Quality*.

Accosted from all sides by people whose names she had already forgotten, Abby was grateful to the musicians for coming to her rescue and striking up the first dance. She was claimed by Lord Evans, the gentleman whom Abby knew her uncle favoured as a husband for her. Not that he would force her into a union against her will, but she was also aware that she had a duty to marry and produce an heir at the earliest opportunity. From her, admittedly limited, observations of the married state, felicity must surely be a matter of chance, so did it really matter whom she chose? Lord Evans was young, well educated, averagely good looking and, most importantly of all as far as her uncle was concerned, of impeccable lineage, with not a

4

whiff of scandal attaching to his name. He was acutely aware of his position, a trifle formal in his manners and stiff in his form of address, and Abby had yet to ascertain whether he was the possessor of a sense of humour. All the same, she considered Lord Evans would treat her with kindness and that she might as well select him as anyone else.

'Good evening, Lady Abigail,' said Lord Evans, his approving expression his only deviation from rigid formality. 'You look exceptionally beautiful tonight,' he added in an undertone, surprising Abby with this uncharacteristic show of spontaneity.

'Why, thank you, Lord Evans,' she replied with a sparkling smile, taking his proffered arm and allowing him to lead her into the dance.

'I see you received my small token,' he remarked, indicating the posy of cream rosebuds attached to her slender waist.

'Indeed I did, sir, and it was my immediate intention to thank you for your kindness.'

'It is thanks enough to see the flowers gracing your person, although they could scarce hope to compete with such natural beauty as your own.'

Abby arched a delicate brow, genuinely surprised: this was not a side of Lord Evans's character she had encountered before. 'Such poetry, sir, I am quite overcome.' And with a saucy smile she twirled away from him and took her position lower down the dance.

Abby, conscious that much of the attention was still focused upon her, was grateful to her seamstress for having risen to the occasion and creating for her debut the most ravishing garment ever to have graced her person. Of the finest silver-blue changeable silk, with a spangled overskirt of silver, contrasting flounces adorning the hem and a small train, it fitted Abby like a second skin, swirling in a froth of lace and petticoats around her ankles as she danced. Fortunately for Abby's fragile composure, she was unaware that it did little to conceal her lithe figure and less still to prevent the lustful thoughts of at least half the gentlemen in the room being directed towards her.

Honey-coloured curls framed Abby's lovely face: a face dominated by laughing eyes which had clearly inspired her seamstress since, like her gown, they were of a sparkling blue, randomly flecked with silver. Temptingly plump lips curved upwards in a sweetly innocent smile, hinting provocatively at passions just waiting to be released. Her mother's sapphire and diamond ear-rings adorned her ears and one of the smaller Penrith tiaras sparkled in her hair.

Abby was swamped by people at the conclusion of each dance and so it was with some relief that she recognized the opening stanza to the evening's first waltz. Not having been presented Abby was not permitted to waltz. Politely disengaging herself from the press of people who appeared intent upon sitting out the waltz with her, she went in search of her cousin, Beatrice. Just one year Abby's senior, she and Bea had shared the schoolroom together at her uncle's imposing country estate in Cornwall: confiding adolescent secrets, exploiting the strict rules laid down for Abby's protection to the limit and forging a relationship that bound them closer than sisters.

'Phew!' exclaimed Abby, flopping onto the seat beside Beatrice in a manner that would have earned her a sharp reprimand from her governess. 'I had no notion these occasions required such fortitude. How do you manage to remain so cool looking, Bea?'

Beatrice smiled. 'This one is a little more crowded than the norm, I suppose,' she conceded, a spark of amusement lighting up her pretty face.

'Is it?' She looked about her with interest, simultaneously attempting to conceal herself behind a pillar in order to gain a much-needed respite from the more tenacious of the gentlemen who were still perusing her. 'Where is Lord Woodley?' she asked, referring to Beatrice's fiancé.

'He has gone to procure me a glass of lemonade.'

'I see.' A commotion near the stairway caught Abby's attention. 'Who are those gentlemen descending the stairs and causing such a stir?'

'That,' said Beatrice, a note of excitement entering her voice, 'is Lord Sebastian Denver, the Marquess of Broadstairs.'

'So that is the infamous rake!' cried Abby, her eyes alight with interest as she chanced surreptitious peeps at the gentleman in question from behind the protection of her pillar. 'He looks just like any other man,' she added, sounding rather disappointed.

'I thought him to be still in France,' observed Beatrice thoughtfully.

'Since when did you take it upon yourself to keep track of the more disreputable echelons within our society?' demanded Abby with mock severity.

'His every move is catalogued in the newspapers,' responded Beatrice reasonably, the innocence of her serene expression brought into question by the mischievous glint in her eye. 'One cannot help but notice his name. And you are quite mistaken, Abby, he is anything but ordinary. Did you ever see such a physique? He has such an air of arrogant disdain about him, which ought to be shocking but which somehow comes across as being rather attractive, I think,' she added on a sigh. 'And his superior height, not to mention that elegant swagger of his, only adds to his distinction.'

'Beatrice, really! I would remind you that you are shortly to be married to Lord Woodley. I am sure it is not at all proper for you to be speculating about other gentlemen in quite such an exacting manner.'

'I have not forgotten that I am promised to Lord Woodley, and I am delighted that it is so. But,' added Beatrice, with a return of her wicked smile, 'that does not mean that I may not appreciate the, er, assets of other gentlemen.'

Discarding her censorious efforts with a speed that belied any true conviction Abby indulged in a gurgle of laughter with her cousin, keeping her eyes trained upon Lord Denver as she did so, observing his every movement. It soon became apparent to her, from the excited snatches of conversations reaching her ears and the sudden frenzied deployment of fans, that half the females in the room were similarly occupied.

'Anyway, Abby,' said Bea, recovering her

composure, 'you are to be congratulated. I believe you are the reason that his lordship has seen fit to attend this evening. You may be sure that in spite of his reputation he will have been invited everywhere, but has not seen fit to show himself until now.'

'Me?' queried Abby, genuinely surprised. 'But he does not even know me.'

'No,' agreed Bea, 'but, just like everyone else here this evening, he most assuredly knows of you, and is curious to have a peep at you.'

Abby lifted her shoulders in a gesture of bewilderment. 'Why, if he is such a lost cause, would he have been invited everywhere?'

'Because, silly, he is rich, titled, handsome and, most importantly of all, eligible. Besides, some of the matrons might well invite him to their functions for reasons of self interest, much as they cite their unmarried daughters as their justification for doing so.'

'Bea, really!' Abby didn't bother to feign shock this time and simply joined her cousin in a fresh bout of laughter.

'It is rumoured that he fought a duel earlier this season,' said Bea in a conspiratorial whisper, although how she could suppose they might be overheard amidst the din in the ballroom, Abby could not begin to imagine. 'Lord Avery called him out after catching him in some indiscretion with his wife.'

'Who won?'

'Well, the weapons of choice were pistols, but could just as easily have been swords. Lord Denver is widely regarded as a first-rate sportsman: a top marksman as well as an expert with a rapier. I understand, however, that both gentlemen fired into the air.'

'Which means they were both willing to accept a portion of blame,' concluded Abby, disappointed, but no longer surprised at her cousin's seemingly unending stock of information about the infamous Lord Denver. 'But do explain, Bea, what indiscretion did he supposedly commit?'

'Oh, I am not entirely sure.' She shrugged. 'The usual, I would imagine.'

'Well, you may be able to imagine but I cannot!' cried Abby, clenching her fists in frustration. 'That is just the problem: I do not know and, what is more, no one ever tells me anything about such matters, nor,' she added, waving an accusatory finger under her cousin's nose, 'do they answer any of my questions on the subject.'

'He is also renowned in the gaming hells hereabouts, so Gerald would have it,' Beatrice avowed, engineering a smooth change of subject without enlightening her cousin as to the nature of the indiscretion in question.

'A gamester as well as a womanizer,' mused Abby, sounding more impressed than shocked. 'I would have supposed a gentleman with such a formidable reputation to be more remarkable in the flesh, but he appears to have nothing in excess of the requisite number of limbs and I cannot see that there is anything special about him at all. It is my opinion that he thinks far too well of himself,' she added, watching him as he kissed their hostess's hand smoothly. Abby tossed her head, causing a tumble of corkscrew curls to dance round her head, and turned her attention to his companions. 'Who are the gentlemen with him?'

'His greatest friends: Lords Jenkins and Trump. Lord Denver is believed to have rescued Lord Jenkins's sister from abduction recently, as well as recovering jewels stolen from the Beaufort household, and who is to say how many other delicate situations he has resolved. He has a reputation for handling such matters with the utmost discretion.'

'Of course! Now I know why his name sounded so familiar.'

Abby fell into a contemplative silence. Lord Denver could be just the person to help her with her own difficulty. But how could she, an unmarried girl who had not yet even been presented, possibly approach such a person and apply to him for his assistance without sullying her reputation beyond recall? It was a challenging conundrum but, as at that moment she was interrupted from her introspective thoughts by the arrival of her partner for the next dance, she accepted that devising a means of gaining Lord Denver's attention would have to be put aside until a more suitable juncture.

★　★　★

Sebastian Denver surveyed the crowded room and made little effort to disguise his boredom. Why he had given in to his friends' cajoling and agreed to attend this crush, when he had been comfortably ensconced in a game of cards at his club, he had not the slightest notion. Both of them were anxious to have sight of the elusive heiress but Sebastian had no interest in juvenile chits fresh out of the schoolroom. His tastes ran to the more exotic.

'It's crowded very early,' he remarked to his friends.

'I suppose everyone else was keen to meet the young thing at the earliest opportunity,' reasoned Lord Trump.

'Yes, damn it!' expostulated Lord Jenkins, thumping his clenched fist against his thigh as his irritation bubbled over. 'We'll never get a look in now, what with this load of jackals having stolen a march on us.'

'Care to have a wager on that?' drawled Sebastian, sensing there might be some sport to be had at this dreary affair after all.

'A monkey,' said Trump with asperity.

'I'll take some of that, too,' offered Jenkins.

'Agreed,' said Sebastian, disguising a yawn behind his hand. 'A monkey says she will dance with me.' He removed his shoulder from the wall that had been supporting it and pulled himself up to his full height. 'Which one is she?' he enquired languidly.

'That one there: the prime piece in blue, having her toes trampled on by Samuels.'

Sebastian raised a brow. 'Not bad. However, she is hardly likely to present me with much of a challenge.' He grinned, offering his friends a brief flash of even white teeth. 'Gentlemen, prepare to surrender your blunt to a worthy cause,' he drawled.

When the dance came to an end Sebastian and his friends contrived to get close to Abby. Fortuitously she happened to be beside her aunt and thus the necessary introduction was accomplished seamlessly. Sebastian hid his surprise behind a calm façade. The child was unquestionably attractive, and not just facially. As if she wasn't in enough danger from her position within society, which would cause any man with an ounce of sense to overlook any defects of nature — none of which was immediately apparent in the specimen before him — the body that her beautifully cut gown was displaying to such advantage would be enough to entice the most discerning of his sex; fortune-hunter or no. All that money, expectation and responsibility resting on such slender shoulders caused Sebastian to feel a moment's concern for the child. Realizing it brought him to his senses. Since when did he waste sympathy on rich, over-indulged heiresses: or on anyone at all for that matter?

Sebastian executed an elegant bow and raised the girl from her curtsey, releasing her hand without inflicting further punishment on her bruised fingers and smiling only in the most perfunctory of manners. 'It is a pleasure to make your acquaintance. I have heard much about you.' But he ensured that the statement sounded merely polite, bordering on the indifferent.

'Thank you, my lord,' she said, her surprise at his casual manner, following so closely on all the flummery she had had to endure during the course of the evening, clearly apparent. Recovering quickly though her eyes lit up with amusement and predictably, a degree of interest. 'And I you.'

She turned towards his companions, who were treating her with much greater civility than he had been prepared to muster, responding to them with a degree of maturity that again surprised him. There was a marked lack of the giggling and simpering he might have expected, and for that he was grateful. If he had to stand up with the baggage for half an hour, the experience would be less painful if she managed to conduct herself with some degree of decorum.

'Your parents were well known to me, Lady Abigail,' he said to her in an aside when the attention of the others was diverted, 'and I know they would be inordinately proud of you this evening.'

Several mentions had been made to Abby of her parents that evening, but Sebastian could not know that none had been expressed in such simple language, without the intention of making any sort of impression upon her, other than one of genuine regret.

'Thank you, my lord.' She turned a dazzling smile upon him, which was the last reaction he had expected, leaving him feeling somewhat disadvantaged; especially as he felt himself responding to it somewhere in the region of his groin. 'You know,' she said in a contemplative tone, 'I rather believe that they would.'

Sebastian inclined his head in the direction of the dancers. 'I believe a quadrille is about to form up. If you are not already engaged, can I persuade you to stand up with me, Lady Abigail?'

Confident that she would acquiesce, he did not wait for her answer but merely reached for her hand.

'Thank you, my lord, but I find myself fatigued and am not inclined to dance again at this juncture.'

Sebastian dropped her hand as though it had scorched him and looked at her askance, his expression of temporary bewilderment soon replaced by one of abject shock. Had she actually just declined his invitation? Impossible! He must have misheard her. Sebastian could not recall the last time a female had rejected his advances, whatever form they might happen to take. He looked at her with renewed interest. Jenkins and Trump meanwhile appeared to be having difficulty maintaining their respective countenances, whilst both Lady Bevan and Beatrice let out small gasps of dismay.

'I beg your pardon,' said Sebastian in a level tone. 'Do I understand you to — ?'

'No, my lord, it is I who must ask for your pardon.'

Sebastian's eyes rested on the flowers at her

waist as he attempted to come to terms with the fact that he had, for the first time ever, actually been cut. His eyebrows snapped together, causing him to look positively lethal, as the truth struck home. He had been cut direct, in the middle of a ballroom and in front of half the *ton*, by a mere chit of a girl.

He watched her as she impulsively made an embarrassing situation worse by plucking a loose bloom from the corsage at her waist and, standing on her toes, slipped it into his lapel. Lady Bevan groaned and clutched her daughter's arm for support. Sebastian, who found the whole situation exceedingly diverting, spared a moment's sympathy for Abby's aunt, well able to imagine the thoughts that must be running through her mind as she observed her niece committing several simultaneous *faux pas*.

'So, my lady,' said Sebastian, recovering and feeling a stab of admiration for the child's courage, 'do you really imagine that you can fob me off with a mere flower?'

'I did not mean to — '

'If so,' he mused, cutting across her explanation, 'you have badly miscalculated.' He was stunned by all he could read in her expression. She clearly now understood the nature of her transgression but far from being contrite she appeared to be having trouble suppressing her mirth. For once a woman had wrong-footed him and he did not know how to rectify the situation. No, not a woman, he reminded himself incredulously, but an unruly child. It was unthinkable. 'I give you due warning,' he continued in an audible undertone, still grappling with his surprise, 'that I do not care to be bested.' He paused significantly. 'At anything.'

He issued his challenge with a raffish smile, intending it as a warning that her victory over him was likely to be both temporary in nature and short in duration. Abby responded, acknowledging his challenge by dropping into a curtsey and offering him the ghost of a sultry smile.

Sebastian bowed and walked away from her, accompanied by his friends. He tolerated their high-spirited joshing with an air of unruffled calm, before escaping in the direction of the card-room and dismissing the incident from his mind.

2

Sebastian was jolted awake when the curtains in his chamber were thrown back, flooding it with more daylight than his jaded constitution could withstand. He shielded his eyes with his hand and glowered at his valet.

'What in the name of Hades do you think you're about, Graves, disturbing me thus? What hour is it?'

'A little after eleven o'clock, my lord.'

'Graves, I left strict instructions that I was not to be roused until midday,' snapped Sebastian, who had not returned to his establishment until daybreak.

'I am perfectly aware of your instructions, my lord.'

'Then why have you taken it upon yourself to disregard them?'

'A lady has called, my lord, and is desirous of an immediate interview.'

This got Sebastian's attention. 'A lady, Graves?' Who would be inconsiderate enough to call at such an early hour? Only his married sisters were likely to attempt it, and if it was one of those sour-faced pusses seeking him out, intent upon berating him yet again

20

for his disinclination to marry, then Graves would know better than to grant her admittance. 'Does this lady have a name?'

'I dare say she does, my lord, but lamentably she declined to disclose it.'

Sebastian sat up, as naked as the day he was born, and rubbed his face vigorously with both of his hands. 'Let me see if I have got this straight, Graves,' he said in a minatory tone. 'An unknown female has called in the middle of the morning, refusing to leave a name or state her business, but you have not only seen fit to admit her into my house but also taken it upon yourself to disturb me over the matter.'

'Exactly so, my lord,' agreed Graves levelly, well accustomed to Sebastian's sarcasm.

'Then I suppose I should enquire next why you have behaved in such a singular fashion,' sighed Sebastian wearily, 'in a manner moreover that is most untypical. You must have a reason to try my patience thus, so, out with it, man, what possessed you?'

'The lady was most insistent, my lord.'

Sebastian rolled his eyes. 'I do not doubt it, but what does that signify? What does she look like, Graves?'

'I really could not say, my lord, since she is wearing a cloak and has pulled the hood close about her face, thereby rendering her features indiscernible.'

Sebastian, more intrigued than annoyed now, raised a brow in surprise. 'Is this mysterious lady alone?'

'No, my lord, she is accompanied by her maid.'

'And what made you suppose that I would even consider receiving this unnamed lady, however insistent she might be?'

'I took the liberty of posing that very question to the lady, my lord, and she asked me to present you with this token.'

Graves offered a silver salver to his master, upon which rested a single cream rosebud. Sebastian let out an oath of astonishment.

'What the devil!' he muttered.

Abigail Carstairs, for it could only be she: what business could she possibly have with him that would cause her to risk her very reputation by calling upon him in such a singular fashion? His mind reeling, Sebastian acknowledged that at least she had had the presence of mind to conceal her features and have a maid accompany her. But still? Intrigued, in spite of himself, Sebastian pushed the covers aside.

'What have you done with the lady, Graves?'

'I took the liberty of showing her into the

morning-room, my lord.'

'All right, Graves, bring up my shaving water, I will see the lady as soon as I have attended to my ablutions. In the meantime, ensure that the door to the morning-room remains closed and that no one enters it, on any pretext whatsoever.'

'I have anticipated your lordship's instructions and set Hodges to guard the door.'

Sebastian grunted his approval, secure in the knowledge that no inquisitive servant would get past his henchman and gain sight of Abby. He slid his arms into the robe that Graves was holding out to him, still pondering upon her ill-advised decision to visit his home, wondering what in the world could have persuaded her to behave so rashly.

★　★　★

Abby could scarce believe she had found the courage to execute her plan, but was fast learning that desperation transcended caution, to say nothing of the rules laid down for the conduct of well-bred young ladies. She sat in Lord Denver's elegant morning-room, nervously pleating the folds of her cloak between her fingers, awaiting the appearance of his lordship with a combination of impatience and trepidation. That a gentleman of his ilk would decline her request for assistance had not previously crossed her mind. But now: now that she was actually here, had somehow found the courage to stand up to his formidable butler and equally severe valet, and gain admittance to his house. What next?

Abby recalled the aftermath of her spontaneous actions at Lady Albion's ball, when she had so negligently cut the most eligible gentleman within the *ton* by declining his invitation to dance, and her face flooded with colour. She had never seen her uncle and aunt so discomposed. Her aunt, by nature a kindly and tolerant soul, had lectured and scolded for a full ten minutes and had been more out of character with her than Abby had ever before known her to be. But it was her uncle's displeasure that she most regretted. He had not railed against her in the fashion of his wife but had merely looked at her reprovingly.

'You have disappointed me, Abby,' he said, his tone only mildly censorious, and infinitely more wounding as a result.

Abby would have given much at that moment to turn the clock back and handle the situation with Lord Denver differently: anything to regain her uncle's good opinion. He had sacrificed so much to bring her to this point and she had repaid him on her first foray into society by behaving with blatant disregard for the conventions.

'Oh, Uncle Bertram, please do excuse me, I did not for a moment intend to bring censure upon us all.'

'I dare say you did not, but you know better than to behave in such a manner with a gentleman of Lord Denver's stature: or any gentleman at all for that matter.'

Abby hung her head, thoroughly ashamed that she had briefly allowed the spontaneous side of her nature to overcome years of stringent training. She was quite unable to account for it herself and so what could she possibly say to her beloved uncle in response to his very justified complaint? She suspected she would have enjoyed dancing with the suave Lord Denver, and it would have provided her with the ideal opportunity to broach the subject uppermost in her mind. So what had made her spurn him so publicly, making an enemy out of him in the process? It defied explanation.

'Yes, Uncle,' she said meekly, 'but some of the blame must surely lie with Lord Denver, too? He invited me to dance and did not even wait for my response. He just *assumed* that I would accept him. It was very arrogant of him!' she added defiantly.

'Indeed it was, child, but what do you imagine you achieved by cutting him so publicly?' When she was unable to make a response, her uncle continued in a more kindly tone, 'You must remember, Abby, that every movement you make will be scrutinized, every action subjected to the keenest analysis. You discovered last night just how anxious people are to take you up. But never forget that an equal number will be looking for the slightest excuse to brand you as aloof and above yourself.' Uncle Bertram paused and fixed her with a gaze of penetrating gravitas. 'Be aware of it, m'dear, and try to behave with more propriety in future.' He kissed her brow to indicate that she was forgiven.

'Oh, Uncle Bertram, I so regret letting you down!' Impulsively she threw her arms around his neck. 'I cannot think what came over me. How can I make amends?'

'There is nothing you can do without making matters worse. But perhaps if Lord Denver should ask you to favour him on another occasion you might think to accept him?' Uncle Bertram twinkled at her, his habitual good humour restored.

'He is surely not the type of gentleman whose attentions you would have me encourage?' queried Abby, puzzled.

'No, indeed! But he is powerful and holds much sway within the *ton*. It would not do to make an enemy of him. And as for presenting him with a flower, well . . . ' Uncle Bertram's words trailed off, his expression of renewed disbelief eloquent in its own right.

'Perhaps I could send him a note of apology?'

'Certainly not!' cried her uncle and aunt in unison. 'That would be an unpardonable transgression.'

Undoubtedly. But, Abby reasoned, her nerves strung as taut as a bow as the waiting appeared to last forever, they had not said it would be improper for her to call upon his lordship and beg his pardon in person: or to crave his assistance with her other concerns either, for that matter.

★ ★ ★

Abby snapped out of her reverie and jumped like a scalded cat when the door to the morning-room was thrust open with considerable force. Lord Denver's intimidating figure filled the aperture. Abby lifted her eyes to his face and gulped as she took in the stony set to his features. He was scowling at her most ferociously, which was hardly an encouraging start. Irritatingly, though, it did little to detract from his lethal form of attractiveness. He was freshly shaved, his rugged features projecting an air of tough resourcefulness, his coruscating eyes amplifying his obvious anger at her intrusion. His expression of thinly veiled hostility would have been enough to terrify a soul less intent upon her purpose but Abby was made of sterner stuff. She squared her shoulders and lifted her chin, desperation coming to her aid and lending her the courage to meet his hostile glare with equanimity. She had beaten the odds by gaining admission to his house and was damned if she would be intimidated just because he was in a bad mood!

Abby chanced a surreptitious peep at his person, trusting that the extravagant sweep of her lowered lashes would conceal her appreciation for all she observed. She was not surprised to notice that he was impeccably attired in a green coat of the finest kerseymere, which displayed his powerful shoulders to considerable advantage. A striped waistcoat in green and cream topped his snowy white shirt and his cravat was tied in a fashionably intricate knot, the name of which escaped her. Close-fitting inexpressibles clung to strong thighs, adding to his allure, and even at this early hour there could be no doubt that he deserved the reputation he had acquired as a formidable sophisticate. Abby's eyes came to rest on his shiny Hessians and it took every ounce of her courage to raise them again and absorb, with every appearance of calm, the full force of the displeasure emanating from his eyes. As he closed the door behind him, and advanced towards her with purposeful strides, Abby shivered and pulled her cloak more closely about her.

'Come with me.'

Abby knew from his tone that it was not an invitation, even before he grabbed her by the wrist, opened the double doors to the adjoining-room and pulled her through them in his wake. Her maid rose to follow but hastily reseated herself when Sebastian barked at her to stay where she was. He left the door slightly ajar but manoeuvred Abby into a position from which they could not be observed by the maid, who was obviously completely cowed by the note of authority in Sebastian's voice and not about to question the propriety of his actions.

Releasing Abby's wrist, Sebastian propelled her until she was backed against the wall and glowered at her. The hood to her cloak had fallen down during the mêlée and her golden curls, now somewhat disarrayed, left no further doubt as to her identity.

'What in the name of the devil are you doing here?'

'I wished to — '

'Do you realize what a risk you have taken?' he continued, not giving her time to embark upon the explanation she had spent so much time preparing. 'By coming here your reputation could be compromised beyond recall. All of your fortune and connections will not be enough to save you if this gets out.'

'I brought my maid with me,' she protested, recovering some of the spirit she had displayed in front of him the previous evening and preparing to fight back. 'Besides, no one could have recognized me beneath my cloak.'

'That is hardly the point,' he countered, moderating his tone slightly. Unbeknown to Abby, it was her courage in the face of his blazing temper that caused him to recall his manners. He did not know many people, of either sex, who dared to stand up to him when he was in such a mood. 'In a household this size it can only be a matter of time before your identity becomes known, and do you imagine that such a tasty *on-dit* would then remain confidential?' His expression was scathing. 'You have much to learn about the ways of society if you do. And all, presumably, because you wish to apologize for your amusing display of immaturity yesterday?' He folded his arms across his chest and looked down at her, his attitude one of blithe indifference. 'Go ahead then, say your piece, get it over with and then get out of here.'

Sebastian was right in one respect; Abby had intended to commence the interview with an apology, if only to soften his lordship's attitude towards her and make him more receptive when she broached the real purpose for her visit. But, in spite of her much greater concerns for her personal safety, something about his derisive treatment of her caused her anger to bubble over. Knowing it would be disastrous to let rip with the words that sprang to her mind regarding his quite shocking want of manners, though, she wisely exercised restraint. But in the light of his arrogant attitude she simply could not bring herself to apologize.

'Indeed you are quite mistaken, my lord,' she told him with a captivating smile. 'I came here with an entirely different purpose in mind.'

He arched a brow in obvious surprise and Abby admitted to herself that she had not been entirely honest with her cousin when she declared him to be nothing out of the ordinary. In such close proximity to him she was acutely aware of his attractiveness. The tensile power in his muscular frame, the expressiveness in dark eyes that reflected anger, and occasionally sardonic amusement, thick black hair spilling over his collar with curly disregard for convention and rugged features that were compelling, caused her pulse to quicken and the breath to catch in her throat. But she dismissed these observations, concentrating instead upon not taking exception to his arbitrary attitude, and reminding herself of her reasons for being in his house; of the risks she had taken to get there, resolving anew to procure his assistance, no matter what the cost to her pride.

'I see,' he remarked, filling a silence which Abby had not realized was stretching between them. 'And so to what, then, do I owe the pleasure?' He bit off the last word, making it clear that her presence in his house was anything but that to him.

Gulping down her nervousness, Abby schooled her features into an expression of serenity. 'I have come to request your assistance with a delicate matter.'

She appeared to have surprised him. 'You need my help?'

'Yes.'

'I do not have the pleasure of understanding you, madam. We met for the first time last night, when you publicly insulted me by declining my invitation to dance, not a dozen words have been exchanged between us and yet you now choose to risk your all by calling upon me and requesting my help.' He fixed her with a gimlet gaze, before shrugging and turning away from her. 'I am unaware what sort of dangerous game it is you think you are playing and can only advise you to reconsider.'

Abby put up her chin. 'You are correct, my lord, in suggesting that I have risked my all in calling upon you thus, and you may rest easy in the knowledge that I would not have resorted to such extreme measures if I could think of an alternative way to resolve my difficulties.'

Sebastian openly sneered at her. 'And what difficulties could a lady in your position possibly have that require my interference?'

'Difficulties of the gravest nature, I do assure you.'

'Even if that is so, what makes you think I would take the trouble to help you?'

Abby swallowed down her anger and disappointment. He really did mean to send her away. This suspicion was confirmed when he pulled her towards the door.

'Come, I will escort you to the side door, where you are less likely to be observed leaving my house.'

'One moment!' She pulled her wrist from

his grasp, desperation lending her added strength. 'I understand you have a reputation for solving problems with discretion.'

Sebastian eyed her with surprise. 'What is that to you?' he barked, neither confirming nor denying her assertion.

She opened her eyes very wide and looked squarely into his face. It was now or never: she would have to tell him the truth, and trust to his instincts as a gentleman, before he made good on his very real intention of throwing her out.

'I fear that someone is trying to kill me, Lord Denver, and I do not know how to go about discovering that person's identity.'

'Good God!' cried Sebastian, surprise clearly taking precedence over good manners. 'You surely cannot be serious.' He looked as though he wanted to laugh but, as his eyes came to rest upon her troubled features his expression underwent a subtle change, settling into one of quiet contemplation. 'Who in the world would wish you any harm?'

'That, my lord, is precisely my difficulty.'

'And a foolish question on my part,' he conceded, his cynical attitude softening a little. 'Given your unusual circumstances I can imagine any number of people wishing to benefit from your demise. Come, Lady

Abigail, let me take your cloak.' Without waiting for her answer he did so, revealing the smart lavender walking dress that she wore beneath it, and glancing at it in what Abby supposed was an approving manner. 'Now', he said, with a sigh, 'perhaps you had better take a seat and tell me all about it.'

3

'Now that I am here I scarce know where to begin.' She fiddled with her reticule and looked down at her hands. 'Suddenly my suspicions seem somewhat tenuous.'

'If you are so concerned that you have resorted to seeking my help then I doubt your fears are completely unfounded, so why not start at the beginning?' suggested Sebastian. 'Calm yourself, Lady Abigail, take a moment to assemble your thoughts and then tell me when you first started to have fears for your safety.'

'Well, as you are aware, my parents' — Abby paused, clearly struggling to overcome her emotions before trusting herself to speak — 'my parents,' she began more forcefully this time, 'died in a carriage accident ten years ago.'

Sebastian inclined his head. 'And you have lived with your uncle and aunt ever since.'

'Yes.'

'And they are kind to you?'

'Indeed, yes! They treat me quite as one of their own.'

'Then why, if they are so good to you, have

you risked seeking my help? Why not apply to your uncle?'

Abby rose from her seat and paced the room, unconsciously displaying her curves for his scrutiny in the process. In spite of the gravity of the situation — Sebastian was fairly certain that any perceived dangers were not entirely a product of her imagination, since it must have taken some courage, much desperation and no little subterfuge for Abby to visit him thus — he was unable to prevent himself from admiring the figure she portrayed.

'Lord Denver, I am the only child of the Duke of Penrith, and heir to my father's considerable estate. I am also, as just about everyone is aware, the holder-in-trust of the title to the duchy. That is why I am under pressure to marry suitably and produce an heir. If I do not do so then the title reverts to the Crown, since my father had no male relations to whom it could pass. Given those circumstances you can doubtless imagine how restricted my life has been. My every movement is closely observed; the suitability of every playmate or tutor thoroughly examined; my activities carefully scrutinized and forbidden altogether if there is the slightest perception of danger; my every outing accompanied by enough chaperons to try the patience of a saint; a sense of duty and responsibility drummed into me at every juncture. Have you any notion just how stifling such an existence can be, even if it is conducted in the utmost comfort?'

'I dare say your uncle has acted solely with your best interests at heart.'

'Yes, indeed he has, and I would not have you think that I am ungrateful. But since coming to Town I have won a few, a very few small freedoms, which are precious to me. If my uncle even suspected that someone was intent upon doing me harm then those freedoms would be withdrawn in a heartbeat and I would be removed to the country.'

'But surely that would be for the best? Would you not be safer there?'

'Since the attempts on my life started in the country I do not see how that would improve my position. Indeed, if whoever is intent upon harming me can reach me in closely guarded, remote locations, then perhaps it is better to be amongst strangers.'

'Possibly. Tell me everything; especially why you are your father's heir, and conveyer of the title.' Sebastian knew the truth but wanted to know if Abby was aware of all the particulars. 'It is, after all, a rather unusual arrangement.'

'Indeed. My great-grandfather was the Marquess of Penrith but the king bestowed a

38

dukedom upon him, for services rendered.'

'I see.'

'It was my great-grandmother, though, who managed to ensure the entail through the female line. I gather,' continued Abby, blushing scarlet to the very roots of her hair, 'that she had much influence with the king's advisers.'

Sebastian was having difficulty keeping his lips straight. Influence *under* the monarch's advisers would have been a more apt description, explaining the unusual arrangement very neatly.

'Your great-grandmother must have been a remarkable woman,' was the only observation he trusted himself to make.

'Undoubtedly. However, I know my parents were hopeful of producing a male heir. My mother suffered the loss of two children before me and the two that followed my birth were still-born. At the time of her demise she was carrying another.'

'She was remarkably brave,' observed Sebastian, strangely moved by the chit's obvious adoration for her deceased mother.

'Thank you. Anyway, today my guardianship, and the management of my affairs, is split equally between my Uncle Bertram and Lord Wilsden.'

'Wilsden was a contemporary of your

father's, I recollect?'

'Yes, he is also my godfather.'

'Then why were you brought up in Lord Bevan's household? Wilsden's estate is closer to the Penrith seat, surely?'

'Yes, and I understand that my godfather argued forcefully at the time of my parents' death for me to reside in his household. But Aunt Constance is my mother's sister, and already had a daughter close to my age, whereas Lord Wilsden's children were both boys, who were already away at school. If I had lived there it would have been a solitary existence and so it was decided that I ought to go to my uncle and aunt at Castleray.'

'But Wilsden has joint custody of you, and your affairs?'

'Yes, as do my father's attorneys, at least as far as matters relating to the duchy are concerned, but I am not privy to the particulars of their involvement.'

'I see. All right, tell me when you first suspected that someone intended you harm.'

'A little over a year ago, my cousin Beatrice and I were walking in the grounds at Castleray. The house was full of guests but it was a fine afternoon and we both craved an hour's respite. You will readily imagine our surprise though,' she said, an impish light illuminating eyes so compelling that Sebastian experienced difficulty tearing his gaze from them, 'when we reached the summerhouse only to find that Lord Woodley, quite by chance, had walked in the same direction as us.'

Sebastian, diverted, treated her to the full force of his smile. She responded by shifting her position, colouring slightly as she fiddled with her reticule and quickly looked away from him, finding something to engage her attention in the arrangement of flowers on a side table.

'But Woodley and your cousin were by then engaged to be married?'

'Not quite,' conceded Abby, 'but an understanding had been reached between them, which merely awaited my uncle's blessing. I was preoccupied with my dogs, who were anxious for their exercise, and so I begged the couple to excuse me. I took a path through the woods, one that I have often used in the past and which is known to be a favourite of mine. It required me to cross a rope bridge, high over a fast-flowing stream, to reach the opposite bank.' Abby paused and Sebastian suspected she was attempting to overcome the fear which the retelling of her ordeal awakened. 'My dog, Marcus, doubtless saved my life, since he forged ahead of me, across the bridge. It gave way, even under his slight weight, and it was only because he had almost reached the opposite bank that he was able to scramble to safety.'

'Rope bridges are subjected to all manner of weather conditions,' remarked Sebastian. 'Could it not simply have been an unfortunate accident, attributable to neglect?'

'That was my immediate reaction, but the head keeper, who came to my aid almost as soon as it happened, informed me that it was in the best of repair and that the rope had been severed almost through: and quite recently.'

'And your uncle took what action?'

'I begged the keeper not to inform him of the incident. I knew what the consequences in respect of my freedom would be if he did, and you must bear in mind that I did not know at the time that someone was deliberately attempting to injure me. I mean, how could they be sure it would be me that used the bridge next?'

'You did say it was a favourite path of yours when walking with your dogs.'

'Yes, but others used it, too. Besides, if I were to tell then my uncle would wish to know why I was alone. You will recall that I am not permitted to be alone: even in the grounds of Castleray. Uncle Bertram would have enquired as to Beatrice's whereabouts and were he to discover that I had left her alone with Lord Woodley, well . . . '

'Quite.' Sebastian smirked his understanding. 'So you dismissed the rope bridge as an unfortunate accident. When did the next incident occur?'

'Two months later, whilst riding on my godfather's estate. A party of us took horses out for the day and stopped for an alfresco luncheon. We were cantering back towards the estate afterwards when my saddle slipped round completely and I was thrown. All of the horses' girths had been loosened when we stopped but my mare's had obviously not been properly tightened when we remounted.'

'Then how were you able to remount at all? Surely the saddle would have slipped when you placed your foot in the stirrup.'

'One of the gentlemen, I forget whom, lifted me back into my saddle.'

'Naturally!' He smiled cynically. 'But whose responsibility was it to ensure that the horses' girths were tightened?'

'My godfather's head groom was with the party and he was adamant that he saw to the matter personally, knowing what particular care was to be taken of me.'

'And so, if he spoke the truth, then

someone undid his work, doubtless conceal-ing his misdeed amid the rumpus caused when the party prepared to remount?'

'Yes, I too came up with that explanation.'

'And the next time?'

'Back at Castleray again a month later. I often use a back stairway in order to reach the side door. It opens straight onto the park and it is a more convenient means of leaving the house to exercise my dogs.' She grinned. 'It saves me a walk that would otherwise take at least five minutes.' Used to living in enormous houses himself, Sebastian nodded his understanding. 'The stairway in question is used only by the domestic staff, but my occasional use of it was no secret. One morning a stair-rod gave way when I was half way down and I fell the rest of the way, spraining my ankle in the process.' Her brow creased with a frown. 'But how could anyone know that I would use the stairs at that particular time? It could just as easily have been a servant and so once again I dismissed the incident as an accident.'

Sebastian now believed Abby was right to have concerns for her safety. Someone who was cunning, resourceful, ruthless and, significantly, running out of patience wished her harm. Someone, moreover, who had free access to her in whatever household she happened to be residing in. That suspicion was confirmed for Sebastian when Abby related the next two incidents.

The first was another attempt to cause an accident whilst she was on horseback, this time at Castleray, by placing a burr beneath her mare's saddle. In spite of Abby's modesty in relating the incident, it was clear to Sebastian that only her proficiency as a horsewoman prevented a more serious outcome than Abby being deposited on her derrière and suffering what she described as insignificant bruising.

The second, and far more serious to Sebastian's mind, was Abby's belief that, since her recent arrival in Town, someone had deliberately set out to poison her. She had partaken of a glass of peach ratafia at the house of mutual friends just a few days ago and had been taken violently ill almost immediately afterwards. Significantly, no one else who took the drink suffered the same unfortunate consequence.

'And so these apparent accidents have become more frequent in recent months?'

'Yes.'

'And so we must infer that someone does not wish you to be presented and embark upon the road to matrimony?'

'It could be interpreted in that manner.'

'Lady Abigail, should this person be successful in doing away with you, who inherits your fortune?'

Abby bristled. 'My Aunt Constance, as my mother's sister and only living relative. My father had no siblings and there is no one, however distantly related, who could hope to make a valid claim. As you are aware, my family does not veer away from the female line inheriting. But my aunt and uncle are independently wealthy and have been kindness itself as far as I am concerned. I could not for a moment consider them capable of such duplicity. Their lives have been completely disrupted by my arrival but not once have they complained. On the contrary, they knew how distressed I was at my parents' demise; how discomposed by my subsequent situation, and have done everything they can to put me at my ease.'

'Calm yourself, Lady Abigail, I merely wish to establish the facts. What happens to the duchy if you are no more?'

'The town house, hunting lodge and other smaller estates are all part of my father's estate and therefore would form part of my inheritance, passing into my aunt's hands. But the title would revert to the Crown, along with the Penrith estate, since obviously the property cannot be separated from the title.'

It was Sebastian's turn to stand and pace the room, deep in thought. He noticed as he did so that Abby remained silent, making no attempt to influence his thoughts. It was highly unusual, in his extensive experience of the species, for any woman to remain silent. However grave the circumstances they always felt the need to fill silences with unnecessary chatter and he applauded Abby's instinct to leave him to his cogitations.

The incidents were becoming more desperate, closer together, and less well disguised. At first they had been ingenious and anyone would have been hard-pressed to attribute any harm that befell Abby to anything other than misfortune. They had occurred in different locations, with a different set of people surrounding her on each occasion.

And so it all came back to the question of whom? And why?

The only answer to the latter had to be her considerable wealth. Someone wanted to inherit before she had the chance to marry and produce an heir. But if she was adamant that her uncle would never stoop to such measures, and had little need of the money anyway, then who else might have expectations?

'I will assist you,' Sebastian surprised himself by saying, 'on one condition.'

'Which is?'

'In return, I require — '

She stood to confront him, eyes blazing with angry disbelief. 'You want payment?'

'Yes indeed,' he responded calmly. 'But not in the monetary sense.'

'Then what?'

'If I solve this tantalizing conundrum on your behalf then I intend to extract payment from you in the form of one kiss.'

'I beg your pardon!'

'Come, Lady Abigail,' coaxed Sebastian, amused, 'I am persuaded this cannot be the first occasion upon which a gentleman has sought to steal a kiss from you?'

'Well, no but . . . ' Her words trailed off but her eyes continued to fire silver daggers of disapproval at him, which bounced harmlessly off his craggy expression. 'Oh, very well then!' She closed the distance between them, stood on tiptoe and placed a delicate kiss on his cheek.

'Satisfied?' she demanded, standing back and glaring at him.

Sebastian chuckled. 'If that is your understanding of a kiss, m'lady, then you really have led a sheltered life. Come here!'

Without waiting for her permission he pulled her against him. Hard. Her body collided against the solidity of his chest, producing a loud exclamation from Abby, and he suspected that only the support of his arms prevented her knees from buckling beneath her in shock. She frowned at him, confusion and alarm evident in her expression.

With a raffish smile he allowed one of his hands to drift to her nape. Long fingers tangled with wayward curls that had escaped their pins. The other framed her jaw, his thumb gently tracing the outline of her velvety lips, causing her to shudder and expel a deep sigh. Her eyes were open wide, making them appear enormous and far too large for the fragile face which they inhabited. But they held curiosity, and Sebastian thought he could detect the first stirrings of passion in their luminous depths. It was a combination that he found completely irresistible.

'So beautiful,' he murmured, his lips closing in on hers, 'such sensuous grace, such innocence.'

His voice was a soft caress, his breath stroking her face as his lips captured hers, not gently or persuasively but with an arrogant presumption that he had every right in the world to ravish her. His tongue forced its way into her mouth, provocatively demanding her complete capitulation. It was not long in coming. A man as experienced as Sebastian was bound to make short work of bending one as vulnerable as Abby to his will. Her body melted against his, all traces of resistance evaporating as she inexpertly attempted to return his kiss.

Her efforts in that regard did what nothing else had been able to manage and restored Sebastian's senses to him. He released her abruptly. What in the name of Hades did he think he was about? He must still be foxed; otherwise he would never have acted so rashly. His suggestion of a kiss had been made on a whim; one which he had not taken the time to think through. He had simply been curious to see if she possessed depth of courage and had wanted to gauge her reaction to his unusual request. He had not been prepared for such ready acquiescence on her part, though. His body had responded to the contact with hers in the time-honoured fashion: that much he had anticipated. He had not, however, been prepared for it to do so with such indecent haste.

His arms fell to his sides but Abby appeared too dazed to stand without his support and stumbled awkwardly. He offered her his arm and assisted her to a chair. His hand briefly brushed the curve of her face as he coiled another escaped curl round his finger, tucking it behind her ear.

'Call that a down-payment for the services I am about to render, if you like, and I will collect the residue when I have completed my work.'

'You are very sure of yourself, my lord,' she said, running her tongue across her bruised lips and slanting him a contemplative glance. 'And what is more,' she added, appearing to regain a modicum of composure and switching to the offensive, 'you are most assuredly no gentleman!'

'My dear,' he responded with a chuckle, 'if you came here in the expectation of finding one such then I regret to inform you that you have been most grievously misdirected.'

'Humph!'

'We need to meet again and discuss the matter further,' he remarked, adroitly cutting off the catalogue of complaints against him which he suspected her to be in the process of dredging up. 'I need a complete list of everyone connected to you, who might have expectations in the event of your death, however tenuous. I also need a separate list of all the people present at each of the attempts on your life, including servants.'

'Very well.'

'Who, by the way, are the attorneys who have control of your affairs?' Abby told him.

51

'Good, I know someone there.'

'Do you need to contact them? Should I write a letter of introduction?'

'Good Lord, no! That would only alert them. Besides, since you are still under age they would take no notice of your missive and simply refer it to your uncle.'

'Of course. I seem to have temporarily given up possession of my wits.'

Sebastian offered her a satirical grin. 'I wonder what could have caused such an aberration.'

Abby glared haughtily and inverted her chin. 'I will prepare the list but it might take a day or two,' she decreed loftily. 'When can we meet again?'

'You are the one under constant guard. That being the case, how did you manage to come here today?'

Abby abandoned her affronted expression and offered up that impish smile of hers that he found so enchanting. 'My aunt and cousin were obliged to call upon the modiste responsible for my cousin's trousseau. She is to be married immediately after Christmas, you understand. Whilst in the modiste's establishment, which most conveniently is situated just around the corner from here, I remembered that my new bonnet would be ready for collection from the milliner's today.

Now,' she continued, a glint taking possession of her dancing eyes, 'normally my aunt and cousin would have been keen to give me their opinion on my purchase, but there was the taxing question of precisely the right sort of lace for Bea's pink evening gown to be considered, and so you will readily appreciate that they could not tear themselves away. They wanted me to delay collecting my bonnet, but I was most insistent that I wished to wear it when we take tea with Lady Makin tomorrow and that I would be quite safe in broad daylight with just Sally for company. I then skipped out before they could think of alternative arguments.'

'I see,' said Sebastian, not attempting to hide his amusement.

'I am to meet them at twelve at Gunter's Parlour for a restorative glass of ice-cream.'

'Then you had better make haste, for it is almost that hour now.' Sebastian picked up her cloak, fastened it securely about her neck and pulled the hood over her curls.

'Presumably you walk in the park?'

'Yes, indeed.'

'Then see if you can lose your protectors on Wednesday morning. Come with your maid to the walk behind the Row: it is always deserted. I will see you there, with your list, at eleven o'clock.' He smiled at her, already wondering quite what he had got himself into. And why. 'Come now, I will see you out.'

He led her through a series of passages in his house. Having checked that the coast was clear he made to usher her through the side door but she stayed him with her hand.

'Lord Denver.'

'What is it now?'

'I feel I must thank you, sir, for listening to my concerns and offering your assistance. I already feel less anxious, knowing you will be working on my behalf.'

'You are entirely welcome,' he offered, briefly touching her face but resisting the temptation to offer her a more personal form of solace. When she looked at him like that, with her fathomless eyes brimming with confidence in him, there was nothing he would not do to quell her concerns. Good God, what a farrago! He was not even touching her and yet she could still arouse him. A mere chit of a girl had no business making him react in such a manner and he turned away from her to open the door, feigning impatience. But Abby was clearly not to be hurried. She looked up into his eyes, her expression deadly serious.

'Be that as it may, I am indebted to you, sir.'

Without a further word she pulled her hood more closely about her head and walked through the door which he was holding open for her, her maid bustling at her side.

4

Sebastian contemplated the extraordinary events of the morning as he wended his way through the seemingly endless maze of service corridors in his house, finding himself in accord with Abby's preference for short cuts when it took him several minutes, walking at a brisk pace, to reach his breakfast-parlour. Entering the room he partook of a healthy repast, scarcely noticing what he ate, his mind still preoccupied with all that his unexpected guest had revealed to him.

Refusing to offer Abby his assistance had not seriously crossed his mind; not once he had satisfied himself that she really was in danger and was desperate enough to turn to a complete stranger for help. Besides, he was bored. It had been some months since an interesting case, one worthy of his vast cognitive powers, had presented itself. Now that it had he was powerless to resist the challenge, even if it did mean that he would have to place himself frequently in Lady Abigail's company. In the brief period that had elapsed since her departure he had already gone a fair way to convincing himself that any grudging admiration he might have of her was merely the result of her courage in making such a daring visit to his home. She was too young to excite his amatory interest: he never dallied with unmarried girls and had no intention of becoming embroiled in a situation that, in all honour, could only end in his becoming leg-shackled.

He was not altogether surprised that his reputation had managed to reach the ears of one as closely guarded as Abby, but could not help wondering how she would react if she knew the truth. He had been one of Wellington's most productive spies, not least because of his penchant for languages, ability to adapt himself to whatever circumstances presented themselves and, most significantly, his reckless disregard for his own welfare.

Settling back into the rigid social structure of life within the *ton* was proving to be difficult. Sebastian found it impossible to take an interest in the latest *on-dits*, or to pander to the scheming matrons and dredge up a show of enthusiasm for their dreary daughters, and so he withdrew behind a façade of haughty detachment. But his position within society, immense fortune and imposing figure were sufficiently good reasons to excuse his contemptuous attitude. Indeed, the more unobtainable he strove to become, the more tenaciously he was pursued by those in possession of sufficient social ambition to ignore his eccentricities.

Abby's trifling difficulty was just the excuse he had been seeking to delay the inevitable. Much as he hated admitting the fact, Sebastian knew that his tiresome sisters were right to remind him of his obligations on the marriage front. It was his duty to produce an heir, thus ensuring the continuance of the Denver dynasty, and he could not invent reasons to prevaricate for much longer. He shuddered as he drew an accurate image of this year's crop of virginal debutantes, prettily deployed for his inspection. He could already anticipate their irksome giggling, lack of intellectual conversation, foolish simpering and childishly flirtatious overtures, all of which, he knew from bitter experience, would leave him completely unmoved.

Feeling totally justified in grasping this most convenient opportunity to temporarily absent himself from the fray, Sebastian returned his thoughts to Abby's plight. In spite of her protestations to the contrary, it was obvious to him that her aunt and uncle must be the prime suspects. No one else stood to gain financially from her demise and since the title would revert to the Crown if

Abby failed to produce an heir, what other motive could anyone have to do away with her?

Sebastian paused in his cogitations, reminding himself that things were seldom as they appeared to be at first glance. People bore grudges and harboured resentments for the most tenuous of reasons. His own first sight of Abby had been a shock; albeit a pleasant one. Wealth, position, beauty and courage: a potent combination that would likely stir up malevolent feelings, and the spiteful desire to even the score, in both sexes.

His breakfast complete, Sebastian made his way to his library and dealt with the matters of business which awaited his attention. He dictated letters, sorted through the pile of invitations that awaited decisions, discarding almost all of them with barely a glance, and reeled off a list of tasks for his secretary to attend to. All this took less than one-tenth of his attention. The rest of his mind was still engaged with Abby's problems, and the best way to go about resolving them.

As afternoon turned to early evening Sebastian, aware that Abby's aggressor was becoming increasingly impatient to finish the job prior to the commencement of the season proper, decided to take immediate action. Putting aside his papers he prepared to leave the house: there was someone he needed to consult regarding Abby's affairs, and he suspected he knew exactly where to find him at this hour.

Presenting an elegant figure, Sebastian sauntered the length of St James's Street. His forbidding expression, far from discouraging passers-by from addressing him, only succeeded in enhancing his attraction in the eyes of more than one female observer. He acknowledged acquaintances and stopped to pass the time of day with several of them, skilfully avoiding anyone who appeared intent upon delaying him for too long. Eventually reaching Whites, he entered the club and had the satisfaction of discovering his quarry ensconced in a leather armchair, engrossed in a newspaper.

'Evening, Anthony,' said Sebastian, taking the chair opposite his friend.

The Honourable Anthony Deverill, youngest of the Earl of Newbury's siblings, put aside his paper and grinned. 'What are you doing about at this Godforsaken hour, Seb?'

'Looking for you.'

Anthony raised his brows. 'What scrape have you got yourself into this time that requires my sharp legal brain to save your skin? Being sued for breach of promise?' he suggested with a grin.

Sebastian laughed. 'Good God, I hope not! My purpose in seeking you out owes rather more to the hypothetical.'

'Then what, hypothetically, can I assist you with?' asked Anthony, raising his hand to attract a waiter.

Anthony and Sebastian had been at Oxford together and were firm friends. Anthony, most conveniently, was now a partner in the law firm patronized by the Duke of Penrith's executors. Sebastian would not ask his friend to reveal confidential information regarding the estate, any more than he would betray Abby's confidence by explaining his interest in the Penrith affairs. Instead he put his faith in Anthony's awareness of his integrity and forged ahead with his first question.

'All right then, consider this. If, hypothetically speaking, you were one of the trustees for a wealthy duchy, a duchy which wanted for nothing, except perhaps a duke, for what purpose would you agree to release funds and to whom?'

Anthony's eyebrows disappeared beneath his hairline. 'I hardly need to enquire whether you have a good reason for your question.'

Sebastian inclined his head. 'Let us just say that it is not the product of idle curiosity.'

'I hardly imagined that it would be. Thinking of falling prey to the parson's mousetrap at last?' Anthony grinned, clearly enjoying himself. 'Or are you simply short of blunt?'

'Come on, Tony, this is serious!'

Anthony drifted into contemplative silence. Sebastian was content to wait him out, already having decided that if his friend declined to reveal the sensitive information he had requested then he would not contrive to extract it from him by unscrupulous means.

'I would imagine that funds would be released from the coffers of your hypothetical duchy for the purpose of routine management, payment of stipends, maintenance of buildings and so forth.'

'Of course, but if there were, say, two trustees, could either one of them make a request for the release of these funds?'

'Yes, but in actuality probably only one would do so. Perhaps, if one were to be located, geographically speaking, closer to the ducal seat, then it might be more practical for said trustee to take it upon himself to manage the estates, and leave his co-trustee to worry about the welfare of the heir.'

'That would be a sensible arrangement,' conceded Sebastian. 'And, presumably, all monies would be meticulously accounted for?'

'Naturally.'

'What if funds were required for something other than routine expenses?'

'We would be applied to, the purpose of the funds would be explained, and we would agree, or not, according to the circumstances.'

'Can you imagine a situation where you would not agree?'

'The hypothetical duchy you refer to sounds as though it would be efficiently managed and, as its legal custodians, we would not have cause to decline releasing funds for bona-fide purposes.'

'I see.' Disappointed to have learned so little, Sebastian brooded upon his lack of progress until Anthony's next words caused him to sit bolt upright.

'The same could be said about personal loans, of course.'

'What, the trustees are permitted to borrow from the duchy?'

'It is not an unusual occurrence in such circumstances,' said Anthony, with a neutral smile. 'After all, the trustees would be giving extensively of their time and expertise to ensure that the estate flourished.'

'Would both trustees require monetary support?'

'I would imagine that the heir's immediate guardian would be comfortably situated and have no such requirement.'

Sebastian breathed a small sigh of relief. This did not absolve Abby's uncle, of course, but went some way to confirming her assertion that Bevan was independently wealthy. But Wilsden, it would appear, possessed no such scruples. Now that was interesting! The man was a common sight at Court, being a prominent member of the Carlton House set, staunchly loyal to the Prince Regent and considered by all who knew him to be beyond reproach.

'For what purpose would personal loans be granted?'

'Were they to be so then their purpose would remain confidential. Only the senior partner would be party to that information.'

Sebastian crossed a booted leg across his opposite knee, took an appreciative sip of Anthony's burgundy and contemplated this latest intelligence. 'Very well,' he said eventually. 'But, tell me, Anthony, do you imagine that these hypothetical loans would always be repaid?'

'Yes,' he said, smiling, 'I would imagine that they would be repaid within the time specified, and with interest.' Anthony looked Sebastian directly in the eye, his expression one of mild concern as he abandoned all pretence at hypothesis. 'But, as to the latest one, that is altogether another matter.'

'Why is this one any different?' asked Sebastian, sitting forward in his seat, alerted by the change in Anthony's demeanour that something of significance had recently occurred.

'Because it is exceedingly large: large enough to arouse my curiosity as to its purpose, and concerns as to the borrower's ability to repay it.'

'You think the borrower might have difficulty meeting his obligations?'

'Most assuredly, but since it was agreed by my senior' — Anthony paused and shrugged his shoulders — 'hypothetically speaking, I can scarce voice my concerns publicly.'

'Anthony, I appreciate this is asking a lot, and you must know that I would not put you in the position, were it not important.' Anthony looked at his friend, his expression now openly curious. 'Are you able to reveal to me how much the loan was for?'

Anthony considered this request for some time before responding in the affirmative, causing Sebastian to let out an oath of astonishment.

'That is a lot! When was it granted?'

'Three months ago.'

'I see.' Sebastian rubbed his chin, pausing to choose his next words with care. 'Anthony, is there any way in which you could discover the purpose of the loan, without compromising your position of trust?'

'Yes, but only if I am prepared to go snooping.'

'Ah well, never mind, I could not ask you to do that. It was just a thought and, anyway, you have already given me much to think about.'

Anthony smiled. 'I will see what else I can discover. I confess to being uneasy about the whole thing myself, although I could not precisely say why. The price for my assistance, however, is that you reveal the nature of your involvement to me as soon as you are in a position to do so.'

Smiling with satisfaction Sebastian offered Anthony his hand to seal their bargain.

★ ★ ★

Abby discovered that life within the *ton* left her with far less leisure time than had been the case in the country. Were it not for the fact that she was scarcely ever on her own, and had little time in which to compile the list that Sebastian had requested, then she would have revelled in her change of circumstances.

Since her appearance at the duchess's ball, the Penrith town house in Belgravia had been inundated with callers. Gentlemen seeking to consolidate their acquaintance with her, ladies looking to include her in their activities, and people calling to issue invitations in person all combined to reduce the well-run household to a state of near chaos. And when they were not receiving callers, or dealing with the latest catastrophe regarding Bea's trousseau, they were themselves taken up with returning calls; taking tea with other ladies; accepting invitations to luncheons; listening to the latest gossip and learning, in the strictest confidence of course, who was about to offer for whom. Too new to it all to find it fatiguing, Abby was fascinated by the depth of interest the ladies took in one another's affairs; by their readiness to indulge in unsubstantiated gossip and the apparent satisfaction they took in branding one another, on the flimsiest of evidence, as being not quite up to the mark.

Abby took refuge in her chamber late at night, when she could at last be assured of privacy, and worked upon her list, shaking her head as she wrote out the familiar names. She knew these people far too well to consider that they wished her anything other than the best of fortune. Besides, none of them had ever shown the slightest sign of envy at her unusual circumstances. On the contrary, they all appeared to take pleasure from her company and had nothing to gain from her demise. As far as Abby was concerned they were, every last one of them, quite simply beyond reproach.

Sighing, she threw her quill aside and stretched her aching limbs, reluctantly conceding that Sebastian was in the right of it when he suggested that whoever intended her harm was motivated by the desire to benefit financially. Accepting the fact, though, did nothing to assist her in identifying the shadowy figure lurking on the edge of her consciousness. It was too fantastic to contemplate anyone close to her being culpable. Besides, if anyone bore her ill-will, she was certain she would have sensed their underlying hostility, however well they sought to disguise it.

In an effort to divert her thoughts from a dilemma that appeared more complex by the minute, Abby turned her mind to the question of Sebastian's kiss. She felt a warm glow spread through her body as she relived the moment. Her cheeks turned scarlet with embarrassment as the glow finally came to rest, pooling in the pit of her stomach in a manner so agreeable that she hugged herself in an attempt to prolong the sensation. She smiled and ran her tongue across her lips in a gesture invested with such a wealth of innocent sensuousness that Sebastian, had he been privileged to witness it, would have been hard pressed to stick to his resolve and keep her at arm's length.

Revelling in the warm aftermath of her first adult embrace, Abby chose not to dwell upon her quite shocking want of propriety in allowing his lordship such licence, justifying her behaviour in the light of her far greater concerns for her personal safety. She could not help but speculate upon his reasons for requesting a kiss in return for assisting her, though. What could he mean by it? If even half of what Bea had related about his past was true then he could hardly claim lack of female companionship as an excuse. And surely he was not desperate enough to dally with her just because she was new to town and the subject of such rampant speculation? Or because he could?

Abby dismissed the idea as ludicrous. It was probably nothing more than a fleeting impulse on his part and, anyway, all this thinking about something that to him probably counted for nothing at all, and which he had doubtless already dismissed from his mind, was making her head spin. She was grateful to Sebastian; grateful to him for offering his assistance, but not for that damned kiss. He had been right to suggest that other gentlemen had tried to kiss her over the years: Lord Wilsden's younger son Charles had twice done so, just last year, but her reaction had been quite the reverse to that which Sebastian's sophisticated approach had managed to stimulate. Being embraced by Charles was about as passionate as being caught in a violent rainstorm. Abby shuddered. Charles engendered no feelings of tenderness within her breast and his attempts to convince her otherwise had been inept; an embarrassment to them both.

Before she left Cornwall Lord Evans had called to bid her farewell, even though he too was making his way to Town. Left alone with her for a few minutes he had surprised Abby by deviating from his formal manners, taking the opportunity to kiss first her gloved hand and then pulling her into his arms and capturing her lips. Although more efficiently executed than Charles's efforts, it had still left Abby feeling unmoved, only adding to her conviction that romantic attachment was overrated.

Abby belatedly understood that ignorance had been bliss. Sebastian, with one practised embrace, had called her firmly held opinion on the matter into question. And she was not at all happy about it. Duty was her byword and she had no intention of allowing her head to be turned by an accomplished rogue with passionate eyes and disgustingly compelling charm.

★ ★ ★

Sebastian arrived at their rendezvous in the park early and seated himself on a bench which afforded him a clear view of the walk in both directions. As he had predicted, it was completely deserted. Fashionable people came to the park to be seen, not to lurk in this quiet backwater.

He had been sitting for just a few minutes when Abby came into his line of sight, two large dogs pulling at the ends of their leashes, the same maid scurrying along beside her. Sebastian stood as she neared him, approving of the fact that she had again taken the precaution to shroud herself in a concealing cloak.

'Good morning,' he said, stepping up to her. 'I trust you did not experience too much difficulty in getting away?'

'It was surprisingly easy,' she assured him, pulling her dogs back, ineffectively preventing them from leaping up at Sebastian. 'Down, Marcus! Leave it, Marius!' The dogs, ignoring her command, continued introducing themselves. 'These are my collies. I am afraid they are rather lively just at the moment, and more than a little disgruntled. You see, they are accustomed to having the freedom to roam the estate in Cornwall and take great exception to being leashed.'

'Collies?' Sebastian raised a brow in amusement as he scratched the ears of first one distinctly non-pedigree dog, and then the other.

'Yes, well, all right, I accept that perhaps they are not pure-bred collies, but they are not aware of the fact and I don't care to offend them by mentioning it in their hearing. They were going to be drowned as puppies because no one wanted them,' she explained, anger flashing through her remarkable eyes. 'Their lineage is hardly their fault, and they were so adorable that I simply could not permit it to happen.'

'I should say not. They are fine beasts.'

'You comprehend my feelings then? And don't forget that Marcus repaid my faith in him by saving my life on that rope bridge,' she declared proudly.

'So he did.' Sebastian smiled at her fierce loyalty for her unlikely looking pets. 'But perhaps your maid could take charge of them whilst we discuss our business? I cannot see that they will allow us to concentrate otherwise.'

'Certainly.'

'Now then, what information have you managed to compile for me?' he asked, watching the maid struggling to remain on her feet as the boisterous beasts dragged her in the direction of nearby bushes.

5

Abby produced her list from her reticule. 'I have made as comprehensive an account as possible, but fear I may not have included all of the servants.' She looked up at him and smiled her regret. 'There are so many of them that it is difficult to recall.'

'No matter, for now I wish to concentrate upon the people above stairs. If servants are involved they will only be so because they are acting upon orders from their masters.'

Sebastian took the pages from her and scanned them, quickly becoming absorbed. Abby sat perfectly still, taking advantage of his preoccupation to admire his noble profile, the evenness of his features and the reassuring intelligence reflected in his eyes. The thick mass of hair spilling across his collar and lifting in the breeze fascinated her and she had difficulty averting her gaze. Strangely disconcerted by his close proximity she focused, with what she hoped would pass for detached interest, upon the elegance of the long fingers which curved around the edges of the paper, embarrassed when she recalled the manner in which those fingers had once so skilfully caressed her face.

Abby was acutely aware of the heat that had invaded her body in response to her inappropriate thoughts. Unable to understand why the sight of Sebastian's muscular thighs encased in tight-fitting inexpressibles should serve to exacerbate her discomfort she moved away from him slightly, extending the already respectable amount of daylight which separated their bodies. Still absorbed by her list, Sebastian appeared far less aware of her presence than she was of his. She had obviously been correct in her assumption that the passionate nature of the kiss they had shared had been nothing out of the ordinary for a man of his reputation. Unlike her it would not have troubled his mind since, and would certainly not have kept him awake at night: wondering, speculating; filling him with longing. Abby assembled the remnants of her dignity as best she could, vowing that he would never know just how extensively his practised embrace had agitated her fledgling passions.

'Let us start at the beginning,' he suggested, his voice jolting her out of her reverie.

'By all means,' agreed Abby, squaring her shoulders and appearing to Sebastian as though she was emerging from a pleasant dream.

'You have commenced your list with your aunt and uncle, who are your guardians.'

'Yes, but as I told you — '

Sebastian halted her protests with a wave of his hand. 'Quite: so we will not concentrate our attention upon them. So who do we have next?' Without waiting for her answer, Sebastian read the next name from the list. 'Lord Tobias Bevan, your uncle and aunt's eldest son and heir, and your first cousin?'

'Yes, and as you will see, Tobias is married to Cassandra. They have two boys away at school and two younger daughters.'

'And they live where?'

'In the summer they reside at Castleray but during the season they live in my uncle's town house in Curzon Street.'

'You are not residing there with them?'

'No, as it is my first season my uncle decided to open the Penrith House in Belgravia.'

'Which is part of your inheritance?'

'Yes.'

'I see. And how does Tobias occupy his time?'

'He has independent wealth, since he inherited money from his grandfather, but he also helps with the running of my uncle's estates, since they will obviously be his one day.'

'And do you enjoy a congenial relationship with your cousin?'

'He is a good deal older than me; over thirty now. When I removed to Castleray he was on his Grand Tour and so I saw nothing of him. When he returned he spent his time in London and married Cassandra one year later. She brought a substantial dowry to the marriage, so I cannot see any reason to suspect either of them. My relationship with them both is entirely amiable and I know of nothing to their discredit.'

Neither did Sebastian, but that hardly exonerated them. 'And your uncle's second son, Harold,' continued Sebastian, consulting her list, 'is a clergyman.'

'Yes, and he now has the living at Penrith, which is a rich one.'

'It being the tradition for younger sons to go into the army, the law or the church?'

'Yes, but in Harold's case his profession was entirely of his own choosing. He too inherited from his grandfather and did not have to do anything, if he preferred to remain idle, but I cannot remember a time when he did not wish to take holy orders.' Abby smiled fondly. 'He is quite one of the best men of my acquaintance.'

'You smile when you speak of Harold. I conclude therefore that you know your younger cousin rather well, and approve of him.'

'Indeed, yes! He is but five years my senior and has been kindness itself to me. He alone appeared to appreciate my turmoil when . . .' Her words trailed off and she quickly averted her gaze.

'Go on.'

'Well, in truth, only Harold seemed to notice just how desperately unhappy I felt when I first removed to Castleray. Everyone else was kind to me but too concerned about the implications for the duchy to pay me much heed. But Harold could see that I was completely lost and more than a little bewildered. I was quite out of character with God, too, for taking Mama and Papa from me far sooner than He had any right to demand their company, and I had lost all faith in Him. I could not understand why He would wish to do such an unfair thing. I mean, Mama and Papa, to my certain knowledge, had never done anyone deliberate harm, and so what purpose could He possibly have? It made no sense at all to a bewildered ten-year-old.' Abby stopped talking in order to dash away tears impatiently with the back of her hand.

'A perfectly natural reaction, I shouldn't wonder,' remarked Sebastian softly.

'Exactly so! But Harold found the time to talk to me about it for hours,' she continued, appearing to have mastered her emotions, 'explaining that God's purpose is not always immediately clear, but that He would not have chosen my parents without good reason. It helped a little to talk to someone who might, just possibly, have God's ear and, what is more,' she continued, with an arch smile, 'his way of putting things was so simple, his faith so unshakeable, that it even made sense to one as angry and confused as I was. That is why, when the Penrith living fell vacant two years ago, I was delighted when my uncle suggested that Harold was deserving of it.'

'And Harold's wife?'

'Mary is an ideal cleric's spouse. She is the daughter of my godfather's late steward, and much spiteful gossip ensued when she married Harold, since it was considered she had brought off a match with a gentleman who was far above her station. But she has proved her critics entirely wrong,' said Abby, lifting her chin in a gesture of defiance that Sebastian was already starting to recognize. 'She has a calm disposition, is quite without malice and is able to connect with the villagers as well as fitting comfortably amongst the gentry, too.' Abby took a moment to reflect, clearly attempting to be fair. 'She is, perhaps, not so obviously beautiful in the way of Tobias's Cassandra, but looks are not everything. Besides, she possesses a unique inner beauty, which those of us who know her well cannot but admire.' Abby paused once again and offered Sebastian a specious smile. 'They have three delightful daughters, who are often at Castleray, and upon whom I dote.'

'And your third cousin is Beatrice; she of the trousseau.'

'Yes, and if you think — '

'Indeed, my lady, I would not dare to harbour such thoughts!' He offered her an expression of mock alarm, to which Abby responded with a reluctant upward turn of her lips. 'Beatrice is engaged to Lord Woodley?'

'Yes, and takes a good dowry into the marriage. Besides, Lord Woodley is very comfortably situated.'

'I dare say you are correct.' Sebastian stretched his long legs in front of him and disciplined himself to abandon his efforts to ignite her laughter. 'All right then, now to your godfather.'

'Lord Wilsden is a widower. Wilsden House is but five miles from Penrith Hall and there has been a friendship between the two families for generations.'

'Hence his being your godfather?'

'Quite.'

'And Wilsden's children?'

'His elder son, Gerald, is married to Elizabeth. They live at Wilsden House and Gerald helps run his father's estates. Since Lord Wilsden spends much of his own time attending to my affairs, or at Court, it is a very convenient arrangement.'

Something about Abby's clipped accent struck a cord with Sebastian. 'You do not care for Gerald?'

'I have little to do with him,' she responded evasively. 'He, like my cousin Tobias, is a good deal older than me and our paths seldom cross. But when they do we are perfectly comfortable with one another.'

Sebastian didn't think she was being entirely candid with him, but let the matter pass. For now. 'And his second son?'

'Charles.' Abby's smile as she pronounced her cousin's name was a warm one. 'He too helps with the running of the estates, and is not married.' When Sebastian looked at her askance, she elaborated. 'My godfather is wealthy and has much property and investments that require supervision. He did not press Charles to pick upon an occupation and, anyway, I am given to understand that Charles showed no interest in any of the usual professions. He does not have the aptitude for soldiering, nor the empathy necessary to make a good clergyman. And as for the law, well, I do not believe that Charles completed his tenure at university.'

'He was sent down?' asked Sebastian, alert to the possibility that he might have hit upon a clue.

'I am unsure. What I do know is that Charles is amusing and surprisingly good company, but does not care to be burdened with too much responsibility, which might get in the way of his other pleasures.'

'Except for you?'

Abby coloured. 'What makes you say that?'

'Am I right?'

'Well, yes, I suppose so. He does try to make himself agreeable whenever we meet, but then we have always been good friends. Besides, many other gentlemen behave in a similar fashion towards me,' she added, her voice laced not with pride but rather a certain note of inevitability. Sebastian felt a moment's anger on her behalf. The wolves could not even let her enjoy her first season before they gathered to fight for her favours.

'Do you encourage his attentions?'

'Certainly not!' Sebastian levelled a steady

gaze at her, compelling her to justify her statement. 'It is like kissing a gaping trout!' she declared, with a moue of distaste.

Sebastian chuckled at her disingenuous display. He also made a large mental mark beside Charles Wilsden's name. 'How does Charles occupy his time, when he is not making amorous advances towards you, that is?'

'He is obsessed with anything related to sport, but then is that not the case with most single gentlemen of means?'

'Quite frequently so, yes.'

'Well, there you are then. Charles's particular passion is curricle racing. He takes it very seriously and devotes much of his attention to it.'

'An expensive pastime,' observed Sebastian.

'Indeed, but Charles is a familiar figure at Tattersall's and prides himself upon being able to recognize good horse flesh. He buys youngsters and breaks them to the harness himself. He loves to hunt, too, and is, so my cousin Bea would have it, a frequent visitor to Gentleman Jackson's Saloon.'

Sebastian upgraded his mild suspicions in respect of Charles Wilsden. Not only was purchasing and maintaining horse flesh an expensive exercise but boxing and curricle racing, of necessity, required a substantial amount of ready blunt in order to indulge in heavy wagers. No one of Sebastian's acquaintance took an interest in such activities without becoming involved with the betting: it simply was not done.

'And these other gentlemen on the list: in what manner are they related to you?' he enquired, keeping his fledgling suspicions regarding Charles Wilsden to himself.

Abby blushed again. 'They are a few of the gentlemen in our circle that I have met on more than one occasion.'

'And who have designs upon marriage to you?'

Abby shrugged. 'Possibly, but I begged my uncle to allow me to be presented and enjoy one season before I settle down and do what is expected of me. He agreed, and so I know he will not entertain any requests of that nature at the present time, and will not enter into any commitments on my behalf for the time being.'

'But Lord Evans finds particular favour with your uncle?'

Abby's shoulders lifted once more. 'I believe so.'

'But what are your feelings for that gentleman?' asked Sebastian, shifting his position in order to gain a clearer view of her features as she pondered the question.

'That he might very well do. If my uncle approves then that is enough for me.'

Sebastian was stunned. Never in all his years had he known a girl of Abby's age who did not harbour grand romantic dreams. With her exceptional beauty she had every right to anticipate being swept off her feet. Damn it, she was only eighteen: she had no business displaying such a mature attitude to such matters! Sebastian itched to change her opinion, to demonstrate to her by deed rather than word just a little of what she was missing, but knew he could not risk starting down that path. He hid his disapproval behind a casual expression and disciplined himself to make no comment, other than asking one simple question.

'But do you entertain feelings for him?'

The glance she cast in his direction was full of wisdom and had no place on such youthful features. 'Does it matter? From what I have observed most married couples within society bear little love for one another. Their unions are often arranged for reasons of monetary gain or social advancement, with scant regard for compatibility, or the finer feelings of either party involved. Anyway,' she added, obviously rattled by the astonishment he was unable to conceal, 'is it not unfashionable for couples to show outward signs of affection in public, or even to be seen at the same assembly together, for that matter?'

'Yes, quite frequently, but — '

'If my uncle is of the opinion that Lord Evans would make a suitable husband for me, then I will be guided by his wisdom. After all he has done for me I owe him not only my duty, but my undying gratitude, too.'

'Does Evans know you feel this way?'

'Certainly not!'

'Hm.'

'And what is that supposed to mean?' she enquired, her eyes flashing with annoyance.

'It means, m'dear, that Evans may not know, but perhaps some of your other suitors have an inkling, which could explain their collective anxiety to pursue you.'

'Yes, but your argument defeats itself since, if they covet my fortune, they would not wish to see any harm befall me. If I am no more, then their aspirations perish with me.'

'True.' He conceded the point with a nod. 'Acquaint me with the rest of these people on your list, Lady Abigail.'

'They are mostly neighbours of ours in Cornwall.'

'Sir Michael Parker. What are your objections to him as a potential husband?'

'Too old and set in his ways.'

'Unforgivable of him!' agreed Sebastian, amused, who knew Parker to be only a little older than he himself was.

'Laura and Simon Graves?'

'More neighbours, with whom we are especially intimate. They are the son and daughter of Lord Sykes and Laura and I are the firmest of friends.'

'But Simon, presumably, wishes to be more than a friend to you? What iniquitous traits does he possess which make you disinclined to return his regard?'

Abby grinned. 'He is excessively portly and already a slave to gout.'

'Lamentable!' sighed Sebastian, charmed by her spontaneous laughter; by the love of life and irreverence she tried so hard to quell, but which sometimes defied her best efforts and broke through anyway.

'What action do we take now?' she asked him, as he scanned her second sheet of paper, which listed the names of some of the servants, and the positions they occupied in the various households Abby moved between.

'I must engineer a way to observe you in a setting that includes all these people.'

Her eyes glittered with triumph. 'That is precisely what I hoped you would suggest! My uncle plans to remove to Leicestershire next week and open my hunting lodge. Will you be travelling to that county to hunt, my lord?'

'Yes, indeed, I have a box there myself and hunt with the Beaufort.'

Abby let out a sigh at the name of the famous hunt. 'Wonderful! Oh, how I wish . . .'

'What do you wish?' he asked with a smile.

'Oh, nothing of consequence.'

'You enjoy hunting, Lady Abigail?' he asked, already suspecting what it was she had stopped herself from blurting out.

'I am sure I would, if only my uncle would permit me to take to the field. If I say so myself, I believe I am sufficiently accomplished as a horsewoman not to disgrace the family name, but unfortunately Uncle Bertram considers it to be too dangerous and refuses me his permission.'

Sebastian hid his disapproval of the restrictions placed upon Abby, and his sympathy for her plight, behind a nonchalant expression. 'I dare say he is right,' he observed casually. 'But as to our previous discussion, I do not see how I can inflict myself, uninvited, upon your uncle's party, without arousing their suspicions.'

'Could you not contrive to break down outside our lodge?' she suggested with the sweetest of smiles.

'It is rather difficult to break down to order.'

'Yes, indeed.' She sounded disappointed and fell into a brief, contemplative silence. 'And I most certainly would not wish any harm to befall your horses.'

'That would be a rather extreme measure.'

'Perhaps you could be taken inexplicably ill during the course of your journey?' she suggested, brightening at the prospect.

'I would be happy to oblige you by falling in with your scheme but, were I to do so, it would be necessary for me to remain in my chamber and nurse my mysterious malady, which would rather defeat the object, do you not think?'

'Oh yes, so it would.' She pouted and looked rather discouraged. 'Inventing reasons for impromptu visits is not as straightforward as I thought.' She frowned a challenge at him. 'Do you have any suggestions to make, my lord? I dare say your experience in such matters is more extensive than my own.'

Several suggestions sprang spontaneously to Sebastian's mind, especially when she regarded him with such transparent confidence in his abilities, but he refrained from voicing them.

'When do you remove to Leicestershire?' he asked her instead.

'Next Wednesday.'

'And all of the people on your list will be there, even the clergyman?'

'Oh yes, it is quite an established tradition. And others will likely be there, too. It will be a jolly party. As for Harold, he enjoys hunting, and can get away easily enough, given sufficient notice.'

'I see. Then I shall endeavour to contrive some ingenious means of inflicting myself upon your party. I am sure I will be able to come up with something convincing before next Wednesday.'

'Oh, do you think you will be able to manage it? That would be splendid! I am indebted to you, sir.'

'Indeed you are,' he agreed, smiling raffishly, 'but your gratitude must wait until a more suitable juncture, since I observe your maid returning and it would appear that your dogs' enthusiasm is in danger of exhausting her strength. Besides, we have risked being in public together for quite long enough.'

'Yes, indeed.' She called her dogs' names and they bounded towards her.

'Lady Abigail.' Sebastian called to her twice before he could attract her attention away from the clamouring hounds. 'One thing more.'

'What is it, sir?'

'Take the greatest of care, m'dear. I do not mean to alarm you, but your assailant would appear to be getting more desperate with the passing of each day and appears now to have surrendered to recklessness, which can only bode ill for you. He has tried everything he can to do away with you, without success, which must be very frustrating for him. Be on your guard at every moment until we meet again and I am in a position to offer you my personal protection.'

So saying he kissed her hand and left her, open mouthed with surprise, in her maid's care.

6

Abby took Sebastian's warning to heart, which was easier said than done, given the hectic nature of the remainder of her time within the *ton*. The initial interest displayed in her showed no sign of abating, leaving her with the disturbing feeling that the pattern of her life was no longer hers to dictate. Having been so impatient to experience all the diversions that society had to offer, they were already starting to pall.

She was disappointed not to see anything of Sebastian during the course of this whirlwind but was rather pleased with the way that she looked out for herself without his supervision. She diligently ensured that she was always within sight of her aunt or cousin at assemblies, never accepting anything to eat or drink unless she observed others partaking from the same dish before she did. She avoided little used corridors, declined all invitations to stroll on terraces, and the ingenious attempts of gentlemen to get her alone.

Arriving in Leicestershire on Thursday of the following week, Abby accepted her uncle's hand as he assisted her from their travelling chaise. She pulled her velvet pelisse more closely about her, grateful for its enveloping warmth. There was a crispness in the air, thick frost underfoot and the promise of snow in the dark clouds which threatened directly overhead. Perhaps that was a good thing? If Lord Denver was as close upon their heels as Abby hoped then he would be able to seize upon the deterioration in the weather as a convenient excuse for breaking his journey.

But the snow did not materialize; no more did Sebastian. Abby hid her disappointment as she greeted the arrival of their guests at various intervals during the course of the afternoon. There was little formality required in this duty, since all were well known to her, and proved to be a useful distraction from her continuous thoughts of Sebastian. When would he arrive? What excuse would he offer and would his presence arouse suspicions in the rest of the party? The waiting, and her growing unease, were starting to tell upon Abby. The knowledge that her aggressor was very likely already in this very room, planning his next attempt on her life, only added to her discomfort. She surreptitiously glanced at the faces of the gentlemen already assembled, trying to detect signs of guilt or calculation in their countenances, observing instead only open friendliness. It was hopeless!

Abby, shaking off her worries, was especially delighted to see her friend Laura Graves again and greeted her warmly. Naturally Laura was far too gentle, and far too loyal a friend, to be involved in any plots against her. Nor did she have any reason to be. There could be no advantage to Laura in seeing Abby dead. But she refrained from confiding in her friend, mainly because Sebastian had impressed upon her the importance of not telling anyone about her suspicions.

Simon remained tenaciously at his sister's side, thereby ensuring that he also remained close to Abby. He was even larger than ever, clearly in pain from the gout, but entertaining company for all that and excessively pleased to see her again. He spoke with enthusiasm, and at some length, about the opening meet on the morrow.

'Will you be able to hunt tomorrow, Mr Graves, do you suppose, since your leg is clearly paining you?' asked Abby, immediately wishing she had not done so when Simon pounced upon the opportunity she had unwittingly created for him.

'I fear not,' he said, with less than convincing regret. 'But, my dear, someone must stay behind and bear you company, I cannot abide to think of you being left to your own devices for an entire day. I should be honoured to keep you entertained.'

'How kind you are, Mr Graves, but I would not put you to so much trouble. My aunt and cousin will not take to the field, and so I shall not want for company. Besides, even though I shall not join the hunt that does not preclude me from riding to the meet and seeing them away. Sadly though, since you are clearly incapacitated, I fear it would not be wise for you to follow my example.'

Simon knew when he had been bested and smiled affably enough, but the exchange left Abby feeling uncomfortable: Simon had never pursued her quite so aggressively before and it was already evident that her first sojourn into society was being treated by her admirers as *carte blanche* to press forward with their claims.

'Lady Abigail.' Sir Michael Parker joined their group and bowed over her hand, holding it possessively and making slow work of releasing it. 'You look ravishing! But, pray do tell me, did you enjoy your time in London? And how many hearts did you add to your growing collection?'

'Sir Michael, really!'

'I hear,' put in Simon, 'that you are to be

congratulated upon giving Denver a well-deserved dressing down.'

Abby coloured slightly but could think of nothing appropriate to say in response. She was appalled that news of her exploits had managed to reach Simon's ears when he had remained in the depths of Cornwall, but was cognizant of the fact that she had just learned a very important lesson: the *ton* was a hotbed of gossip and intrigue. Had she not already discovered that nothing anyone did went unnoticed, or was deemed too insignificant to warrant animated discussion? Abby understood then that Sebastian had not been exaggerating when he had advised her to proceed with caution and trust no one with her confidences.

'Lady Abigail behaved with perfect decorum, and indeed one would expect nothing less,' remarked Lord Evans, gliding up to her side.

'Oh, quite so!' agreed Simon. 'Denver is far too big for his boots anyway. Thinking he's above everyone else and behaving just as he pleases. Did you know that Lady Redford confided to — '

'Yes, thank you, Graves. Save it for later,' suggested Lord Evans, with a meaningful glance in Abby's direction.

Simon coloured and fell silent. Abby

detected an undercurrent between the two gentlemen, unaware that Lord Evans had just prevented Simon from blurting out a risqué story in respect of Sebastian's mistress. What she did know was that Simon's criticism of Sebastian seemed unjust and she had had to fight off the impulse to defend him. Why a single man of independent means should be censured for pleasing himself about his activities she could not begin to imagine, but had the good sense to keep this thought to herself.

Abby was next accosted by her godfather, who was in company with his son Gerald, Gerald's rather aloof wife, Elizabeth and, naturally, Charles.

'How did you enjoy the *ton*, my dear?' asked Lord Wilsden, smiling and kissing her cheek. 'I hear you were quite a sensation, but then that hardly came as a surprise.' Before she could regale her godfather with the anecdotes she had already trotted out several times, Lord Wilsden spoke again. 'No, my dear, I must beg you to excuse me, since I believe your uncle is trying to attract my attention. Tell Charles all about it instead,' he invited, glaring significantly at his son. 'He is impatient to hear all your news, is that not so, Charles?'

'You are in the right of it, sir,' responded

Charles, displaying a marked lack of enthusiasm at the prospect of being admitted to Abby's company. 'How are you, m'dear?' he enquired, casually kissing her fingers and not appearing the slightest bit interested in any response she might have to make.

★　★　★

As the party gathered at the lodge partook of dinner that evening, Abby wondered if her recent visit to town had heightened her awareness in respect of such matters or whether things had always been thus, but there could be no doubt that Sir Michael and Simon Graves were openly competing against one another for her attention, whilst Lord Evans was fending them off with a display of possessiveness, which Abby supposed was intended to imply a prior understanding between them. She was vexed by it; he had certainly never behaved in such a fashion in the past and his pristine manners had been one of the things she most admired about him. Had there been other unattached gentlemen present she would have made a point of singling them out, just to show Lord Evans that she did not care for the assumptions he was making, but short of encouraging Sir Michael and Simon — or,

God forbid, her cousin Charles — there was little she could do, other than attempt to put a distance between herself and Lord Evans: something he did not appear to notice, disregarding the coolness of her responses to his questions and taking every opportunity to pretend an intimacy between them which did not exist.

Abby wondered what had caused Lord Evans's attitude towards her to undergo such a marked change. Perhaps her visit to London, when he had seen her in such demand? Even if he and her uncle had come to an understanding, Lord Evans would be aware that it also required her agreement and could easily imagine the situation causing him some uneasiness. He was a gentleman who would only ever be truly comfortable with order and method in his life, not caring for issues of import to remain unresolved.

Abby breathed an inaudible sigh. Did he but know it, against her better judgement and every last vestige of common sense, her heart was engaged elsewhere. Abby smiled at the impossibility of it all. If Lord Evans were ever to guess at her infatuation, then he would also comprehend that he had nothing to fear: Sebastian Denver was unlikely to show an amatory interest in her. And even if she had not taken heed of the rumours about his legendary exploits, which Bea was only too pleased to expound upon at every opportunity, she had seen with her own eyes at the duchess's ball that he favoured the more experienced lady. It was laughable really. Abby, without being unduly boastful, knew she could have virtually any man she set her heart upon. Oh, not for reasons of any physical attractiveness on her part, but rather more because of who she was, and the fortune under her guardianship. Unfortunately the only gentleman she had met who could stir her passions did not appear to have any need of her fortune, no interest in matrimony and even less interest in her.

Throughout the meal Abby listened for the sound of unexpected arrivals. But Sebastian did not appear and, as a result, the evening seemed as dreary as it was interminable. The gentlemen continued to shower her with their attentions until she was ready to scream. Only with the greatest of difficulty did she prevent herself from walking outside, in spite of the cold and the fact that it was pitch dark. Sebastian's dire warnings rang in her head and she resisted the temptation to escape, only to regret her decision when Sir Michael won the battle to partner her at whist. She soon came to the conclusion that she would rather have taken her chances with her antagonist. Whist was a game she enjoyed and played well, but at which she and her partner fared disastrously, entirely due to the fact that Sir Michael's attention was all for her, leaving little to spare for his cards.

The evening eventually drew to a close, but only after she had reluctantly accepted the offer of Charles's company to ride to the meet with her the following day. It was an offer made by her cousin in response to much prompting and hint-dropping by her godfather; an offer Charles appeared as reluctant to make as Abby was to accept it. Charles enjoyed hunting enormously and the paltry excuse he offered for not riding to hounds the next day, just because his own hunter had not yet arrived was, to Abby's ears, just that: a miserable stratagem. A definite contrivance to be alone with her if ever she heard one, since everyone knew she had a splendid string of hunters here at the lodge, which were entirely at her guests' disposal.

Something else occurred to Abby as she was preparing to retire; something she had not realized before and which gave her pause. Charles was not interested in pursuing her, his heart was definitely not in it, and he was clearly only doing so at his father's behest. Now that was interesting! Something she must relate to Sebastian as soon as she had the opportunity. It also raised a whole new range of possibilities. Why was Lord Wilsden so anxious to have Abby married to Charles? Was it because he wished to form a permanent connection with the only remaining relative of his best friend? It seemed a rather tenuous explanation, since Abby was on the best of terms with Lord Wilsden, but she could think of no other reason. What she did know, however, was that she would bear Sebastian's warning in mind and take her own groom with her when she rode with her cousin on the morrow. Not for one moment did she suspect Charles of culpability — he was far too lazy and not nearly clever enough to dream up the scheme — but still, she could not risk exposing herself to any danger, however slight.

Charles made not the slightest objection to Abby's groom accompanying them, a circumstance which gave Abby heart, since she particularly did not want Charles to be involved in the plot against her as she was inordinately fond of him. She watched carefully as her dapple-grey mare, Sonnet, was saddled. She checked the girth herself, leaning her weight on the saddle to ensure that nothing had been placed beneath it, and carefully examined the stitching on her bridle before mounting. Charles raised a brow in evident amusement as he observed these precautions.

'Lightning don't strike in the same place twice, Abby,' he remarked.

'What do you mean?'

'Lord, Abby, you employ enough grooms and what have you, to make a chap's head spin. I can't begin to imagine the scolding that was dished out when your saddle slipped that day on our estate. Rest assured, no one will be that negligent with you again; not if they value their livelihoods.' He lifted her into the saddle, offering her a raffish grin. 'Now come on, let's go see the fun.'

'Race you there!' challenged Abby, abandoning all caution, her eyes flashing with spirited rebellion as she cantered from the yard.

As they set off, Charles became himself again; the young man whose company Abby found so conducive. He tore along at her side, laughing across at her, obviously not prepared to give any quarter, as most gentlemen in his position would have done, for which Abby was grateful. Away from his father's influence he relaxed, chatted to her amiably enough and made no attempt to flirt with her.

At the meet an atmosphere of anticipation fizzled, stirring Abby's blood but adding to her regret that she could not form part of this most traditional of events: the opening meet of the season. The pink of the huntsmen's coats; the baying of the hounds, fresh and anxious for the off; the horses, caught up in the excitement, too, pawing at the ground and fighting their riders for their heads; the cheerful exchange of greetings as the stirrup cup was passed; intense discussions about the conditions underfoot: all of these things combined to make her feel like an outsider, excluded and unnoticed on her own land.

Some people did observe her arrival and enquired if she intended to take to the field. When she replied in the negative, they mostly lost interest in her. Even Lord Evans had little time to spare for her; such was his enjoyment in the sport. When the master blew his horn to signal the off Abby did not wait to see them go. Instead, depressed, she turned Sonnet and headed in the direction of home. She should not have come: it only made her more aware of the crippling restrictions placed upon her.

Abby endured the rest of the day, taking refuge in her sitting-room, where she was joined by her aunt and cousin, who had little interest in any topic of conversation other than Bea's forthcoming wedding. Abby tried to join in, but knew she was making a poor show of taking an interest in a subject which had already been exhausted between them. She also felt morose and restless. Mr Graves was pacing the house like a caged tiger, just waiting for her to appear. He would not dare to invade her privacy in this room, but anywhere else in the house she would be considered fair game and politeness would dictate she bear him company, falling prey to his well-meant attempts to make an impression upon her.

It was only as she dressed for dinner that evening that her mood lightened. Somehow she knew that Sebastian would appear before the end of the meal. Abby took great care in the selection of her gown, already berating herself for her foolishness, but donning her new silver-blue brocade just the same. Sally brushed her hair until it shone and then secured it at her nape with a simple diamond clip, leaving it loose to bounce about her shoulders, framing her lovely face and accentuating her sparkling eyes.

She delayed her entrance to the drawing-room, where the rest of the party was already gathered, and was gratified by the reception she received. Once again Lord Evans elected himself as her protector, but she mostly ignored him and listened with genuine interest, but less than half of her attention, to the others, who were discussing the day's sport.

And she listened for the sound of wheels on gravel, too.

In spite of her alertness, she did not hear Sebastian when he actually arrived. It was only when she detected a commotion, and unfamiliar male tones, coming from the hall that she realized he was here at last. She felt the colour flooding her cheeks and made a huge effort to remain calm. The door opened, everyone naturally turned towards it and watched as Abby's butler approached her uncle, presenting him with a card upon a silver salver. Lord Bevan took the card, his face reflecting surprise as he read the name printed upon it.

'My dear,' he said to Abby, 'it would appear that we have an unexpected guest to whom we must extend our hospitality. Lord Denver's coachman has been taken suddenly ill and they seek shelter beneath our roof.'

7

Gasps of astonishment preceded the hush which fell over the company.

'Now this should be entertaining,' predicted Charles in a cheerful undertone to his brother.

'It should certainly liven up the proceedings,' agreed Gerald, glancing at Abby. 'Think what you like about the man but life is never dull when Denver's abroad.'

'Do not keep Lord Denver standing about in the draughty hall, Rogers,' said Lord Bevan, with a smile of reassurance for Abby. 'Show him in at once.'

Before the occupants of the drawing-room had the opportunity to recover from their collective surprise, or to comment upon the awkwardness of the situation from Abby's perspective, Lord Denver strolled across the threshold and headed towards Lord Bevan. Lord Evans took up a position close to Abby.

'Do not concern yourself about the man's presence, m'dear, but in all Christian charity your uncle cannot avoid inviting him to join our party; at least until his man has recovered. I realize you have the good sense to mistrust him and that for someone who possesses such a sensitive nature as yours there must be a degree of embarrassment when you recall your last meeting. But, rest assured, his tenure beneath your roof is likely to be of short duration. I cannot persuade myself that his coachman is afflicted with anything other than the most trifling of ailments. However, you may rest easy in the knowledge that I shall be on hand to protect you from Denver's scathing tongue.'

Abby suppressed the urge to stamp her foot in frustration. The last thing she required was Lord Evans's protection and, knowing he was more than capable of making good his intention to remain beside her, saw any opportunities she might otherwise have contrived for private discourse with Sebastian rapidly slipping away. All that aside, Lord Evans's attitude irked her. Lifting her chin in a manner that he should have known spelt trouble, she delivered a prettily worded rejoinder.

'I thank you, my lord, but no such sacrifice on your part is necessary, I do assure you. I am well able to withstand Lord Denver's scrutiny. Besides, he is now a guest in *my* house and, I dare say, too well mannered to mention that which is best forgotten.'

'M'dear, I did not mean to imply — '

But Abby, acutely aware of Sebastian's gaze resting upon her, never did discover what Lord Evans did not mean to imply, since she was no longer paying him any heed. Her attention was all for Lord Denver; she could not help herself. His demeanour was charming as he was made welcome by her uncle and aunt, the latter of whom was going out of her way to assure him that his presence was of no inconvenience whatsoever.

'Your coachman will receive the best possible treatment for his maladies whilst he remains beneath this roof,' finished Aunt Constance, who looked rather flustered.

'I am indebted to you, ma'am,' responded Sebastian with a dashing bow.

Belatedly aware that the rest of the party were openly observing her, Abby's courage rose to the occasion. She ignored the feeling of exhilaration which Sebastian's arrival had engendered and stepped forward to greet his lordship.

'Lord Denver,' she said, dropping into a curtsey. 'I trust the illness that your coachman has unfortunately contracted is not of a serious nature?' Abby regretted the words as soon as they escaped her lips, since she was certain that the devilish mood which had taken her over must be apparent in her expression. Everyone was still watching her closely, and she was conscious of their surprised reaction to her gracious reception of a man they supposed her to dislike. Schooling her features into an impassive expression she spoke again. 'Our housekeeper is an expert with herbal remedies and you may rest easy in the knowledge that whatever ails your man will be speedily identified by her. She will have him back on his feet in no time at all.'

She realized her expression must still be giving her away when Sebastian smiled a warning into her eyes: eyes which she suspected were alight not only with mischief, but relief too, at finally having this most unlikely of protectors beneath her roof.

'Thank you, Lady Abigail. It is an inconvenience to me that Hodges should choose such an inopportune time to become unwell, I cannot deny the fact.'

'I dare say it is a trifle disagreeable for him, too,' responded Abby mischievously, 'but I wager he did not do so simply to disoblige you.'

'I dare say he did not,' drawled Sebastian, choosing to frown a warning at her on this occasion. 'Nevertheless, if he must be ill at all, it is fortunate for him that his care has fallen into the hands of your most capable-sounding housekeeper.'

Sebastian was claimed then by her aunt, who made the introductions to those in the company not already known to him. Abby observed him as he circulated the room, perfectly at his ease, the air of insouciance she had detected in his manner on more than one occasion replaced now by an unreadable mask as he dispensed gallantry and charm with an even hand. If the sigh which escaped Laura Graves, now standing at Abby's side, was anything to judge by, then Abby was not the only lady in the room who found herself overwhelmed by his presence. This was confirmed as each lady straightened her spine and polished up her smile when it was her turn to be introduced. The gentlemen — in spite of the comments they had made about him the previous day — appeared, almost to a man, to be seeking his ear for a variety of reasons that Abby did not comprehend.

Apparently oblivious to the stir he was creating, Sebastian moved about the room, his quicksilver charm and dry wit apparently inexhaustible. The lithesome grace which commanded his movements was all the more impressive since it clearly owed nothing to contrivance and everything to an innate natural elegance. Abby had never met anyone quite like him. He fascinated her: not least because danger and intrigue appeared to follow in his wake, only adding to his attractiveness.

Having him firmly ensconced amongst them made Abby feel giddy with relief as she surrendered responsibility for her well-being into his hands, supremely confident in his ability to keep her safe.

'Were you out of your senses, Abby,' enquired Laura softly, as she leaned towards her ear, 'to refuse to dance with such a man?' Laura chuckled in a decidedly unladylike manner. 'Just give me the opportunity, that's all I ask!'

'Laura!' exclaimed Abby, amused and annoyed at the same time by the man's ability to charm absolutely everyone he met so effortlessly.

'Well, you must admit that we have never encountered anyone quite so sophisticated before, what with being hidden away in Cornwall all the time.'

'True,' agreed Abby contemplatively, 'but the gentleman is far too full of his own importance and deserved to be put down.'

'Well,' mused Laura, 'from the way he is surreptitiously observing you, I can see that by denying him you have also managed to excite his curiosity. Are you sure that you are not in league in some way?'

'What do you mean?' cried Abby, alarmed

that her perspicacious friend might somehow have detected Sebastian's true purpose for being here.

Laura shot her an appraising glance. 'Fear not, Abby, I know nothing to your discredit. I was merely speaking in jest.'

All the same, Laura continued to contemplate her in thoughtful silence for what seemed like an age and Abby was only saved from further embarrassment by the announcement that dinner was served.

* * *

Sebastian escorted Lady Bevan into the meal but was seated too far away from Abby for there to be any possibility of conversation between them. He had deliberately intended that it should be so. He had observed suspicion on the faces of some of the gentlemen at his unexpected arrival; especially Lord Evans's. That gentleman had stuck as closely to Abby as the proprieties permitted, and had escorted her into dinner. When Sebastian made no attempt to single out Abby, though, he could sense a slight lessening in the antagonistic attitude he had detected earlier and would contrive an opportunity for private conversation with her only when the rest of the company had relaxed its collective guard.

Upon entering the drawing-room his eyes had automatically sought Abby out and he had scarce been able to disguise his relief at seeing her hale and hearty. Other than being able to assure him that she had been in perfect health upon arrival at her hunting box, the spies Sebastian had set to observe her movements had been worse than useless. They had been unable to gain access to the well-guarded estate itself to continue their watch over her and the twenty-four hours Sebastian had deemed it wise to wait before presenting himself had felt like the longest period of his life. A man of action, he hated to be idle, even if his enforced stay in town had produced some very interesting information from Anthony Deverill in respect of the loans made to Lord Wilsden, and the purpose for which they had been granted.

His reaction to the sight of Abby had rocked him to his toes. She looked excessively beautiful and perfectly composed, but the relief that flashed through her eyes as she observed him enter the room did strange things to him. She was clearly still terrified of what might lie in wait for her, but could not keep the mischievous expression from her eyes when she addressed him. Much as he enjoyed this latest display of her spontaneity, she had been foolishly incautious: something Sebastian would warn her about as soon as he had the opportunity to speak with her alone.

The card tables were not placed this evening and when the gentlemen rejoined the ladies the instrument was opened. Beatrice, Elizabeth and Laura succeeded one another and entertained the company with performances that were, thankfully, both light-hearted and well executed. Whilst Laura played, Sebastian took the opportunity to move beside Abby, who was seated at the rear of the room, Lord Evans predictably at her side. He stiffened as he observed Sebastian's approach and made a great show of patting Abby's hand. Sebastian stifled a snort of amusement, already sufficiently in tune with her character to appreciate her likely response to such an overt display of possessiveness, and accepted the seat which Abby indicated to him on her other side.

'Are we to look forward to your performance next, Lady Abigail?' he enquired, deliberately pitching his voice so low that Evans could not hear him.

'Alas, no. I fear I do not play.'

'I am astounded.'

Her eyes twinkled with a liveliness which she appeared to reserve just for him. 'I wish it were otherwise but, lamentably, three of the best music instructors in succession have quite given up on me as a hopeless case.'

'Then, doubtless you compensate by having an excellent singing voice?'

'Whenever I open my mouth to sing I succeed only in making the dogs howl.'

'Then your talents must be of an artistic nature. Presumably you paint and sketch?'

'Regrettably not.' Sebastian raised a brow in mock astonishment. 'I once attempted to capture Beatrice's likeness, but when she saw the result she quite took offence and did not speak to me for a full two days.'

'I have it!' exclaimed Sebastian, matching her devilish mood and not caring who noticed. 'You embroider beautifully and provide half your households with fire screens and exquisite linens.'

Abby shook her head, a saucy smile on her lips. 'I fear that my aunt and cousin have quite given up on me in that regard, too. I cannot seem to set a stitch without first attaching it to my finger. I applaud your efforts to find an occupation that I lend distinction to but unfortunately, Lord Denver, I think it only fair to warn you that you are destined to failure.'

'I cannot accept that,' he responded, his voice now easily carrying to Lord Evans. 'You are too modest. There must be something you are not revealing.'

'Indeed, with all my advantages it ought to be the case, but to my mortification I cannot think of a thing.'

'Unless, that is,' put in Lord Evans, 'you discount the fact that Lady Abigail speaks four languages fluently, has a passion for, and extensive knowledge of, Greek mythology, and an aptitude for mathematics that would put most gentlemen to shame.'

'Fie, Lord Evans!' cried Abby, causing Sebastian to suppose that she did everything she could to disguise her passion for pursuits that were considered unsuitable for a lady. 'I was unaware that you were privy to such information.'

'I am the possessor of a great deal of charming information about your abilities, m'dear,' he said, lowering his voice to an intimate drawl which merely served to amuse Sebastian since there was a decided air of desperation about it.

'Then you will also be aware,' she responded haughtily, 'that such matters are not for general discussion. My aunt has often impressed upon me that it is not at all proper to boast of such talents, or even to mention them in polite society at all, for that matter.'

'For fear of discouraging gentlemen of

lesser ability, presumably?' suggested Sebastian in fluent Greek, correctly surmising that if she was passionate about Greek mythology that it was most likely one of the languages she spoke. As he did so he laughed with genuine mirth at the thought of callow youths sensitive enough to feel threatened by her intellect: all too aware that many would be so.

'I fear so,' agreed Abby, proving his earlier assumption correct when she responded in Greek as fluent as his own, leaving Lord Evans with an angry frown upon his face.

Lady Bevan chose that moment to invite Lord Evans to sing, a request which in all politeness he could not ignore, and Abby and Sebastian were, at last, left alone.

'I am relieved to see you here in such robust health, Lady Abigail,' he whispered.

'You would have been impressed with the way I adhered to your instructions, had you been in a position to observe my behaviour over the past few days for yourself,' she assured him, unaware that a note of faint injury had entered her voice.

'Indeed?' he remarked in a lackadaisical drawl. 'Then pray do enlighten me as to why you became detached from the rest of your party in the park last Thursday and walked with just Mr Braithwaite for company?'

'Where did you gain that intelligence?' she

queried, her voice rising.

Several heads turned in their direction and Sebastian silenced her with a warning look. 'You imagine that I left you unprotected?'

'You were having me watched?'

'Naturally!'

'Mr Braithwaite is an old acquaintance of my aunt's. He has never visited us in Cornwall and was not present at any of the attempts on my life, and so I was confident that he could not be involved. We were discussing the newest botanic gardens at Kew, upon which he is an authority. What possible risk could he represent to me?'

'Braithwaite is a renowned botanist, it is true, but what you may not be aware of is that he also has pockets to let. Never underestimate what a man might do to obtain funds, Lady Abigail, especially when he is passionate about a pursuit and requires the blunt to maintain his interest.'

'You suspect Mr Braithwaite of being in league with my enemies?'

'I have no reason to suspect Braithwaite: I am merely demonstrating a point.'

'All right, sir, but would it not have been easier, rather than going to the trouble of having me watched, for you simply to attend the same assemblies as me?'

'What, events I would not normally be seen

dead at?' he asked in a horrified tone. 'What purpose do you imagine that might serve, other than to alert your enemy to a possible connection between us?'

'Oh yes, I did not think.'

She faced him with admiration she was too inexperienced to conceal shining from her eyes. Sebastian's body reacted instinctively and he cursed under his breath. He needed to keep his wits about him if he was to keep her alive and the effect her guileless innocence appeared determined to inflict upon him was the sort of distraction he could well do without.

'It was ingenious of you, my lord, to hit upon the idea of having your coachman be taken ill. But will he be convincing, do you suppose?'

Sebastian's lips quirked. Hodges was far more than a mere coachman: he was Sebastian's right-hand man and had been his eyes and ears during those exhilarating years he had spent spying for Wellington. He had helped his master escape from tight situations on more than one occasion and had been responsible for saving his life at least twice. He now acted as Sebastian's coachman, general purveyor of information and substitute valet. It was he who had arranged for a watch to be kept over Abby. In all their years together though, agreeing to feign a complaint of the stomach was the first time Sebastian could recall him voicing serious objections to one of his schemes: Hodges was inordinately fond of his rations.

'Hodges will not be found wanting. He is suffering from severe stomach cramps even as we speak.'

'Oh dear!' sighed Abby, her eyes brimming with laughter.

'What is so amusing?'

'Poor Mr Hodges! I was once the unfortunate recipient of Mrs Burton's herbal remedy for an upset constitution. I am mightily relieved that I am not in Mr Hodges's situation. Nothing could ever compel me to ingest such an evil potion again.'

'Fear not. We planned our campaign well. Hodges will not drink any remedies given to him; he is a master at dissimulation.'

'But will he not be hungry?'

'We thought of that, too. He has supplies hidden in the folds of his driving coat.'

'Ah good, but I will see if I can procure something a little more substantial for him and arrange for it to be sent to his quarters when the household has retired.'

'Believe me, if you can manage that then Hodges will lay down his very life for you.

There is no faster way to that particular man's heart than through his stomach.'

'Leave it to me, then. But, my lord, we must talk privately. I have gained some intelligence which I am anxious to share with you.'

Sebastian held up his hand in warning. 'Not here!'

Lord Evans had completed his song, was politely declining to entertain the company with another and casting frequent glances in Abby's direction. Others, too, were looking towards them with increasing frequency, presumably wondering what two people who disliked one another found to talk about in such an animated fashion. Noticing it, Sebastian realized that he had made an elementary error, and cursed his stupidity. His pleasure at being in Abby's lively company had caused him to be incautious. He vowed to conduct himself, whilst in public with her, with greater circumspection in future.

'Shall you hunt tomorrow?' he queried.

'You know that I am not permitted to join the field.'

'Good. Everyone will assume Hodges will be recovered by the morrow and that I will depart. Regretfully, I fear he will take a turn for the worse overnight, forcing me to trespass upon your hospitality for a little longer.'

Abby's sympathetic smile would have been quite convincing, had she been able to keep the mischievous glint out of her eye. 'Mrs Burton's cures have sometimes been known to take days before they become effective. But she will not accept defeat and I dare say will not recommend that Mr Hodges departs until he is completely himself again.'

'There you are then. By the time it is discovered that Hodges is still too unwell to travel, the rest of the party will have departed for the hunt. You and I will then be at liberty to ride out together and converse at our leisure.'

'So be it,' she whispered.

8

The heavy sky was insufficient to deter the hunting party from riding over to the next valley the following morning, where they were to be the guests of Lord Braisher, Master of the Mindon Valley Hunt. Charles's hunter had arrived and it was immediately apparent that he did not mean to miss a second day's sport. Anything his father might have had to say on the subject of missed opportunities, or his attempts to bully and then cajole his son into remaining behind to entertain Abby, had clearly fallen upon deaf ears.

All to the good, thought the lady in question, as she waved the hunters a cheerful farewell. Lord Evans was the last to leave, lingering to assure her that Sebastian, a renowned sportsman in his own right, would be anxious to reach his own hunting box and was sure to continue his journey today, whatever the condition of his coachman. He confided to Abby, his tone one of measured reassurance, that he had appraised her uncle as to the inadvisability of having one such as Denver amongst their number, oversetting Abby with his raffish behaviour and total disregard for the proprieties, and had recommended that he offer one of Abby's own grooms to drive his lordship's conveyance on its way. Abby, who was unaware — that is to say a mite disappointed — that Sebastian had not displayed any behaviour of a raffish or unsuitable nature, arched a brow at Lord Evans in frank surprise.

'There is no need to thank me, my dear, I was thinking only of your comfort. You need not fear that you will encounter his lordship during the course of our absence, and feel the need to entertain him, since I am convinced that even now he must be preparing for his departure.' Lord Evans paced the room, his hands clutching the lapels of his beautifully tailored hunting coat. 'The man really does think far too well of himself!' he blurted out. 'Turning young girls' heads with his rather obvious charm, just because he can. He might consider it to be a harmless means of passing the time but he has not stopped to consider that young ladies, ill-used to the habits of the *ton*, might take his flirtatious manner seriously, causing them to harbour unrealistic expectations, forgetting to whom they owe their duty and neglecting their other guests. Really, it is just as well that he will soon be on his way, or else I should not be able to help giving him a piece of my mind.'

Abby was rendered speechless by this display of interference, so unlike the man she thought she knew, and could only gape at him in astonishment: a circumstance which he clearly misinterpreted as gratitude, causing him to depart with a smile on his lips.

Alone now in the dining-parlour, since the ladies not forming part of the hunting party breakfasted in their chambers, Abby toyed with a slice of toast and wondered when Sebastian would put in an appearance. She did not have to speculate upon the matter for long since the door opened almost as soon as Lord Evans quit the room and Sebastian, resplendent in a blue coat and patterned silk waistcoat, stood before her. Ignoring the surge of excitement that lanced through her veins, she concentrated instead upon his brooding expression, and the merest tantalizing hint of challenge she thought she could detect in his eye, as he bade her good morning.

'Good morning, my lord,' she responded evenly. 'I trust you slept well?'

'I thank you, yes.'

'And how is poor Mr Hodges this morning?'

'I regret to say that his condition has not improved.'

'Oh dear!' remarked Abby, refusing to meet

his eye, being conscious of the servants in the room and knowing they would be listening to their conversation with avid interest. 'But I did warn you that Mrs Burton's remedies often take time to become effective.'

'Indeed you did.' Sebastian strolled towards the sideboard, which contained an extensive array of covered dishes for his inspection, and devoted his attention to the selection of a substantial breakfast. Satisfied, he returned to the table and seated himself directly opposite Abby. 'Your uncle kindly offered me the loan of one of your grooms to drive me to my hunting box,' he informed her quietly. 'He was concerned that I would be missing the best of the sport, what with it being the opening week of the season. He suggested that Hodges remain here until he is recovered, and that your groom should return with my carriage for Hodges to drive on when he is recovered.' Sebastian paused and moved a fork laden with sausage towards his mouth. 'You know,' he remarked in a speculative tone when he had finished chewing, 'if I did not know better, I would think that someone was anxious to be rid of me.'

'Lord Evans,' responded Abby with asperity. 'What makes you say that?'

Abby related the substance of her earlier

conversation with that gentleman. 'He did appear most anxious that you get to your hunting box,' she remarked, thinking it better to keep to herself his lordship's less generous remarks in respect of Sebastian's character.

'I dare say he would not be sorry to see me gone, leaving the field clear for him.'

'What do you mean?' Abby's eyes opened very wide as a startling thought occurred to her. 'Surely you do not suspect Lord Evans of wishing me ill?'

'Not at all.'

'Then pray tell me what is in your mind.'

Sebastian regarded her for some time before responding. 'He will perhaps be pleased to see me gone, since he will no longer have serious competition for your favours: at least whilst you are under the same roof together,' he suggested at length.

Abby blushed scarlet to the roots of her hair. Sebastian observed her with amusement, and a mounting desire to pull her into his arms and kiss her witless. His hands itched to caress those enticing curves of hers, which even her high-necked morning gown made a poor job of concealing. Remonstrating with himself, he returned his attention to his breakfast.

'Are you planning to ride this morning?' he enquired.

'I was about to change for that very purpose.'

'Then if you can provide me with a mount from your stables I should be pleased to accompany you.'

'But, of course!'

Abby excused herself, motioning Sebastian back into his chair when he made to stand, and headed for her chamber.

It was discovered, upon arrival at the stables, that all of Abby's string had been claimed by her guests, whose own mounts had suffered a series of mishaps the previous day — a lost shoe, a case of a strained fetlock and one of an open saddle sore. The only mount remaining was Warrior, an irascible stallion whom few could master and who was in a particularly foul mood, since he had just recovered from a swollen hock but had not been considered sound enough to withstand a full day's hunting. The creature in question took singular exception to his exclusion and was kicking at his stable door like a beast demented, tossing his head and rearing up when any of the lads attempted to approach him. He had energy to expend, clearly resented being cooped up and was in danger of inflicting further injury upon himself if he continued with his rebellious behaviour.

'Let me have a look at him?' said Sebastian.

'I would not recommend it, my lord,' caution the head groom. 'He can be a tricky devil when he's riled.'

Nodding his understanding Sebastian stationed himself sideways-on in front of Warrior's door, just out of range of his wildly snapping teeth. He made no attempt to touch the horse but simply stood stock still, whispering quietly to the animal, his eyes lowered and unthreatening. Warrior appeared to understand that this latest human wasn't about to be intimidated and his irritation gradually turned to curiosity. He stopped attempting to remove chunks of Sebastian's arm and instead dropped his head, snorting his confusion, weaving to and fro in the confined space of his box. Sebastian continued to speak soothingly to the horse and offered him the flat of his hand, which Warrior inspected thoroughly. Having satisfied himself that Sebastian passed muster, Warrior permitted him to enter the box and place a saddle on his back.

'Stay here for a moment,' he said to Abby, as he led the horse out.

Abby nodded her agreement. 'Take care,' she cautioned, as Sebastian prepared to mount. 'He has a tendency to deposit all his would-be riders on the ground.'

He flashed her a cocky grin and swung his leg over the horse's back. Warrior took off at a flat-out gallop before Sebastian could secure his second foot in the stirrups. Sebastian made no move to check him and simply sat firmly in the saddle, permitting Warrior to run in the direction of the open paddock gate. Confused not to be confronted by the battle of wills he had obviously expected, Warrior lowered his head and put in an almighty buck, which lifted Sebastian, still with only one foot in the stirrups, straight into the air. A collective groan emanated from Abby and the gaggle of grooms who were watching the display: there could be only one outcome to this confrontation.

But amazingly Sebastian maintained his seat. With a roguish grin he scrambled to find his other stirrup and, with a slight twitch of the reins, turned Warrior in the opposite direction. They were now circling the paddock with the horse leading with his off-fore, the direction which he did not favour, causing his flat-out gallop to slow to a more manageable canter. Gradually Sebastian reined him in. His calm acceptance of the stallion's bad behaviour caused the horse to remember his manners at last and when Sebastian asked him to slow to a trot he complied with something akin to docility.

'That was very impressive, my lord,' remarked the head groom, who was standing at the gate beside Abby.

'Are you ready to ride now?' she enquired sweetly, clearly having no intention of advising him whether she, too, had been impressed. Heading for the mounting block she sprang lightly into Sonnet's saddle and preceded him from the yard.

'Do you wish to ride to the next valley and watch them move off?'

'No!' responded Abby without hesitation.

'But why? I was of the opinion that you enjoyed the spectacle.'

'I did, once. But I discovered yesterday that it has lost its allure. What is the point if I cannot participate?'

Sebastian experienced a moment's sympathy for the chit as she struggled to conceal the extent of her disappointment. All of the ladies in residence at her hunting lodge, with the exception of Abby's aunt and cousin, had taken to the field today, even Mary, the rector's wife. Sebastian had observed their departure from his chamber window. Having now seen how at home Abby was in the saddle he was prepared to wager that she was a far superior horsewoman to any of her guests and was of the opinion that Lord

Bevan's well-meant caution in respect of his niece's safety was a mite stringent.

Sebastian did not voice his thoughts and made do with inclining his head in compliance with her wishes. But he had made up his mind. Today, just for an hour or two, Abby would forget all about the restrictions placed upon her; about duty, honour and expectation; about the people who looked upon her with murderous intent, too. Instead she would disregard the rules and enjoy being carefree, with nothing more taxing on her mind than the obstacles she would soon be asking Sonnet to clear.

Today she would cease to be an outsider and would follow the hunt.

'Which coverts are they likely to draw first?' he enquired innocently.

'The tradition is to move south, towards the edge of our land here, and follow the trail to Finders Bottom.'

'I see.'

They rode along side by side, Sebastian seeking ways to distract himself from the growing attraction he felt towards this most unlikely of females, whose haunting beauty had been responsible for his recently disturbed repose. Annoyed by his apparent inability to dislodge images of her flashing eyes from his sub-conscious, Sebastian placed the blame squarely at her door. Indeed, whenever she appeared at her most vulnerable, as she did at that moment, he was powerless to prevent his mind from wandering in any number of grossly unsuitable directions. He reminded himself that he had one purpose, and one purpose only, for being here and vowed anew to discover the identify of her foe, without inventing reasons to procrastinate. He would ensure her safety, remove himself from her life and forget all about her.

'But tell me,' he said to her now, 'you have information to impart, I believe you said.'

'Yes, about my cousin, Charles.'

'Go on,' he encouraged, when her words trailed to an abrupt halt.

'Well, it probably means nothing at all.'

'And I cannot know what it means unless you tell me. Lady Abigail, you must think it important, otherwise you would not have mentioned it.'

'All right.' She turned to look at him, the quiet strength of character he now knew she possessed evident in her expression. 'You will recall my telling you that my cousin has, on two occasions, tried to alter the nature of our relationship by attempting intimacies?'

'Indeed, he of the wet fish kisses, if memory serves.'

She offered him an impish grin. 'Quite! But

when my godfather and his family arrived yesterday I noticed the strangest thing. Charles had no particular wish to single me out — '

'A fact that would have been immediately apparent to you, since the rest of the unattached gentlemen, I venture to wager, most certainly did.'

'Well, yes, but that is not the point.'

'Then what is?'

'It was my godfather who quite blatantly pushed Charles in my direction, even insisting that he miss the opening meet yesterday in order to remain with me. It was obvious that he would have much preferred to take to the field and, what is more, as soon as we were alone together we immediately fell back into our friendly relationship of old, with no attempts on his part to flirt with me and, thankfully, no kissing!'

'Now that is interesting, Lady Abigail! Well done for making the connection.'

'But what does it all mean?'

'That your godfather wishes you to make an alliance with his son.'

'Yes, even I had managed to comprehend that much,' she informed him, with a haughty toss of her head. 'But why?'

'Why indeed?'

Sebastian considered this latest news, in

conjunction with the information Anthony had supplied about the purpose of Lord Wilsden's loans from the duchy, wondering if there could be a connection. But none of it made sense to him. Yet.

Abby gasped with surprise. Sebastian had deliberately engaged her attention so comprehensively that she had only just realized they had taken a path that would lead directly towards the first covert the hunt was likely to draw. The distant sound of the field in full cry caused her to look at Sebastian in confusion.

'We have taken the wrong path,' she said, making to turn back.

'Not if you wish to join the chase.'

'You know very well that is not permitted.'

'Do you always do as you are bid?' he asked her lazily, a taunting edge to his voice. He observed hunger for excitement in her expression as she gazed her regret in the direction of the field. Her blood was up and there could be no doubt that she wanted to be part of the chase. He suspected it would not take much for her to capitulate and did not hesitate to push home his advantage. 'Who will notice if we join the back of the field for an hour? Come, Abby,' he whispered, his voice a provocative challenge as her name escaped his lips for the first time. 'Shake off the shackles and be yourself for a while. Your uncle is right to protect you, but he has overestimated the dangers of the hunting field. You are a far better horsewoman than all of your female guests and you will come to no harm; not with me at your side.'

'But what if I am observed?' she asked, biting her lip with indecision.

'There will be too much confusion down there for anyone to take notice of us.' He could see that she was still vacillating and openly goaded her. 'Come, Abby, where is your courage? What has become of the young lady who not only risked her all by calling alone at a single gentleman's house, but also dared to accept his kiss?' He broke off and devoured her features with eyes that unquestionably wanted, forcing her to return his gaze. 'The young lady,' he continued softly, when he was satisfied that he had her full attention, 'who enjoyed being in that gentleman's arms.'

Abby, making no attempt to deny that she had enjoyed his embrace, appeared to come to a decision. Lifting her chin she offered him a riotous smile and spontaneously spurred Sonnet forward.

'What are we waiting for?' she asked, turning back to laugh at him over her shoulder.

Catching up with her, Sebastian ensured

that they remained at the back of the field and watched her closely. He suspected this was the first time in her life, apart from calling upon him in London, when she had flagrantly disregarded the rules laid down for her protection, and he could see at a glance that she was enjoying the experience enormously. She sat erect in her side-saddle, clearing hedges and open ditches with elegance and style; the occasional whoop of pleasure escaping her lips as she landed safely and caught his eye, sharing her exhilaration with him. No one existed in Sebastian's universe at that moment, except Abby. Her face was flushed with excitement, her eyes glowing with triumph. Sebastian's attention was caught by her breasts, rising and falling against the tight confines of her habit as she fought for breath. He was staring at her, compelled by the picture she presented, his manhood responding to her unconscious display of femininity: something stronger than his own will preventing him from looking away.

They were approaching of an especially high obstacle — a hawthorn hedge that had not been cropped — which forced his attention back to the field. Many riders were going round the side, or coming spectacularly to grief. Sebastian noticed that virtually all of the ladies had chosen to take the safer route and indicated to Abby that she should do the same. But, fully committed now, she was having none of it.

'I may never get an opportunity to do this again,' she yelled to him across the distance that separated them. 'And so I do not intend to waste this one. Sonnet can clear that hedge easily!' she assured him, her laughing eyes brimming with confidence.

Sighing at her stubbornness, and wondering now if he had acted wisely by encouraging her to rebel, Sebastian's worries were compounded when he noticed that those who had attempted the hedge had naturally converged on the lower end, and consequently there was now a tangle of fallen riders littering the ground. He and Abby would have no choice but to aim for the high part of the hedge. He turned Warrior in that direction and with Abby at his side they set the horses at the obstacle on a collected stride. Both of them cleared it with ease.

It was only as Warrior's hoofs hit the ground that Sebastian glanced to one side and noticed that one of the fallers at the fence was not a stranger to him. Lord Evans was even then picking himself up, his breeches caked with mud and his coat torn. Annoyingly he happened to look up as the last of the horses cleared the hedge. His mouth fell open, slack with shock, as he recognized the familiar figure of Abby streaking away from him, bubbling with laughter, Denver at her side.

Sebastian glanced in Evans's direction and offered him an ironic salute, knowing that Abby's act of rebellion could not now remain a secret and that he would have some awkward explaining to do. But, glancing at her animated features, listening to her musical laughter as it floated towards him, he decided it had been worth it.

9

After the incident at the hawthorn hedge Sebastian deemed it wise to withdraw from the field. Not having seen Evans, Abby was unaware that her presence had been observed and it was with obvious reluctance that she complied. Sebastian scrutinized her as they walked their horses back in the direction of her lodge. She was mud-splattered and dishevelled, but there could be no mistaking the fact that she had enjoyed her moment of rebellion royally. He knew he was unlikely ever to forget the way she had appeared whilst soaring so elegantly over the hedges, displaying a flair for horsemanship which vindicated his decision to join the chase.

He looked heavenwards in an effort to disguise his growing desire and noticed that the clouds which had threatened that morning were darkening and rapidly closing in.

'It looks as though we might have some snow,' he remarked.

'Good, I love snow!'

'Do you now?' he said, smiling softly at her. 'And what so attracts you about it?'

'Oh, I do not know precisely, but it looks so pretty,' she said, sighing. 'And romantic, too, when it covers the trees and turns the landscape into a wonderland of white.'

'Romantic?' questioned Sebastian in amusement. 'I thought there was no room in your life for romantic notions.'

'Remind me never to reveal more of my secret thoughts to you,' she rebuked, turning back to issue this retort and facilitating the accident which tearing hell for leather across the hunting field had been unable to accomplish. A low branch glanced against the back of her head and, with a gasp of surprise, she slid from her saddle and landed on her derrière in the middle of the muddy path they were following.

Sebastian dismounted and was at her side in seconds. 'Abby, are you all right?'

She lifted her head, moved it experimentally from side to side and retrieved her hat, which had also finished up in the mud. She grinned at him in mock reproach.

'That is what happens when you provoke me,' she scolded, her laughter soft and sultry.

As Sebastian had already learned, she was hopelessly inept when it came to concealing the more passionate traits of her character, and it was obvious to him that she was more affected by his close proximity than concerned about the likelihood of having sustained any injuries. He pulled her to her feet and, without pausing to consider the wisdom of his action, into his arms. In spite of her inexperience she should know better than to regard him with such invitation in her eyes.

'And this is what happens when you look at me like that,' he responded, lowering his head. Pulling her closer his lips seared into hers, passion burning like a ravenous hunger through his body as he plundered her mouth, slowly sating his appetite. She made not the slightest attempt to resist his advance, winding her arms around his neck instead and closing her eyes in anticipation.

His swirling tongue probed the recesses of her mouth almost lazily, taking his time to become familiar with the taste of her. Releasing her prematurely, since she appeared to be having some difficulty in drawing breath, he nibbled gently on her lower lip and traced the outline of her mud-stained cheek with his forefinger, his eyes never once leaving her face. As she looked up at him her expression was invested with such a wealth of refreshingly innocent curiosity that his own needs escalated, causing him to regret his impulsive action. He should have known better than to have kissed her: if his friends were to hear of it they would be hugely diverted to discover that an inexperienced chit was so effortlessly holding him in her thrall.

He leaned his back against the tree which had so inconveniently dislodged Abby from her saddle, creating a situation which he ought to have avoided like the plague. But it was too late for thinking: the damage was already done. Never one to waste time on remorse Sebastian pulled her more closely against him, forcing his hands to remain at her waist as he kissed her for a second time.

★　★　★

Abby felt the full force of his lips searing into hers, causing her pulse to quicken and her breath to come out in uneven gasps. Feeling her body responding to his, she was reminded of the dangers of allowing such an experienced sophisticate to enthral her. But, overwhelmed by her surging emotions, the voice of reason went unheeded. She felt dizzy and desperately gulped air from the mouth that covered hers, convinced that he must be able to hear the thud of her heart as it crashed its irregular beat against her ribs. His tongue darted inside her mouth on a fresh sortie, forcing her lips apart ruthlessly,

144

demanding and easily receiving her complete capitulation. It was too much! All thoughts of over-loud heartbeats vacated her mind as a tide of surging pleasure coursed through her, its ambiguous nature transporting her to a place beyond rational thought.

'You have twigs in your hair,' he remarked, gently releasing her as he broke the kiss.

'Have I?'

'Come,' he said, his voice taking on a brisk edge. 'We should get back before the onset of the snow.'

He rounded up the horses, which were grazing on a patch of grass close by. Helping her into her saddle, he mounted Warrior and fell into step beside her.

'You should be aware,' he remarked lightly, 'that due to the grossest misfortune our presence at the chase was observed by Evans.'

'Oh no!' Abby's hand flew to her face, her dazed expression replaced by one of naked alarm. 'Why did you not tell me at the time? This is disastrous! I thought you said we would remain undetected at the back of the field.'

'And so we would have, had Evans not disobliged us by falling at that hawthorn hedge and then chancing to look up just as we were clearing it.'

'I shall be in for it now,' she predicted gloomily.

'That is why I gave you advance warning: to enable you to prepare your explanation. But you must place the blame at my door and convince them that I persuaded you to join the chase against your better judgement.'

'Since you speak nothing less than the truth, that is obviously what I shall tell them,' said Abby with a dignified toss of her head, reconciled to the fact that an ugly scene with her uncle was now inevitable. Knowing how much Lord Evans disapproved of Sebastian, she could hardly hope that he would keep his intelligence of her misdemeanours to himself.

'And they will have no difficulty in believing your account.'

'My uncle will be more concerned by the fact that I rode out with you unescorted.'

'I dare say,' he agreed, grinning raffishly. 'But they will be able to see for themselves that I have not taken advantage of you and ravished your person, tempting though that prospect might be. Besides, no one else need ever be privy to the information that we rode out alone, so no lasting harm has been done. Once your uncle recovers from his annoyance, I feel persuaded that he will see the matter in that light. This is hardly the *ton* and the rules are less stringent in the country.'

'Only to a degree and, besides, Lord Evans is aware that we were alone together.'

'Yes, but it would not suit his purpose to broadcast the fact. And as to your uncle, what other approach can he take, apart from evicting me from the house and ordering you never to speak to me again?'

Sebastian's apparent unconcern at the prospect of being deprived of her company caused a dull ache to take up residence in her breast and her temper to bubble over. 'If he does that,' she said, treating him to a quelling glance, 'then how are we supposed to discover who it is that intends me harm?'

'We shall find a way.'

'Humph, that is easy for you to say!' Really, the man was insufferable. She lifted her chin as they rode into the stable yard and tried for a dignified expression. 'You are far too sure of yourself, my lord.'

'Sebastian,' he whispered in her ear as he placed his hands on her waist and lifted her to the ground.

The first fat snowflakes were falling from the sky as Abby and Sebastian made their way towards the house and he predicted, correctly as it transpired, that by the time the rest of the hunting party returned the snow would be at least two inches thick.

'This is most convenient for our purpose,'

Abby remarked. 'Are you even able to bend the weather conditions to suit your purpose?'

Sebastian's grin was disgustingly wayward. 'I do not have the pleasure of understanding you.'

'You know very well what I mean,' she complained, the train of her riding habit, heavy with mud, making a slow job of following her movements and almost tripping her over as it tangled with her feet. With a squeal of irritation she swung it over her arm, causing wet mud to fly in Sebastian's direction. 'If the weather closes in and makes the roads impassable you will be unable to leave, even if Mr Hodges's condition should happen to improve, providing you with an excellent excuse to remain with us.'

'Hodges will be most gratified,' predicted Sebastian. 'He will be able to make a remarkable recovery and mingle with the rest of your guests' retainers in the servants' hall. You would be amazed how much information is to be gleaned from such a source, if one knows what questions to ask.'

'I dare say.'

'Oh, I almost forgot, Hodges asked me to send his grateful thanks to you for the gift of the chicken pie your maid managed to smuggle to him last night.' Sebastian flashed her a wicked grin. 'And for the gift of the maid herself, for that matter.'

'Sally?' queried Abby, perplexed. 'I trust she did nothing to offend your man?'

Sebastian winked at her. 'I believe she gave complete satisfaction,' he said, looking vastly amused.

'Good, since as you are aware, she is the only person whom I have taken into my confidence in respect of your true reasons for being here. Since she accompanied me to your house, and to my meeting with you in the park, I could scarce do anything less.'

'Indeed, I am sure she is entirely to be trusted.'

'Naturally! She is devoted to me.'

'Hodges also thanks you for the substantial breakfast Sally provided him with this morning,' he added, chuckling.

'He is most welcome. I would not wish for him to be uncomfortable on my account.'

Sebastian's chuckle turned into a rumbling laugh. 'You may rest easy on that score.'

Entering the house by a side door, Abby took advantage of the deserted hallway to scamper up the stairs and change her muddy attire, before she was noticed and awkward questions, the answers to which she would much prefer to delay, were posed to her.

Clean and freshly gowned, Abby joined her aunt and cousin, exchanging covert glances of sympathy with Bea, as her aunt continued to bewail the deterioration in the weather. Anticipating the ructions to come when her presence at the hunt was revealed, Abby sought to ingratiate herself with her aunt by paying particular attention to her unending lamentations about the conditions under foot and the adverse affect they were likely to have upon their guests' abilities to attend Bea's wedding.

'I knew we should have delayed and made it a spring wedding!' she bemoaned so often that even Abby, determined to be on her best behaviour, wanted to scream.

'Calm yourself, Aunt,' soothed Abby, rising to her feet with unusual alacrity when the luncheon gong sounded, 'or you will render yourself unwell. I am sure the arrangements will not be inconvenienced when the time comes.'

'Oh, Abby dear, you are such a comfort to me!' Aunt Constance clutched at her niece's proffered arm as they walked slowly from the room, her jowls wobbling as she continued to mull over her anxieties. 'And how have you occupied your time this morning, my love?'

Abby was able to avoid answering the question she had been dreading by the arrival of Sebastian himself at the door to the dining-room. He bowed to her aunt and, with the suggestion of a wink in Abby's direction, begged permission to escort her into luncheon.

After the meal Aunt Constance retired to her chamber to rest, whilst Bea headed in search of her sketch book. Abby and Sebastian were once again alone.

'I should find some occupation, my lord,' she said, not quite able to meet his eye.

'Sebastian,' he reminded her. 'Say it,' he commanded imperiously, leaning towards her as they traversed the hall together. 'I want to hear my name pass your lips.'

'Certainly not: that would not be at all proper. Let me go!' she hissed, attempting to free herself from the arm that had snaked its way round her waist.

'Say it and I will release you.'

'No!'

His only response was to tighten the arm that held her and cock a challenging brow.

'Oh, all right! Sebastian,' she whispered, feeling the heat rising to her cheeks.

'There, you see, it was not so hard, was it?' Keeping his side of the bargain he removed his arm. 'Now then, what shall we do this afternoon?'

'I am not sure that I should do anything in your company. I am already in enough trouble as it is, thanks to you.'

'Nonsense! Anyway, I am your guest and so it is your responsibility to keep me entertained.' He smiled that annoyingly smug smile of his, clearly confident in the irrefutability of his argument.

She narrowed her eyes at him. 'Should you not be searching for clues, or whatever it is that you do in order to solve mysteries?' she asked in a tone that would have deterred a lesser man from his purpose.

'Not possible until the rest of the party return from their day's sport. It is their attitudes, and behaviour towards you, that I most particularly wish to study. Besides, you will be gratified to learn that Hodges has already made a remarkable recovery and is even now consorting with the other servants. I would wager half my fortune that he will uncover something to interest us before the end of the day.'

They passed the open door to the billiards-room. 'Do you play billiards, Abby?'

'No, of course not! It is for the gentlemen.'

'That is where you are quite wrong,' he told her, steering her into the room and closing the door behind them. 'Several ladies of my acquaintance are very proficient players.'

She offered him a withering glare. 'I daresay they are.'

Sebastian chuckled. 'You have taken to the hunting field for the first time today. Why not continue with your rebellious turn and try your hand at another new game?'

Abby observed the dangerous glint in his eye and could not be entirely certain that he was alluding only to billiards. 'I have better things to do with my time,' she told him haughtily, but could not help biting at her lip with indecision. She was sorely tempted and Sebastian obviously knew it.

'What things? Embroidery, sketching, practising your performance at the pianoforte?'

'Now you are just being ungentlemanly, picking on my lack of accomplishments in such a bold manner.' She turned away from him, hurt that he would choose to use information imparted in a rare moment of spontaneity against her. His hand brushing across her shoulder forced her to turn and face him.

'Not at all, m'dear, I was merely attempting to prove to you that you have no pressing matters awaiting your attention and can, for once, afford the luxury of pleasing yourself.'

'Maybe so, but what makes you suppose I want to play billiards?'

'You want to!'

His erudite expression and tone of voice, which resonated with supreme confidence in his ability to read her mind, made her want to strike him. Even so, the temptation to transgress again, to spend a little more time in the presence of this accomplished roué who could, with one carelessly bestowed kiss, rouse her to a state of such unbridled passion that she was prepared to disregard all her most dearly held principles, was compelling. Making up her mind, even though she knew her decision was not a wise one, she turned to face him and nodded her head.

'Very well, since you insist.'

'Good girl! Now what do you know about the rudiments of the game?'

Upon receiving her confession that she knew little or nothing, Sebastian succinctly outlined the aims, whilst efficiently setting up the balls.

'The skill lies in striking the cue ball crisply, exactly in its centre, whilst lining one's shot up with the pocket one intends to sink the ball into. The key is to hold one's cue correctly. Like this.' He struck the cue ball dead centre, sending a red shooting smartly into the pocket opposite. 'Now come on, you try.' He ushered her to the side of the table and handed her his cue. 'First decide which ball you intend to pot.'

'That one over there, perhaps?' she suggested sweetly, pointing out an easy shot.

'Good choice. Now then, you hold the cue by sliding it between your thumb and index finger, making a groove in your hand for it to rest upon.' She experimented and earned a nod of approval from Sebastian. 'That's right, but it is vital that you look straight down the cue, in the direction that you intend to send the ball.'

'A bit like throwing your heart, metaphorically speaking, over a jump before your horse takes off?'

'Exactly so.'

'What next?' she asked impatiently.

'You must line your body up in accord with the cue. In fact the cue should almost touch your person. Line it up with your chin. No, no, move a little more to your right.'

She did so. 'Is that better?'

'No, you still are not properly aligned.'

Standing behind her he placed his hands on her hips in the most brazen fashion and Abby froze. Her bottom was now within scandalous proximity of his groin. Surely she should put an end to his unseemly conduct? But, feeling his hands gently caressing her hips as he straightened her position, she forgot all about propriety, and tried to concentrate upon the game they were playing, no longer quite so sure that it went by the name of billiards.

'That's better.' His voice, purring in her ear, brought her back to her senses. But not for long. 'A useful way to remember how to line up your shot is to say to yourself chin, breast and hip, since that is the line it should most closely follow.'

Abby gasped, not so much at his outrageous words, but at the fact that he was running his hand down the cue as he spoke, brushing it against the anatomical points in question to emphasize his words. She let the cue fall from her hand, and it hit the floor with a loud clatter as she turned to give him a piece of her mind. It was either that or allow him to continue taking liberties, and Abby could not altogether trust her resolve if she did not call a halt to his amusements immediately. Just the feel of his fingers brushing against the side of her breast was enough to . . . but no, this must stop, now!

'Lord Denver, you really should not — '

'I know,' he said, the penitence in his tone at direct variance to his predatory expression, which allowed not the slightest room for remorse, 'but you only have yourself to blame. You are entirely too enticing for your own good.' She opened her mouth to upbraid him further but he silenced her by picking up her cue and handing it to her. 'Now come on, stop tarrying and try potting that ball instead.'

She scowled at him. 'It might be nothing to you.' Sighing, she turned her scarlet countenance away from him. 'I will attempt to pot the ball only if you agree to stand aside and not touch me.'

'Why? You like me to touch you.' His dark eyes held hers and refused to release them. Spellbound, she could feel them burning into her own, defying her to deny his assertion. She was incapable of doing so and remained silent, a piquant thrill rippling through her as he continued to observe her, incandescent desire reflected in his eyes. 'You did not seem to have any objection in the woods this morning.'

'You took shameful advantage of my misfortune,' she declared hotly, knowing it was untrue. 'I was dazed after my fall and did not know my own mind.'

He raised his hands in surrender. 'All right, Abby, all right, you have my apology and I agree to your terms. Now, about the game, shall you continue?'

Irrationally annoyed that he had given up on her so easily, Abby put all of her irritation into the shot, lining it up with precision and potting the ball cleanly.

'Well done! But that was a rather simple

shot. Try that ball over there next if you really want a challenge.' She attempted to line up for the shot. 'No, no, you are already forgetting what I have taught you; your body is not behind the cue. Come now,' he encouraged, his hands taking possession of her hips once again, 'swing a little more this way. That's right, now aim and slide the cue smoothly, as I have taught you.'

His hand brushed against the side of her breast — and remained there. The breath caught in her throat and, too shocked to move away and give him the trimming he undoubtedly deserved, she remained rooted to the spot, the cue slipping from her hand as she surrendered to his touch. The explosive amalgamation of conflicting emotions which bubbled inside her as his thumb expertly caressed the swell of her breast was beyond anything she had ever before experienced. All thoughts of the inappropriateness of their situation left her head as she unashamedly revelled in the sensations he was deliberately creating within her. Every inch of her body was assailed by wave after wave of dizzying shock, overwhelming her with a torrent of pleasurable feelings.

What did he intend to do next? She should not stay here and compliantly wait to find out; really she should not. But curiosity won the day and she didn't move, willing him to cover her lips with his own as he continued to stir her passions by moving his hands to once again rest on her hips.

On the point of capitulating to whatever he had in mind, some sixth sense, some deep-rooted awareness of duty and propriety, prevented her, but it took every last vestige of her willpower to move out of range of his magical fingers. Not trusting herself to speak, or to reprimand him for a situation which she should never have permitted to develop in the first place, she reclaimed her cue and, putting all her frustration into her shot, lined it up and watched the ball tumble crisply into the opposite pocket.

'Well done, m'dear!' he remarked suavely, as though nothing of an inappropriate nature had occurred between them. 'You have commendable powers of concentration.'

Sebastian looked up as he spoke and espied Lord Evans standing in the now open doorway, wearing an expression which was, if anything, even more outraged than the one he had bestowed upon Sebastian at the hunt.

'Oh dear!'

Abby, who had not yet seen Evans, turned towards Sebastian, smiling victoriously.

'What concerns you, sir?' she asked, observing his angry frown. 'Are you fearful, all of a sudden, that I might be able to best you at this silly game? I am willing to wager . . . '

Sensing a presence behind her, Abby turned and her words trailed off as she too gazed in horror at Lord Evans.

'Now I am really for it!' she predicted to Sebastian in a gloomy undertone. 'And,' she added, waggling an accusatory finger at him, 'it is all your fault.'

10

Abby fled the billiards-room, brushing past Lord Evans without pausing to beg his pardon. Sebastian's languid drawl vaguely registered with her as she made good her escape and she could only hope that his air of unruffled complacency would not further antagonize Lord Evans, causing him to act foolishly in defence of her honour.

'Is there a problem, Evans?' she heard him enquire in a tone of mild derision.

The sound of cue striking ball reached her ears and she could easily imagine the stuporous expression in Sebastian's eyes, too obvious to ignore yet too innocuous to take exception to. Lord Denver had mastered the art of expressive innuendo.

Abby spent an inordinate amount of time attending to her toilette, expecting at any moment to receive a summons to attend her uncle and offer an explanation for her behaviour. When it did not come she could not decide whether she was relieved at the delay, or disappointed not to have got the scolding over with. When she could defer her arrival in the drawing-room no longer she descended the stairs on leaden feet, wishing she had done something to justify her guilty conscience. If she was to be taken to task for behaving improperly with Lord Denver — feeling the full force of this unjust accusation and conveniently forgetting about the two occasions upon which she had permitted him to kiss her — then she rather wished that she had something to truly repent.

Upon entering the room her eyes instinctively sought Sebastian, and easily located him. He must experience difficulty in making himself inconspicuous in a crowd, she decided, because there was something about him: an indefinable something which made it impossible to overlook his sophisticated presence in a room full of equally sophisticated people. Abby could see that he was not making any attempt to draw attention to himself, but she felt mesmerized by him none the less. For her there might just as well have been no one else in the room.

She paused in the doorway, taking a moment to observe him, before her appearance was noticed and she was obliged to enter the fray. He was engaged in conversation with Harold and Mary, the only person to appear perfectly at his ease in a room that was resonating with tension. There was an element of suspicious resentment in the way that some of the other gentlemen darted wary glances in his direction but Sebastian appeared oblivious to their animosity. Abby wondered how it could be so when the charged atmosphere was almost palpable: as though everyone was waiting for something to happen. Surely he must have noticed it?

But Sebastian presented a picture of unruffled calm as he listened to Harold, who was speaking to him in an affable manner, displaying not only his very obvious suitability for his chosen profession, but superiority of breeding, too. The thinly veiled hostility demonstrated towards Sebastian by some of the company had obviously not gone unnoticed by Harold and Abby felt grateful to her perspicacious cousin for going out of his way to make him feel welcome, his actions negating much of the acrimony that seemed to hover in the atmosphere.

Abby persuaded herself that she was reading too much into what had after all only been a moment's scrutiny of her guests. Perhaps her nerves had got the better of her and it was nothing more than the inclement weather, which would keep the company off the hunting field until it improved, that was casting a pall over the proceedings?

She observed Mary smiling almost coquettishly at something Sebastian murmured to her in a private aside and her lips twitched as she accepted that even dear, caring Mary — who had earlier kindly warned Abby to be on her guard when in the presence of such a rogue — was not immune to Sebastian's gallantry.

Uncle Bertram turned at that moment, caught sight of Abby and beamed in her direction. Abby, nervously clenching her fingers around her fan to prevent her hands from shaking, was confused. She understood that her uncle could not take her to task in front of their guests, but she had not expected him to greet her in quite such a convivial manner; not when he must be furious at all he would by now have learned about her conduct during the course of the day.

What was happening? She felt Sebastian's eyes resting upon her, and from the significance of his expression knew he was trying to warn her that something of import had occurred and, in a blinding flash, she understood what it must be: Lord Evans had not chosen to inform her uncle of his discoveries. Not chosen, or had been dissuaded from his purpose by Sebastian? Abby suspected it must be the latter, since Lord Evans's standards never deviated from the rigidly correct and he would have felt honour bound to report what he had seen.

Abby had not considered her suitor's manners in that light before: indeed she had never had occasion to, since her behaviour had always been as punctilious as his own. But now that her eyes had been opened, could she really marry such a man? She looked in Lord Evans's direction, trying to keep the enquiry out of her expression. He was conversing with Laura and Elizabeth but looked over their heads and frowned at Abby, shaking his head in a gesture which managed to convey his disappointment. Then she understood. Sebastian had not persuaded him to keep silent: he had done so for fear of losing favour with her. She experienced only a moment's gratitude before realizing that she was far from exonerated. If nothing else, his lordship's grim expression told her at least that much. What in heaven's name would it cost her to purchase his continued silence? What promises would she be expected to make: what assurances would she be required to give? Irritation superseded the fleeting gratitude she entertained towards him. Whatever she might have done to provoke his displeasure, Lord Evans still presumed too much and his attitude was starting to rankle.

Thrusting her grievances to the back of her

mind, Abby moved to join Harold and Mary, linking arms with the latter, and smiling at Sebastian.

'Lady Abigail.' Sebastian bowed to her with rigid formality but set her senses reeling by offering her a fleeting wink as he raised his head.

'Lord Denver.'

'His lordship has been telling us about his recent visit to Italy,' explained Harold. 'It is a country I have never set foot in but one that boasts such a rich religious history that the desire to experience it first-hand must, I own, tempt any man of God. I would not be averse to making a visit.'

'Nor I,' agreed Mary, with a wistful sigh.

'Mary!' exclaimed Abby, genuinely surprised. 'This is the first time I have ever heard you express the slightest interest in setting foot outside of England.'

'Perhaps but, Abby dear, I would give much to see the wonderful architecture and museums of Florence, travel the canals in Venice and experience the splendours of Rome, which Lord Denver has described for us so eloquently.' She sighed again and looked almost pretty. 'Lord Denver has made it all sound so romantic.'

'I, too, did not know that you yearned for such adventure, my dear,' remarked Harold.

'We can all dream, Harold, but that is all it is, merely a yearning,' said Mary, somewhat acerbically. 'I am well aware that it will likely come to naught.'

Harold looked upon her with genuine concern; as did Abby. They were both well aware that it was quite out of character for Mary to complain, however obliquely. Indeed, she wanted for nothing, was adored by her husband, and it was difficult to imagine that she might have anything to complain about.

'Then one day I will take you, my dear, upon that you have my word.'

'I do not see how you will be able to keep that promise, my dear, but I thank you for making it all the same,' she remarked mildly, her old self again as she curtsied to Sebastian, excused herself and crossed the room in answer to a signal from Lady Bevan.

'What was that all about?' asked Harold, a look of genuine bewilderment upon his face.

'What indeed?' echoed Abby. 'I am quite at a loss to explain it.'

'I must shoulder the blame,' confessed Sebastian, his demeanour one of thoughtfulness rather than contrition. 'Perhaps my descriptions of Italy were a little too colourful and caused your wife to acquire a yearning for foreign travel that I had no right to excite. I apologize if I have overset her, Bevan, and unwittingly created difficulties betwixt you.'

'Think nothing of it, sir. I am sure it is nothing at all. But perhaps, if you will excuse me, I had best ensure that she is all right. She did not look at all the thing just now.' And he bustled off, full of concern for the welfare of his precious spouse.

'Circulate,' whispered Sebastian in Abby's ear, 'we are being observed.'

Abby obeyed, delighting the eagle-eyed Lord Wilsden by joining Charles, who was in the midst of describing to Sir Michael the added complexities of phaeton racing when a high-perched conveyance was involved. Barely pausing to acknowledge Abby's presence, he continued to explain the importance of possessing a perfectly matched pair.

'Knew a chap once who spent a small fortune on a well-bred pair, but they didn't work right together, don't you see. One of them just wouldn't take near-side corners on the right leg. Overset the entire rig and cost the chap another fortune to put it right.' Charlie waved his arms about, almost knocking the glass from Abby's hand in his enthusiasm. Hastily, she backed out of his range. 'It is far more important to make sure your pair are properly schooled, and completely in tune with one another. Flighty horses don't always make the best teams. Give me sturdier beasts, built for endurance, any day. Proved the point this autumn when I beat Fenwick in our race to Brighton. His pair was much better bred but ran out of steam and didn't last the distance.'

'Will you let me drive your pair sometime, Charlie?' asked Abby sweetly, knowing in advance what the answer would be.

'Not a chance, Abby!' he responded with asperity. 'Too dashed valuable, and too much time invested in them, to risk them at a woman's hand.'

'I say!' interposed Sir Michael. 'That's a bit rich. Have a care, Wilsden; I happen to know that Lady Abigail is a first-rate whip.'

'Sorry, Abby,' said Charles, patting her hand but not looking sorry at all. 'I know you are an adequate driver — '

'For a woman? Is that what you were going to say, Charlie?'

He grinned at her and twitched her nose. 'Of course!' he concurred, making her laugh and forget her indignation.

Dinner was announced and Abby congratulated herself at having successfully avoided Lord Evans's efforts to have a private word with her. Her relief was short lived though because he materialized at her side, offering her his arm to escort her in. She had let her guard down whilst sparring with Charles and had not seen him coming. Reluctantly she placed her hand on his sleeve.

Matters were even worse in the dining-room. Sebastian had been claimed by Laura and was at the other end of the table, where he would not be able to help her out of any difficulties. Almost as though he recognized the fact and was using it to extract revenge, Lord Evans played upon her taut emotions by making no immediate mention of all he had observed throughout the day. There were ample opportunities for him to do so, since those around them were engaged in conversations of their own, paying Abby and Lord Evans little attention. A dozen times Abby steeled herself, convinced he would broach the subject at that particular moment. Instead he engaged her in light conversation, saying nothing to offend; nothing that she could take exception to, and seeming to go out of his way to make himself agreeable. If his plan was to string out her nerves then he was succeeding better than he could know; she was as jumpy as a rabbit, had no appetite at all and a concentration span which was inferior to that of Mary's young daughters.

The interminable meal was almost at an end and Abby was starting to relax a little, thinking she might be safe after all. As though reading her mind, Lord Evans chose that very moment to break his silence.

'What were you thinking of, taking to the field with Denver today, when you know your uncle expressly forbids you to hunt?' he asked her in a fierce undertone.

'What makes you suppose I was on the hunting field?'

'Do not make the mistake of thinking that I speak out of turn.' He eyed her with a combination of disapproval, unmistakable affection and annoyingly possessive intent. 'I saw you, and that rogue, with my own eyes. You could have been hurt, Lady Abigail, and I could not bear to think of you being harmed, or worse, just for the sake of a few hours' sport. I suppose he wagered that you did not have the courage?'

'You saw me?' Abby tilted her head, pretending to consider the matter. 'Where? I do not recall the occasion.' She paused and chewed daintily at her lower lip, still feigning misunderstanding. 'Oh, was that you, crumpled on the ground by that unclipped hedge?' She offered him a seraphic smile. 'I do hope you did not sustain any injuries.'

Lord Evans coloured slightly. 'None at all, I thank you. But do not think to change the subject. It is your conduct under scrutiny at this moment. Quite apart from allowing that scapegrace to talk you into hunting, you must also have ridden with him this morning, unaccompanied. That is not something you consent to do, even with me,' he accused her, a note of ill-usage entering his voice. 'You should not — '

'I thank you for your concern,' said Abby, who felt she had displayed commendable restraint and that it was time to call a halt to his lecture, 'but I assure you that nothing of an inappropriate nature occurred and, truth to tell, I had a perfectly splendid time.'

She offered him a smile that did not quite meet her eyes, intended as a warning to leave the subject alone. But Abby had not made allowance for the jealous and possessive nature of a man who sees the object of his passion being wooed away from him on the capricious whim of a scoundrel.

'Nothing inappropriate, you say!' he cried harshly, causing those near him to look round in surprise. He checked himself and continued in a more moderate tone. 'If what I observed in the billiards room is not your idea of inappropriate behaviour it only serves to demonstrate just how comprehensively he has already turned your head.'

'Lord Denver was teaching me to play billiards,' she informed him with an air of composed indifference.

'Is that what he called it?'

'You forget yourself, my lord. You are an old and a valued friend, but I need hardly remind you that my behaviour is none of your concern.'

'A friend. Oh, Abby,' he cried passionately, 'do you really only think of me as such?' When she looked at him, incomprehension in her eyes, he forged ahead. 'You should be aware that I have already spoken to your uncle. He insists that you be presented, as is only proper, and enjoy your season before you consider your future. But there is an understanding in place between your uncle and I, which merely awaits your approval.'

'I know nothing of this, my lord. My uncle, at least, has had the goodness not to mention it to me, having given me his word that I might enjoy my season without thinking beyond it.' Lord Evans flushed deeply in response to her rebuke. 'I should be obliged if you would refrain from mentioning the matter to me again.'

'You know me too well to imagine that I had any intention of spoiling your pleasures!' he cried, a hint of desperation in his tone. 'But I cannot stand by passively and observe Denver turning your head.' He glanced down the table to where Sebastian sat between Laura and Cassandra, his expression a mixture of censure and disdain. Both ladies were laughing with abandon at something Sebastian had just said to them. 'See what I mean?' he said, his lip curling with disapproval. 'He does not seem to be able to help himself. Abby, the man enjoys the most dreadful reputation. He is possessed of good looks and coercive charm, it is true, but it is merely a sport for him, an amusing way to occupy himself when he has time on his hands. And after he has seduced a lady it is well known that he deserts her without a moment's regret, or second thought for her welfare, either.' Lord Evans focused a gaze of immense gravitas upon her. 'He has excited your passions, perhaps, but my recommendation is that you remain on your guard. It represents little to a man of his ilk, other than an opportunity to boast to his acquaintances of his dalliance with you.'

'My Lord, I hardly think this a suitable — '

Clearly impassioned, Lord Evans did not give her the opportunity to complete her statement. 'Oh, I acknowledge that he must seem glamorous to you, but I beg you not to be fooled by his sophisticated manner. Do not permit yourself to be taken in by him!' he beseeched, touching her arm. 'Nothing good can come out of having your name associated with his and I would not have scandal attaching to your spotless reputation simply because you have been led astray by an experienced rakehell.'

Lord Evans looked at her, love and entreaty plainly apparent in his eyes, and Abby privately acknowledged that he must firmly believe what he was saying. She was not to know that he was tormented by images of Sebastian standing so closely behind her, having the temerity to hold her hips almost against his own body, on the shoddy pretext of teaching her to play billiards. No more could she comprehend that he was even more desolate whenever he recalled the expression on her face as he entered the room and she did not immediately realize he was there. She was laughing at Sebastian, without inhibition, not taking the least exception to his shocking behaviour. But it was the look in Abby's eye at that moment, as she glanced over her shoulder and smiled at the rogue, which would forever haunt him. She had never once looked at him in such a manner.

'I have not discussed the events I observed today with your uncle,' he continued gently, 'and would simply caution you not to allow yourself to be alone with the brute again.' He looked towards the heavy curtains, as though he could see through their thickness and observe the snow, which was still falling steadily outside. 'Blast this weather! Were it not for the conditions the fellow would have been on his way again tomorrow and we could be ourselves again.'

'Indeed, it must be most inconvenient for him, and even more so for his coachman,' agreed Abby, rising with alacrity to join her aunt and the rest of the ladies as they left the table. 'I dare say he is as anxious to be gone as you are to see him depart.'

11

Sebastian was in a contemplative frame of mind as he stood and waited for the last of the ladies to leave the dining-room. The gentlemen then congregated around Lord Bevan's position at the head of the table and the port was circulating before the last of them had resumed his seat. Sebastian, draped in an elegant sprawl, accepted the decanter and filled his glass. He observed the rest of the party through hooded eyes and answered the questions directed at him with a nonchalance designed to conceal the true nature of his thoughts.

Only Lord Woodley, Beatrice's intended, was not in attendance. That was of little consequence since Sebastian agreed with Abby's assessment, at least in so far as Lord Woodley could have no possible reason to wish her harm.

The remaining gentlemen partaking of Bevan's excellent port were an eclectic mix. Lord Bevan was playing the part of the genial host with no ulterior motives that were immediately apparent to Sebastian. He would be the most visible beneficiary of any misfortune that might befall Abby, it was true, but that would also ensure that suspicion would be universally focused upon him. Gossip and innuendo would inevitably follow and society would certainly not refrain from condemning him simply because they lacked definitive proof. Sebastian could not bring himself to believe that a gentleman of honour, who possessed such a refined sense of familial responsibility, would risk bringing such censure upon his name, no matter how perilous his personal circumstances might be.

Bevan's elder son, Tobias, Viscount Bevan, was a humourless and dour individual, appearing suspicious and disapproving of Sebastian's presence, and having little of consequence to say to him. But that hardly signified since he did not appear to make much effort to converse with anyone else either. He was completely wrapped up in the management of his father's estates and, if only half of what the vivacious Cassandra had implied during the course of dinner was to be believed, neglectful of his lovely wife, too. But did he have the cognitive ability to devise such a convoluted campaign to bring about Abby's demise? He would ultimately benefit from her death, since anything his father inherited would eventually fall into his hands. It didn't seem likely that he would go to such lengths but Sebastian knew from experience just how dangerous it could be to discount any possibility, however tenuous.

Harold Bevan was altogether another matter and, unless Sebastian's ability to assess character had somehow become impaired over recent months, was exactly what he appeared to be: a dedicated and compassionate man of God with no ambition to accumulate additional personal wealth. Indeed, from remarks made during the course of the evening, Sebastian had been left with the impression that Harold was generous to a fault with his own funds, often assisting those who had fallen upon hard times from his own pocket. Sebastian agreed with Abby's assessment of Harold's character and was glad for her sake, since she obviously held her younger cousin in high regard.

Sebastian's brooding gaze rested next upon Lord Wilsden. Now there was an interesting character, if ever he saw one! With a great sense of his own importance, Wilsden was completely dedicated to the Prince Regent and regarded as one of his closest confidants. He gave no indication that he was anything other than financially sound, but that had not prevented him from borrowing several times from the Penrith estate: increasingly large amounts which he required for a very interesting purpose. Artful and calculating, he would have been Sebastian's first choice as the mastermind behind Abby's accidents, were it not for the fact that he was patently anxious to see his son Charles wedded to her. And even if that were not the case, what possible advantage would there be in it for him to see Abby dead? In his case, it was in his best interests to keep her alive, and to do everything in his power to ensure that she remained so, in order that she might be persuaded into a union with Charles, whose company she obviously found entertaining. Besides, if Abby were to die then Wilsden would no longer be able to borrow from the estate and further his other driving ambition.

Wilsden's elder son, Gerald, was affable enough. He spent a lot of time in the *ton* and was already known to Sebastian. He enjoyed society, had a carelessly affectionate relationship with his wife, Elizabeth, and Sebastian's sixth-sense told him that Gerald was exactly what he appeared to be; a harmless individual of limited intellect, with no murderous intentions towards Abby. In any event it would require a massive leap of faith to imagine him in possession of both sufficient wits, and the devious turn of mind necessary, to invent such a multifarious plot, much less the energy to put it into practice. And even if

Sebastian had underestimated his intellectual capabilities, he appeared a little too fond of the port — his penchant for the ruby liquid amply demonstrated at that precise moment as he took Evans to task for delaying the decanter's journey — for what wits he did have to remain sharp enough to collude in his cousin's demise.

Sebastian did not imagine that Sir Michael or Simon Graves were culpable, since they too were both intent upon winning Abby's hand, and gaining access to the Penrith fortune into the bargain. That they were discomfited by Sebastian's presence, and regarded him malevolently, was not in question. But Sebastian thought this was due more to the fact that they saw him as a direct threat to their marital aspirations, rather than to any more sinister reason. Should Abby depart this world then they would both see the comfortable futures they aspired to disappearing into the ether.

Evans was no less anxious to see Abby remaining hale and hearty. Sebastian suspected she was right to assume her uncle favoured him as a husband for her: that much had become apparent to him, even in the short time he had been in Evans's company. It was equally clear that Evans despised Sebastian, and after his observations today, who could blame him? Evans, gentlemanly to a fault, was now brooding over his port, lifting his head occasionally only to shoot looks of pure vitriol in Sebastian's direction: looks which Sebastian amused himself by parrying with a derisive expression.

But Sebastian knew he had unwittingly made an enemy out of an honourable man, and could not but lament the fact. Short of breaking his promise to Abby, though, and explaining to Evans that he had nothing to fear from his arrival amongst them, there was naught he could do to set matters right. He could only hope to resolve his business quickly and leave the field clear for Evans.

Sebastian had observed Evans deep in conversation with Abby during the latter part of dinner, his expression oscillating between irately severe and volcanic passion. Sebastian hardly needed Abby to confirm the nature of that conversation when they were next able to exchange a few private words. It was obvious that Evans cared deeply for her and was the only one of her suitors who wanted her for herself, rather than for the pecuniary and social advantages to be derived from possession of the Penrith estate. Sebastian felt his respect for Lord Bevan racket up a notch. A sharp brain, which clearly held Abby's best interests at heart, resided behind a façade of vague amiability which might cause people to underestimate him. But Sebastian was not fooled. The fact that he had already detected in Evans the qualities necessary to make a suitable consort for Abby was insight enough into the perspicacious nature of Bevan's mind.

Sebastian did not care for the sharp pang of jealousy which shot through him as he grappled with this thought. To his certain knowledge he had never once, in all of his thirty years, lost so much as a wink of sleep over a member of the fairer sex. Abby was an enchanting little minx, it was true. He enjoyed her company, admired her courage and pitied the situation she found herself in; but she meant nothing more to him than that. He was here for one purpose only, and that did not involve unravelling her uncle's carefully laid plans for her wellbeing.

Sebastian's speculative gaze came to rest upon Charles Wilsden. He was in full flow at that moment, entertaining the table with a risqué story about a curricle race, which involved a lady of questionable morals being paid by his opponent to distract him. He was a natural raconteur and kept the party amused with his light-hearted account.

'What could I do?' he asked, shrugging his shoulders and spreading his hands in helpless supplication. 'The lady literally threw herself at me and, let me tell you, she was deuced attractive. Not the sort of invitation a chap could turn down. Couldn't have afforded to pay for her services from my own pocket, you see, so I was dashed obliged to my competitor. Anyway, I got the better of him in the end, and enjoyed the lady's company into the bargain, since Fanshaw's leader went lame ten miles out from Brighton and I tooled past him not one hour later, promising him a full account of my experiences at the lady's accomplished hands when we reached our destination.'

'Where do you procure your cattle, Wilsden?' enquired Sebastian, as the laughter and raucous comments died down, curious to see if his answer corresponded with the information Abby had already provided him with.

'Tattersall's,' he responded, without hesitation. 'Mark my words, there's no place better. I pride myself on having a good eye for horse-flesh. I pick 'em young and break 'em myself. Upon my honour, 'tis the only way to be sure of their mettle, and damned good sport it is, too. I make a little extra, by selling some of 'em on.'

The conversation turned to horses in general but Sebastian played little part in it.

He was still curious about Charles Wilsden: he was the obvious candidate for the role of Abby's assailant. He was charismatic, popular and easily his brother's intellectual superior. But he was also idle, reluctant to take on any responsibility which would distract him from his sporting endeavours, and an enthusiastic gamester to boot. In spite of his suggestion that he recouped part of the funds he expended on his horses by breaking them and selling them on, Sebastian doubted that would provide him with sufficient blunt to support his expensive activities. Had he not just unconsciously confirmed the fact by confessing that he did not even have the wherewithal to procure the services of a high-class whore? But what did he have to gain from seeing Abby dead? Frustratingly, nothing whatsoever was the only answer Sebastian was able to come up with. Whichever way he looked at it, Charles Wilsden, younger son of an earl, and no blood relation of Abigail Carstairs, could have no expectations in the event of her demise.

Sebastian reached for his glass. This enigma was proving to be more baffling than he had at first imagined would be the case, but was also just the sort of pithy conundrum he most enjoyed and he was damned if he would permit the solution to evade him for long.

'How is your man faring, Denver?' enquired Lord Bevan graciously, jolting Sebastian's mind from his introspective thoughts.

'He appears to be almost entirely recovered, I thank you.'

'How fortunate!' remarked Evans acerbically, placing his glass aside to speak for the first time since the ladies had left the room.

'How right you are, Evans,' responded Sebastian equitably. 'He was in a great deal of distress but Mrs Burton's herbal remedies have greatly reduced his suffering.'

'Glad to hear it, Denver: only too pleased to have been able to help,' put in Lord Bevan.

'Shame about the weather closing the road down like this,' remarked Charles amiably. 'I dare say you're anxious to be on your way, Denver, and not miss any more of the sport.' He grinned. 'Know I would be if I was in your shoes. Saw that chestnut hunter of yours out with the Belvoir last season and was mightily impressed.'

'Thank you,' returned Sebastian who, in spite of his suspicions in respect of Charlie, was starting to like the man. 'You must try him out when you join our hunt the next time. But as for the weather, it would appear that I must trespass upon your hospitality for a little longer, Bevan, at least until the roads are passable again.'

The derisive snort from Evans's direction went undetected by all, except Sebastian.

'How fares His Royal Highness?' enquired Sebastian of Lord Wilsden with a lightning change of subject, designed to offer Wilsden little time to formulate a reply. 'Does he plan to remove to that monstrosity of his in Brighton in the spring?'

'He does not confide all of his plans to me,' responded Wilsden stiffly.

'I hear he gave a gastronomic banquet of unparalleled proportions at the Pavilion recently,' remarked Lord Bevan. 'His French chef is rumoured to have surpassed himself. It must have been quite a spectacle.'

'Over a hundred courses,' said Wilsden, unable to keep the pride from his voice. 'Naturally, I was there and it was a triumph for His Royal Highness. Never before has such opulence and good taste been demonstrated on such a lavish scale. Our overseas guests were quite overcome by it all.'

'More likely to be overcome with indigestion, I shouldn't wonder,' remarked Charlie irreverently to Sebastian.

'How could one be sure to partake of a

particular dish, with so many to select from?' enquired Tobias, jolted out of his introspection by a subject so dear to his heart.

'His Royal Highness's staff is proficient in the execution of its duties,' responded Wilsden, his affronted expression demonstrating his complete lack of humour in all matters related to the prince.

The gentlemen rejoined the ladies soon after this exchange, the card tables were placed and Sebastian found himself just about as far away from Abby as it was possible to be. Lady Bevan had placed Abby at a table with Laura Graves, Sir Michael and, predictably, Evans. Sebastian found himself in company with Charles, Mary and Elizabeth, a circumstance which was most convenient since he was anxious to study at least two of his card-playing companions at unguarded moments, as well as keeping a discreet eye on Abby. From his current position he was likely to achieve both objectives without drawing unnecessary attention to the fact that his mind was engaged with anything more taxing than partnering Elizabeth Wilsden in a winning rubber.

By the end of the evening he and Elizabeth had achieved their objective and relieved Mary and Charles of a modest sum, which

Charlie grumbled about good-naturedly. Since Abby had also come through unscathed, Sebastian counted the evening as a success.

Retiring only after discreetly hovering to ensure that Abby reached her own chamber without mishap, Sebastian entered his room and found Hodges awaiting him.

'Well, Hodges,' he remarked, throwing aside his coat, 'you will be pleased to hear that your remarkable recovery is a cause for great joy in the drawing-room.'

'It's a cause for great joy for me, an' all, I can tell yer. That Mrs Burton is a sly one, all right. She didn't trust me to take her potions in me own time, which would have meant I could have chucked 'em out the window without her being any the wiser, but insisted upon standing by me and watching me down the lot.' He pulled a hard-done-by face. 'It tasted vile enough to make me ill for real, I can tell yer.'

'Doubtless there were other comforts to be derived from your enforced bed rest?'

Hodges responded with a smug grin. 'Yeah, that Sally is quite a girl! The quiet ones are always full of surprises.' He shrugged his massive shoulders. 'Let's hope that the weather keeps us here for a bit longer.'

'It most likely will. But tell me, Hodges, were you able to take time away from your amorous conquests to make the enquiries I asked of you?'

Hodges looked offended. 'Have I ever let you down, m'lord?' Without waiting for a response he commenced regaling Sebastian with gossip from the senior servants' hall. 'Lord Bevan is considered to be a fair and tolerant master, and Lady Abigail is universally liked, as well as being pitied, because of all the responsibility resting on her shoulders. They all think she should have a bit more freedom, and the chance to enjoy being young before she's obliged to settle down, so they're glad she is to have a season.' Hodges rubbed his stubbly chin and looked thoughtful. 'I find it difficult to believe that any of the servants in her household could be bribed into facilitating her murder: they love her. Apparently she addresses them all by name, remembers the names of their children, too, and ain't too high and mighty to concern herself with their affairs.'

'Hm.' Sebastian followed Hodges's example and rubbed his own chin in thoughtful contemplation.

'But what I did find out from Mr Wilsden's man is that he is fiercely enamoured with a certain lady in Cornwall. He confides in his man, who does not seem to understand how to respect that confidence,' said Hodges, the disgusted edge to his voice making it clear what he thought about such misplaced loyalty.

'Is that supposed to be news?' enquired Sebastian, his brows locked together in annoyance. 'Are you sure you did not spend all of your time dallying with Lady Abigail's maid and are now making this up in an attempt to cover your neglect?'

'If you would just allow me to finish,' said Hodges huffily, 'I was about to inform you that the object of Mr Wilsden's passion is not Lady Abigail.'

Sebastian's head shot up: Hodges had his full attention now. 'Then who, in the name of the devil, is she?'

'I was getting to that,' complained Hodges, clearly reluctant to be deprived of his moment of glory. 'She is Lady Isabel Lawrence.'

'Earl Cowper's daughter? I know her.'

'That doesn't surprise me,' remarked Hodges sarcastically, displaying his usual scant regard for the disparity in their respective ranks. Sebastian reminded himself that Hodges was first and foremost a hard-bitten soldier, most at home on a battlefield. Hodges fulfilled whatever role Sebastian asked of him with competence and discretion. That he tended to forget his position and treated Sebastian as an equal was, in the circumstances, easily overlooked.

'Has he offered for Lady Isabel?' Sebastian enquired sharply.

'The word is that he wishes to do so but his father won't give him leave.'

'Which would explain everything,' said Sebastian slowly, voicing his thoughts as they occurred to him. 'A man in the throes of passion will go to any extremes to get his way. Wilsden won't give his consent because he wants Charlie to marry Abby, but if Abby were out of the way there would be no reason for his father to continue withholding his consent. I understand that Wilsden still holds the purse strings, until Charlie is five-and-twenty at any rate, and so he wouldn't have the blunt to marry without his father's approbation.' Sebastian grimaced, disinclined to think ill of the charismatic Charlie, in spite of all the evidence he was gathering against him. 'I knew Charlie was involved somewhere.' He paused. 'Pity, because I rather like the man, but there you are.'

'Are you sure it's 'im? What about Lord Wilsden and all that money he's borrowed from the duchy?'

'I haven't forgotten about that any more than I have discounted the possibility of a lady's involvement. If Charlie is to blame then he must have had help, since he has not been present at all of the incidents. No one person has.' Sebastian shrugged. 'Well, no one whom I consider suspicious, anyway.'

'What do you make of the females above stairs then, m'lord?'

'Lady Bevan and her daughter are blameless, as is Laura Graves. Cassandra Bevan is a saucy baggage, not averse to forgetting her wedding vows if the opportunity presents, if I read the signals she was sending me at dinner a'right.'

Hodges chuckled. 'I doubt you would have got 'em wrong, m'lord. Heaven knows, you've had enough experience of 'em.'

Sebastian ignored his henchman's irreverence and continued with his cogitations. 'Elizabeth Wilsden is rather vacant, completely self-obsessed and, I venture to suggest, not involved in the attempts on Abby's life. Which leaves Mary Bevan. Now, she has attracted my attention for very different reasons than the norm.' Sebastian paused to marshal his thoughts, drawing on the mental image he had filed away of demure Mary Bevan: everyone's friend and no threat to the rest of the ladies, given her unexceptional appearance and apparent satisfaction with her lot. But Sebastian was well aware of just how deceiving appearances could be, especially in a creature as easily over-looked as Mary, whom no one would ever suspect of being the least bit duplicitous.

'She married well above her station and gives every impression of being satisfied with her situation.'

'The perfect clergyman's wife in every respect, then?'

'Ostensibly, but I would wager she's playing some sort of dangerous game, which no one else is party to.'

'Well, you ain't usually wrong about these things,' remarked Hodges, brushing Sebastian's discarded coat almost reverently, his large, coarse hands, which ought to have been clumsy, managing the task with delicate precision.

'I was talking to her about Italy, a perfectly suitable topic of conversation, you would have thought. But her reaction was beyond anything I have ever known such an innocuous subject to inspire. The longing in her voice, the ill-concealed envy as she expressed her desire to see that country, should have no place in the expressions of a lady who knows she has made an advantageous match and ought to be grateful. Furthermore, when she thought she was undetected I saw a look of pure loathing briefly flash through her eyes as she observed

Abby's gown. She herself wears sober colours, as befits a clergyman's wife, but I believe she secretly yearns to change that state of affairs.'

Sebastian knew he was right. Reading the tell-tale nuances in peoples' expressions, and acting spontaneously upon what he detected there, had saved his life on more than one occasion during his occupation as Wellington's spy. There was more to meek Mary Bevan than met the eye, and Sebastian was a fair way to being certain that behind those plain features lay not only a vindictive personality but also a calculating brain occupied with felonious schemes she would have few qualms about executing ruthlessly.

She had secrets she did not choose to share with her family, too. He had been sure of it before he sat down to play cards against her: absolutely convinced by the time the card party broke up. But did those secrets have anything to do with the plot against Abby? And was she really in league with Charlie? If so, she was extremely efficient at concealing her involvement, since not by so much as a flicker of an eyelid did she give herself away whilst partnering him at whist. If anything she appeared annoyed with him for playing recklessly, causing them to lose. And as for Charlie, he regarded her with nothing more than affable indifference.

Sebastian snapped out of his reflective mood, cursing roundly enough to cause Hodges to start. 'I must have taken leave of my senses!' he growled, scowling at nothing in particular. 'I have grown soft, Hodges, and am losing my edge.'

'What is it then, m'lord?' enquired Hodges, unmoved by Sebastian's sudden change of mood, presumably because he was accustomed to it.

'Lady Abigail has just retired, am I not right? Indeed, I observed her enter her chamber with my own eyes.'

'Indeed you did, m'lord.'

'Please tell me that you have an assignation with Sally, when she has seen her mistress safely to bed.'

'Well, yes, as it happens, but what — '

'Excellent, Hodges! Station yourself outside Lady Abigail's chamber immediately; but remain in the shadows and ensure that you are not detected. When Sally emerges send her straight back in again.'

'Hey, hold on a minute! I was going to — '

'I know what you were going to do, Hodges. But the fact remains that I have been an idiot. Too concerned about who might wish Lady Abigail harm to ensure that she is properly protected in the interim, thus giving her would-be assassin every opportunity to strike at leisure. She must not be left alone at night until we have got to the bottom of the matter. Sally must sleep in her room. Tell Sally when you send her back in to inform her mistress that she is acting upon my orders.'

'But, m'lord, if you suspect Charlie Wilsden, I can't believe that he'd try to murder the young lady in her bed. Even if he waited until the small hours he still couldn't be certain of avoiding detection. He can't be sure that Lady Abigail will be soundly asleep, or that she won't manage to scream before he can silence her. There are just too many possibilities for failure for him to take the chance. You said yourself that he ain't stupid so, however desperate he might be feeling, I doubt he'd risk anything so bold.'

'It is not Wilsden I am concerned about, Hodges, it's Mary Bevan. If she chose to visit Abby, for some innocuous reason of her own invention, Abby would not suspect her for one moment and would grant her admittance without hesitation.' Sebastian, who had been pacing out his agitation in front of his fire, waved Hodges to the door. 'My presence here, coupled with my reputation as an investigator, cannot have been lost on the perpetrators of these outrages. They were desperate enough before, but if they consider I have any knowledge of their intentions, they are likely to step up their efforts.'

'Why? Would it not be safer for them to await your departure?'

'Possibly; but they are as arrogant as they are desperate and have probably convinced themselves that I pose little threat. Either that or they wish to make a point. Go now, if you please, Hodges, and ensure Sally is safely ensconced in Lady Abigail's room. And make sure she locks the door firmly behind her before you retire yourself.'

'Consider it done, m'lord,' responded Hodges with a martyred sigh.

12

When Sebastian entered the breakfast-parlour the following morning it was his misfortune to find only Lord Evans in occupation. Mindful of his suitability as Abby's future spouse, and disinclined to further the antagonistic state between them, Sebastian greeted him warmly and attempted to engage him in light conversation. But it soon became evident that Evans was not in a conciliatory mood and he made no effort to be even superficially polite. Instead, elbows rudely planted on the table, he rested his head in his hands and toyed with a dry piece of toast.

Sebastian shrugged, satisfied that he'd done all he could to pacify Evans, and having broken his fast at his leisure went in search of the other gentlemen. He found them assembled in the billiards room; all but Bevan and Evans, who had apparently taken refuge in the library. Of the ladies there was no sign but Sebastian was not unduly concerned. He knew that they would be together somewhere, doing whatever ladies did to pass the time when the weather was inclement. He had no specific concerns for Abby's safety, since even Mary Bevan would have more sense than to attempt staging an accident in full view of the rest of the party. She might well have been responsible for the incident with the peach ratafia but that had taken place in someone else's household and had been attributed to an unfortunate case of food poisoning. Sebastian was counting on the fact that she would be too fearful, in a house full of servants who always knew precisely where everyone was, to risk any misfortune befalling Abby under her own roof and have the finger of accusation levelled in her direction.

Sebastian earned Charlie's derision when he missed an easy shot, making it evident that his mind was not on the game of billiards in progress, but few present would have guessed that the female with whom it was currently preoccupied was Mary Bevan. He was more convinced than ever of her involvement in the plot against Abby; every shred of evidence, as well as his dependable sixth-sense, pointed to the fact. But unlike Charlie, whose motivation was now plain to Sebastian, he could not think of a single reason to account for Mary's participation. Unless Charlie knew something to her discredit and was using it to force her co-operation? It did not seem likely but he had exhausted all other possibilities.

Amiably admitting defeat and surrendering his cue to Tobias, Sebastian gazed out of the window, still deep in thought. It had ceased snowing and the dark clouds of yesterday had been replaced by brittle winter sunshine. Rays reflected off the snow, caused it to sparkle like multi-faceted diamonds, transforming the garden into a mythical kingdom. He hoped that Abby had observed it too, recalling how much she enjoyed snow.

Shouts of mirth from the side of the house caused him to move to another window and the sight that greeted him made him smile. Three small girls — Harold and Mary's, presumably — were building a snowman, demonstrating more enthusiasm than skill for the project, under the watchful eye of a severe-looking governess. But that was not what held his attention: it was Abby, Beatrice and Laura — bundled up against the cold and hurling snowballs at one another, laughing as they argued about the number of direct hits — which held him in thrall. Sebastian smiled again: he should have known that Abby would not have remained indoors at such a time. Her dogs were there, too, only adding to the mayhem by chasing one another in clumsy circles and then streaking off in tandem after the snowballs.

Suddenly the walls of the house felt as

though they were closing in on him and Sebastian could not bear to be indoors for a moment longer. If nothing else, perhaps the frosty air would help to unscramble his brain. Slipping unobserved from the billiards-room, he fetched his caped driving coat and gloves and stepped out into the garden.

Abby, cheeks flushed rosy red, the remnants of a snowball dripping from her sodden curls, held a deadly-looking mound of snow in her gloved hand and moulded it purposefully, her eyes dancing as she took aim.

'I give you due warning, Bea; I will have my revenge for that last one.'

Laughing, she lifted her arm and let fly, but Bea dodged at the last moment, taking refuge behind the half-constructed snowman, leaving Sebastian directly in the line of fire. The snowball landed fullsquare in the centre of his chest and slithered down his coat.

'Oh dear!' exclaimed Abby, clasping a hand to her mouth, clearly trying not to be too obvious about the fact that she was laughing with satisfaction. 'Pray excuse me, I did not see you approaching, Lord Denver.'

'Evidently not.'

'We are assisting my nieces with their snowman,' explained Bea, grinning as she poked her head out from behind the creation in question. Deeming it safe to emerge again she stood up and brushed snow from her knees.

'But we got distracted,' added Laura.

'Please allow me to present Megan, Alice and Ellen, and their nurse, Miss Frobisher,' said Bea politely. 'Girls, this is Lord Denver.'

Megan and Alice curtsied, but Ellen took fright at the sight of this enormous stranger and hid behind the humourless Miss Frobisher.

'Your servant, ladies,' said Sebastian, bowing low and causing the older two to giggle.

'We are making a snowman,' explained Megan importantly, her pinched features a mirror image of her mother's. 'Would you like to help us? Aunt Bea and Aunt Abby were helping, too, but then they stopped to play with the dogs,' she added accusingly, backing away from Marcus and Marius who had gambolled up to join the group, tongues lolling from the sides of their mouths, tails wagging in expectation of more games.

'Well,' said Sebastian, hunkering down to their level, 'it just so happens that I enjoy building snowmen enormously.'

And he proceeded to prove his point by supplying vast handfuls of snow, far bigger than the children could have accomplished with their tiny fingers, for them to wedge into place. He supervised the construction, making helpful suggestions when the whole edifice appeared to be in danger of toppling over, but didn't once attempt to take over from them. The children were soon so comfortable with him that even little Ellen was persuaded to rejoin her sisters.

Miss Frobisher maintained an expression as frosty as the conditions, clearly unimpressed with grand gentlemen who had nothing better to do with their time than to play at children's games, and jumped with lightning speed upon any of her charges who dared to exhibit the slightest signs of spontaneity. They became unusually subdued the moment the woman spoke, almost as though they had temporarily forgotten her presence but knew their brief spell of freedom was too good to last, and Sebastian wondered how someone with Harold's compassionate nature could condemn his daughters to long hours under the forbidding eye of this dragon. Only by reminding himself that Mary would be the one to take responsibility for the employment of her children's governess did it start to make any sense.

'What do you suppose he lacks?' asked Sebastian, standing back with Abby and the girls to examine the result of their labours.

'A nose, of course!' exclaimed Megan, a note of scorn in her voice.

'And eyes.'

'You are quite right,' agreed Sebastian. 'But do you suppose that his head might be a little chilly, and his neck, too? Should we not procure a hat and scarf for him? After all,' he added, twinkling at Alice and reducing her to giggles again, 'we would not wish him to catch cold, would we now?'

'Snowmen cannot catch cold,' said Megan disdainfully, displaying traits of the ungenerous nature that her mother had most likely learned to keep under closer guard.

'They most certainly can,' contradicted Sebastian, trying to make allowances for this rather unpleasant child's manner. 'Just look, his nose is already running!'

This produced more giggling, even from Megan, and Sebastian pressed home his case. 'What do you say, girls, shall we make him more comfortable?'

'Yes, yes!' cried Ellen, all shyness forgotten, as she jumped from foot to foot in excitement. Sebastian swept her into his arms and swung her over his head, causing her to giggle and beg for more.

'I would prefer it if you did not agitate her so, my lord,' said Miss Frobisher, the haughtiness of her tone belying her humble situation. 'She is prone to sickness when she becomes over-excited.'

'Really!' remarked Sebastian, raising a brow and suffusing the word with a wealth of superior arrogance. Appearing to remember her place, Miss Frobisher retreated to the seat which the children had cleared for her on a stone bench, sniffing with indignation.

'I must return to the house now,' said Bea, 'since Mama will be wondering what has become of me. But,' she continued, bending to address the children, 'I will beg a carrot from cook for our snowman's nose, find buttons for his eyes and see if Richards can find an old hat and scarf to keep him warm.'

'Yes!' cried three enthusiastic voices. 'Hurry please, Aunty Bea.'

'I will go too,' said Laura, 'but I shall return directly with our snowman's wardrobe.'

But in fact it was a footman who delivered their treasures, Laura having decided she was too cold to venture out of doors again. As soon as the snowman had been adorned with his final touches Miss Frobisher lost no time in ushering the reluctant children back into the house. Sebastian, alone now with Abby but anxious not to be seen to be so, turned away from the windows of the house.

'Stroll this way with me for a moment, if you will?'

'Indeed I will!' responded Abby, with asperity, 'since I most particularly wish to speak with you. What did you mean by insisting that Sally share my chamber last night?'

'Only that I felt safer knowing she was bearing you company, rather than entertaining Hodges,' he responded evenly, devilishly intent upon shocking her out of her annoyance.

He was not to be disappointed. Abby covered her mouth with her gloved hand, but not before he had seen her lips shape themselves into an astonished *oh*.

'Sally is a good girl and would not do such a thing!' she declared, abandoning her grievances in favour of defending her maid's honour.

Sebastian cocked his brow in stark amusement. 'Would she not?' When Abby remained stubbornly silent, Sebastian spoke again. 'Hodges can be very persuasive, you know, and enjoys a great deal of popularity with the opposite sex.'

'Lord Denver, this is hardly a suitable topic of conversation between us.'

'Is it not?' he enquired mildly. 'I should have thought that you would find it intriguing.'

Abby lifted her chin and changed the

subject. 'What discoveries have you made?'

'That Lord Evans does not care for my company,' he responded, determined not to reveal his suspicions in respect of Charles and Mary.

Abby giggled. 'Indeed he does not! He warned me quite forcefully to avoid your company.'

'Did he indeed!'

'Most assuredly. You should be aware that he considers your reputation to be irretrievably lost,' she advised him with a glittering smile. 'And I dare say he knows what he is talking about. He is also fearful that I might become tainted by association if I spend too much time with you. He accuses you of befriending helpless ladies, taking shameful advantage of them, and then deserting them.'

'Really?' remarked Sebastian, perfectly unruffled. They had wandered beneath the shelter of a stand of trees and, both of them being hatless, were falling victim to the thawing snow as it dripped from the overhanging branches. Sebastian pulled the hood of Abby's cloak close over her damp curls. 'And does he suppose that I intend to seduce you, do you suppose?'

'That, or something worse.'

'What worse fate could possibly befall a young lady?'

'It is difficult to imagine one, I grant you,' she conceded absently, but the gaiety had gone out of her voice and she appeared preoccupied.

'What is it?' he asked her. 'What troubles you?'

'Oh, it is nothing, I am just being foolish.'

'Tell me,' he invited gently.

'Oh, it is just this tree,' she confessed, indicating the bare branches of the magnificent oak tree they were standing beneath. 'I was just thinking that I have never once seen it in full leaf.'

'Because you only come here in winter for the hunting?'

'Yes, but this tree is special to me for reasons of greater import than that. I was standing under it when I saw my father alone for the last time. He had just returned from a day's hunting. I heard him return, escaped my governess and ran out to meet him. We stood under this tree, just as you and I are doing at this moment. My father talked to me like I was a grown up; telling me all about the excellent day's sport he had enjoyed.' She paused, her face averted from his. 'It was almost the last occasion upon which I shared a private word with him: three weeks later they were both dead.'

She turned to look at him again, one fat

tear running down her face, her valiant efforts to maintain her composure igniting Sebastian's compassion. Her childhood had come to an abrupt end at the age of ten, and she had been attempting to deal with grief, and live up to people's expectations of her, ever since. In the eight years since the death of her parents Sebastian suspected that the only occasion upon which she'd shown the slightest sign of rebellion had been yesterday, when he had persuaded her to transgress.

Fighting an inner battle with his conscience, he vowed that it would not happen again. He wiped the tears from her face with the back of his thumb. She responded by leaning her head against his chest as she struggled to find her composure. She was trembling; a circumstance which he suspected was not entirely attributable to the weather conditions, and had little choice but to envelope her within the heavy folds of his coat, trapping her breath in her throat as securely as he was trapping her body in his arms. Determined to stick to his earlier resolve, though, he did not trust himself to look at her and searched for a question that had little to do with the reason for her distress.

'Would you care if Evans was right about me?'

'Don't be ridiculous!' she snapped, some of her former spirit once again evident in her tone. 'Our relationship is one of expediency.'

'Ah yes, so it is.'

'Lord Evans informed me at the dinner table last night that he has already sought my uncle's permission to pay court to me.'

'Did he now! It was very bad-mannered of him to mention it.'

'That is what I told Lord Evans.'

Sebastian chuckled: he did not doubt it. 'But you cannot have been altogether surprised. Is it not what you expected?'

'Yes, I suppose . . . '

'But?' he prompted, when her words trailed off, placing a finger beneath her chin and tipping it upwards until she was forced to meet his gaze. What he saw there caused him to curse beneath what little breath he had remaining, reminding him more forcefully than ever that he had no business toying with her affections. He had led her into an improper situation on the feeble pretence of discussing the investigation with her. In the process he appeared to have caused her to question the plans that had been made for her future by a man with greater wisdom about these matters than he was ever likely to possess.

'I no longer know what to think about Lord

Evans,' she admitted candidly. 'He does not excite my passions.'

'And what do you care about passion? I thought it had no place in your life.'

A charming blush crept up her cheeks. 'Perhaps I was mistaken.'

'Abby, oh Abby, what am I do to with you?'

When she looked at him like that, her eyes still artlessly reflecting her blind faith in his abilities; when she all but admitted that he had awoken her passions and aroused her curiosity, he was profoundly moved. Her sensuality was like a beacon, drawing him towards her with licentious intent, testing his resolve in the light of his recent crisis of conscience to the limit. It roused his jaded spirit, overwhelming him with a torrent of protective feelings and reinforcing his determination that no one would ever get close enough to cause her harm.

Realization of what mayhem he had caused in her well-ordered life served to reinforce his own will. He simply would not make matters more complicated for her. But Abby clearly had other ideas and, before he realized what she was about, her arms had worked their way round his neck and her lips were seeking his. She tasted of apples, fresh air and everything that was pure, touching an area inside him that no other female had managed

212

to invade, removing a healthy wedge of his cynical attitude in the process.

It took every molecule of his self-discipline to break that kiss before it could become more impassioned. They were both breathing heavily as he moved slightly away from her, their heated breath swirling above them and rapidly cooling in the frosty air. Sebastian knew that cooling his rising ardour would not be so easily accomplished. Framing her rosy cheek with his hand, he smoothed the hair from her forehead and smiled into eyes which had flown open in protest when he broke the kiss.

'So much beauty,' he murmured, unaware that he had spoken the words aloud.

He groaned at her artless expression, the invitation in eyes that sparkled with a rare combination of provocation and innocence, wondering afterwards what would have happened, had Abby's dogs not bounded up at that precise moment, almost knocking them both from their feet. What in the name of Hades had he been contemplating doing? Putting her aside from him with unnecessary force he suggested they return to the house.

'Enough of this amusement,' he drawled laconically. 'The hour for luncheon approaches and I find I have the most fearsome appetite.'

She astounded him by stretching out a

hand and touching his face, eyes alight with a fiery passion as she uttered just one word. 'Please!'

'No,' he said, turning abruptly away from her.

'That is unfair,' she protested.

'I apologize, I should never have — '

'Perhaps not, but I have always wanted to know about such matters. No one would ever enlighten me, though, and that is why I was of the opinion that emotional attachment was overrated. Perhaps now I am of a different frame of mind, but I cannot say with certainty until I learn more. And you,' she continued, smiling up at him with supreme confidence, 'are going to teach me.'

'No, Abby, I am not!' Alarmed by her determination he attempted to move away from the tree, but short of literally pushing her aside there was no method by which he could extricate himself. 'We should never have started this.'

'Sebastian, please!'

Her imploring expression and, more especially, the sound of his name slipping so naturally from her lips, almost persuaded him. She was right; he was to blame for her current state of frustration. He had never considered the matter before but it must be extremely vexatious for young ladies, especially those with natures as passionate as Abby's, to be denied even a rudimentary education in amatory matters.

He felt sympathy for her plight but could not risk prolonging this dalliance, even though it would be no easy matter to dissuade her from her purpose. Appearing to sense his hesitation she seized the moment, and his neck, pulling his head downwards with considerable force as she set her lips upon his in a searing kiss. Her enthusiasm sent fire lancing through his veins, but guilt overpowered even that dizzying sensation and he pulled away from her, aware now that the only way to overcome her determination was to be cruel to her.

'Come, we will be late for luncheon,' he said brusquely.

Her eyes flashed with bewilderment. 'I do not understand.'

'Then you have a lot to learn.'

'But I thought — '

'Abby, you know very well that we have transgressed. You really must learn to master your impetuous nature if you wish to be respected.'

She gasped, shooting him a look of such injured confusion as to make him feel like crawling beneath the nearest rock. Recovering her poise quickly she put up her chin, anger radiating from her eyes as she called to her dogs and headed for the house.

Sebastian let her go, knowing he had been to blame for the entire incident and fully deserving of her displeasure. He should have known better than to try and comfort her when she became distressed about her parents, which had resulted in his adding to her distress with deliberately cruel insults. Not having been troubled by its existence for years, Sebastian's conscience made its presence felt again for the third time in ten minutes.

What a farrago! Sebastian did not know his own mind at that moment. This inexperienced chit had turned his world on its head, stirring his passions until he thought he would go out of his mind: making him think the unthinkable. He vowed never to allow Abby to gain intelligence of how greatly her innocent curiosity had affected him. She was young and impressionable, almost half his age, and had no place in his life. Better that she should despise him than learn the true nature of his feelings.

Abby pointedly ignored him during luncheon, saving her smiles instead for Lord Evans. Sebastian tried to congratulate himself upon steering her in that direction but his heart was having none of it. This situation was dangerous: very dangerous. He vowed to redouble his efforts to reveal the identify of her aggressor and put a safe and permanent distance between himself and the object of his desire at the earliest opportunity.

He idled the afternoon away playing piquet with some of the gentlemen. Lord Evans did not join in the game and Sebastian wondered if he had chosen to remain with the ladies; an excuse to be close to Abby. Had he not heard some suggestion mooted during luncheon that he should read aloud to them? Be that as it may, not prepared to take any further chances when it came to her safety, Sally and Hodges had orders to keep her under surveillance at all times and not leave her unattended for a moment.

Afternoon turned to evening and Sebastian started to feel uneasy when Abby had not appeared in the drawing-room by the usual hour. He was about to go in search of her when, standing in the hall, he espied her descending the stairs, looking particularly lovely in a peach-coloured gown of embroidered brocade. She saw him observing her and doubted that she could have mistaken the admiration that he was singularly failing to keep from his expression. When she bestowed a brief, scornful glance upon him, Sebastian's suspicions were confirmed. He had foolishly given her cause to entertain expectations he could never fulfil and she had every right to feel humiliated and slighted. But instead of falling into a fit of the sullens, it would appear that she had already recovered her spirit and was ready to exact revenge by torturing him with this instinctively provocative display of her femininity.

She could have no notion of how comprehensively she was succeeding, Sebastian decided, grinding his teeth in frustration. He stood spellbound, continuing to drink in the sight of her as she progressed towards him. With a ghost of a smile directed somewhere above his head one small, prettily-shod foot appeared from beneath her froth of lace petticoats and, toe pointed daintily, she took a slow step downwards. And then the other foot followed suit. Abby appeared intent upon prolonging the moment, satisfied that her captive audience was incapable of tearing his eyes away. Another step downwards: a tiny, imperious smile playing about her lips. As the little witch got closer, so his discomfort increased but Sebastian ignored it, reminding himself that he only had himself to blame for the torture she was inflicting upon him.

Lost in a world of lascivious thought, his brain was slow to realize that the piercing scream which suddenly rent the air had come from Abby. He could only watch in helpless frustration as she tumbled the rest of the way down the stairs, landing in a tangle of limbs at his feet and lying there, completely motionless.

13

Everyone streamed out of the drawing-room, stopping just short of Sebastian, who was bending over Abby to ensure that she was still breathing. His own breath was coming in short bursts, the fear he had felt as she tumbled making his movements at first slow and ungainly. Her eyes opened and she blinked at him, more in surprise than in pain, he realized, relief washing over him.

'Are you all right?' he asked her, supporting her raised head as he felt for her pulse.

'Yes, I think so. What happened?'

But he could see from her shocked expression that she already knew. Another attempt had been made on her life: and not just in front of her relations, but in his presence, too. Had she descended the stairs at her usual rapid pace, knowing she was inexcusably late, the accident could have been so much worse. It was clear to him that she had only slowed her progress when she became aware of Sebastian prowling in the hall below her. She had put the amatory lessons he had tried not to conduct to good use and staged a provocative display for his benefit, trailing her hand along the rail — something which she would not normally have troubled to do, he suspected — and was able to hold on to it as she tumbled, breaking the worst of her fall.

'Do you suppose you can stand?' Sebastian asked her, struggling to disguise the anger bubbling inside him as he reflected upon her narrow escape. An audacious attempt had been made on her life, in spite of his presence, but his head had been too full of salacious thoughts to have properly considered this very real possibility. He was responsible for Abby's welfare; she had entrusted herself to his care and he had almost failed her in the worst manner imaginable. His expression became thunderous as he reflected upon the nature of his negligence. He had been so preoccupied with the child's charms that he had forgotten the dangers that surrounded her: forgotten his very reason for being here.

'I will try.'

Sebastian offered her his hand and pulled her gently to her feet. The moment she attempted to place weight of her left foot though she cried out in pain and would have crumpled to the floor again, had not Sebastian's arm been supporting her. Wordlessly he swept her into his arms and ascended the stairs, several of the ladies trailing in his wake, lamenting the accident and discussing it in shocked under-tones.

'We should send for the doctor,' said Aunt Constance who, predictably, was weeping.

'He will not be able to get through the snow,' answered Sebastian, not the slightest bit out of breath, in spite of the burden of Abby's weight. He continued upwards with swift strides, taking the stairs two at a time, making it necessary for the ladies following him to lift their heavy skirts and scamper in order to keep pace with him. 'Best advise Mrs Burton. She will likely be able to help.'

'I will seek her out,' volunteered Laura, who still appeared to have her wits about her.

Sebastian laid Abby on the couch in her chamber, her left leg supported by several cushions. He removed her shoe and, ignoring the proprieties, gently examined her ankle, holding it between his long fingers, probing with a gentle touch as he persuaded her to rotate it in both directions, if she was able. She was, even though it was painful, proving that it was not broken but badly sprained. Satisfied that her injury was not life-threatening he squeezed her fingers, winked his reassurance and ceded his place at her side to her hovering aunt.

Offending shoe still in his hand Sebastian

slipped from the room, unobserved by the concerned crowd of well-wishers. Prominent amongst them, and openly expressing her horror, Sebastian was disgusted to notice Mary Bevan. The ladies had recovered from the first effects of shock and, realizing it was the same ankle Abby had sprained when she fell down the stairs previously, reached the obvious conclusion that there must still be a weakness in it, which would account for this second accident. Sebastian did not put them straight.

Alone in the corridor, he examined the shoe. It had a high heel, which had come loose and caused Abby to fall.

But, of course, the fall had not been the accident that everyone supposed.

Looking at the shoe more closely Sebastian could see that the heel had been meticulously loosened at the edges, leaving it hanging by the merest thread in its centre. Abby's weight would need only to have shifted slightly to one side to cause the heel to snap off completely and who when descending a staircase, especially in a rush, keeps their weight central?

But Abby would surely have noticed when she put her foot in it and moved about that the heel was not secure? Unless? Unless she was running late. Everyone knew her uncle was a stickler for punctuality and that tardiness in his own family was one of the few things guaranteed to test his congenial temperament. That being so, she would have put her shoes on in haste at the last minute — did not everyone leave their shoes until the end when dressing? — and rushed from her chamber without concerning herself about a slightly wobbly heel. Which meant that someone must have deliberately delayed her.

Sebastian moved back into Abby's sitting-room, discovered Sally hovering on the edge of the crowd, and beckoned to her. Back in the corridor he quizzed her for several minutes and then, grim faced, returned to his own room, where Hodges awaited him. Flinging the offending shoe towards the bed, Sebastian faced his henchman, the magnitude of his fulminating anger clearly apparent in his expression.

'Unimaginable evil resides beneath this roof,' he prophesied grimly.

'It ain't like you to get so riled,' remarked Hodges, looking pensive. 'What's so different about this case that's got you so worked up then?'

'The lady was depending upon me and I almost failed her in the worst manner imaginable. It was only by the purest chance that she survived this attack.'

'Don't let fly with your temper at me; that won't help. This one's special to yer, is she?' Hodges grinned, apparently oblivious to his master's chilling glare. 'And her just a chit of a girl.' He chuckled. 'Who would have thought it? The great Marquess of Broadstairs brought to heel by a mere child. Still, she is fearful handsome, I'll give yer that.'

'That will do, Hodges. As always, you forget yourself.'

'If you say so, m'lord.' Hodges shrugged, clearly unrepentant. 'So how did it happen then, the accident, I mean, not your falling for the lass?'

'The heel of her shoe was loosened.'

'How come Sally didn't notice?'

'That is what I just asked her. She informed me that she always lays her mistress's clothes out for the evening whilst she takes tea with the other ladies. She is adamant that the shoe was sound at that time because she checked it thoroughly herself whilst retying the ribbons.'

'So, someone tampered with it between then and when Lady Abigail put it on.'

'Exactly! Someone who understands her routine and knew her attire for the evening would be laid out during tea, when anyone could slip away unobserved for a few moments. Sally is waiting upon some of the other ladies in residence, including Mary Bevan, who does not have her own maid, and so has much to occupy her. But she is aware of the danger Lady Abigail is facing and is being extra vigilant.'

'The heel must have been pretty loose if it was meant to snap when she had only got as far as the stairs,' remarked Hodges.

'That was what I thought. But someone detained her and presumably she did not concern herself with the shoe for fear of being even later than she already was.'

'It could have happened that way,' remarked Hodges, thoughtful in his turn, 'but it would require some precision of timing.'

'Yes indeed, and a cool nerve, too, but nevertheless that was how it was achieved. I can speak with certainty because I asked Sally.' Sebastian paused, cold, hard fury blazing from his eyes. 'It would appear that Miss Frobisher called upon her with little Ellen, just as Abby was finishing dressing. Ellen was supposedly fractious after her energetic day playing in the snow, unwilling to settle and anxious to see Abby. Naturally, Abby, who makes no secret of the fact that she adores the children, was unable to resist playing with the little girl, which is what caused her to be late.'

'Ah, very clever,' conceded Hodges.

'Quite so. Hodges, I want you to seek out Miss Frobisher, bombard her with your legendary charm and see if you can find out who sent her to see Abby. I know who it was, of course, but need confirmation. I am persuaded that a woman of her ilk would not be dictated to by a mere child, but could hardly ignore a direct order from her employer.'

'Aw, God, m'lord, have a heart. That woman's got a face like a stewed prune, a body that looks like it's been pummelled by a flat iron and the most spiteful personality I've ever known. All the servants shun her as much as they can.'

Sebastian managed a brief chuckle but, in his present uncompromising mood, it came out more as a bark. 'Then look upon it as a challenge, Hodges. Besides, this is for Lady Abigail, and you would do well to remember that it was she who thought to supply you with sustainable vittles during your supposed illness.'

'Yeah, there is that, I suppose, but still — '

'And sent Sally to deliver them.'

'Yeah, all right then, I'll do it. But only,' he added mulishly, 'for Lady Abigail's sake. Nothing else could induce me to have anything to do with that old hag.'

'Good man!' said Sebastian absently. 'We

must all make sacrifices occasionally.'

Hodges humphed. 'I don't see you making any. But what of you, m'lord, what do you plan to do whilst I attempt to soften the heart of a woman who probably hasn't got one?'

'Me?' Sebastian drew himself up to his full height, looking exceptionally grim but resolute. 'I plan to seek an immediate interview with Lord Bevan. Things have reached the stage when Abby's uncle must be informed of the danger she is in. She will not be happy that I have betrayed her trust but, given the circumstances, I can see no alternative. Besides, I have an idea how we might resolve the matter, but it can hardly be attempted without Bevan's prior knowledge and consent.'

★ ★ ★

The commotion caused by what everyone still supposed to be an unfortunate accident gradually calmed down. Mrs Burton took charge of Abby, making her comfortable and pronouncing her injury to be superficial. She treated it with a poultice composed of her special herbs and predicted that she should be back on her feet again within a week, provided she rested and did precisely as she was told. Abby pulled a face behind her back, making it abundantly clear that her instructions were unlikely to be complied with.

That she could still retain her sense of humour, when she must be aware just how close to succeeding this latest attempt on her life had been, said much for her strength of resolve. It did little, though, to aid Sebastian in his endeavours to withstand her appeal, or to evict her from the special place she appeared to have taken up in his heart.

The rest of the party headed for the dining-room, but dinner was a rather desultory affair, with everyone lamenting the accident, speculating as to its cause and exclaiming over and over again just how fortunate Abby had been not to have sustained a more serious injury. Sebastian made little contribution to the conversation, enduring a meal that seemed interminable, and rather flat without Abby's sparkling presence. He bore it with ill-disguised impatience, scarcely noticing what he ate and savouring the excellent wines in a contemplative frame of mind, which discouraged people from addressing him. Even Cassandra, who appeared to be especially determined to flirt with him this evening, eventually conceded defeat.

Anxious to explain to Lord Bevan the

nature of the malevolent acts being perpetrated against his niece, Sebastian's opportunity came only after the port and cigars had been lingered over for an inordinate amount of time. Lady Bevan attempted to liven up proceedings when the gentlemen re-entered the drawing-room with some music and Sebastian seized his chance to join Bevan in his library.

With the door closed to discourage those who might otherwise seek them out, Sebastian prepared his lordship for a shock. Commencing with Abby's first approaching him, but deliberately keeping the circumstances of that first meeting vague; he outlined the whole of Abby's concerns. To say that Lord Bevan appeared stunned would be a gross understatement. He was completely shocked, ghostly white and quite unable to speak for a full two minutes. Moving to a console table, Sebastian poured substantial measures of brandy for them both, pressed Bevan's glass between his slack fingers and waited for him to recover his power of speech.

'Do you mean to tell me, Denver, that this has been going on for months and she did not see fit to enlighten me?' He downed his brandy in one and handed the glass to Sebastian for a refill. 'My God, when I consider the danger . . . of what could have happened if fortune had not favoured her.' He thumped his clenched fist on the arm of his chair. 'My poor darling, when I think what agonies she has already endured. Who could possibly wish her harm? And whatever could she have been thinking of? Why did she not see fit to confide in *me*?'

'I think because she was not altogether persuaded that anything actually *was* happening to her,' responded Sebastian, attempting to address all of Lord Bevan's questions simultaneously in an effort to immediately reassure. 'By stretching her imagination she was able to brush the separate incidents off as misfortunes, since that is what she wanted to believe. And I think that she dreaded losing her freedom even more than she feared for her personal well-being.'

'Maybe so, but to confide in a complete stranger: why would she do that? Have I wronged her to such a degree that she no longer has faith in me?' Bevan rubbed his face in his hands, appearing truly distressed by the notion. 'I have moved heaven and earth, neglecting my own estate, my own concerns, my family even, in order to secure her future. Do not imagine that I am complaining, since I have done so with a gladness of heart, out of compassion for her singular situation. It was not only a duty but a pleasure to do my best to see her happily established, and to ensure that the duchy remains in good shape. My family has done everything in its power to make her responsibilities rest as lightly as possible on her shoulders.' Lord Bevan stared fixedly at Sebastian. 'She cannot possibly believe that I have anything other than her best interests at heart.'

'Not at all. I believe she approached me merely because she had been informed that I had a reputation for solving mysteries and acted impulsively upon that information. I do not believe that her disinclination to involve you owed anything to mistrust. She loves and respects you, feels she has caused an unnecessary disruption in your lives and did not wish to make matters worse by burdening you with additional worries.'

'Perhaps she did not confide in me because she thought I might be involved in some way. After all, were she to die then I would inherit the bulk of her estate.'

'She does not believe that for a moment,' Sebastian told him with firm conviction. 'But she is aware of the sacrifices you have made on her behalf and dreads earning your bad opinion. The problem is, however, that she does not believe that anyone else close to her can be responsible either. She is hopelessly naïve and trusts them all implicitly.'

'And so,' said Lord Bevan, starting to recover from the shock of Sebastian's revelations, 'your arrival here was not a coincidence at all.'

'No. And I regret the necessity to deceive you, but I was of the opinion that in order to gain further intelligence it would be advantageous to see the likely culprits together, in her company. I was intent upon travelling to my own hunting box this week anyway and Abby told me you would all be gathered here. It seemed too good an opportunity to ignore, especially as I believe that the dangers are only likely to pick up pace, now that your niece has started to appear in society and is generally supposed to be thinking in terms of matrimony.'

'I see. And I presume that your reason for confiding in me now is that you suspect Abby's fall down the stairs this evening was not an accident?'

'I know it was not.' Sebastian briefly explained about the loosened heel. 'I also know that the persons who wish to see her dead are becoming more desperate by the day. They are quite ruthlessly determined and, as Abby is now being openly courted by more than one gentleman and could marry at any time, passing her fortune into the hands of her new husband in the process, they are stepping up their campaign.' Sebastian appeared exceptionally grim-faced as he paused to sip his brandy. 'Since whoever wishes her harm is someone whom she trusts I cannot hope to keep her out of harm's way for every second of the day and so, with your permission, I propose to set a trap to draw the culprits out.'

'You keep saying *they*, Denver. Do you suspect more than one person?'

'I do.' Sebastian explained how difficult it would have been for one individual to stage all the accidents, without drawing unnecessary attention to himself: even if he did have servants assisting him.

'And presumably you now have an idea who those people are?' said Lord Bevan, anger and steely determination underlying his tone, affording Sebastian a telling glimpse of the real man lurking beneath that congenial façade. 'Perhaps now is the time to share that information with me.'

'Indeed.' And Sebastian, preparing Lord Bevan for more shocking disclosures, told him all he had surmised in respect of Charles Wilsden — and Bevan's own daughter-in-law, Mary.

Lord Bevan took these revelations more calmly than Sebastian might have supposed, pondering upon them for some moments without speaking.

'You could be in the right of it,' he eventually conceded, 'much as I hate to admit it, but your logic appears irrefutable. But what is your plan for finding them out.'

'The scheme that has occurred to me is riskier than I care for, but I can think of no other. It also requires absolute secrecy. With your permission we will put it into play at once but no one, no one at all apart from the two of us and Abby herself, must be aware of what we are doing. If I am wrong about the identity of the perpetrators we could unwittingly alert the true villains.'

'I understand. But before I agree to anything perhaps you had better tell me, Denver, precisely how it is you intend to draw them into the open.'

Sebastian did so, succinctly and without discernible emotion. Lord Bevan, grim faced, nodded his agreement, adding a few conditions of his own.

'Evans will likely become suspicious and attempt to intervene,' warned Sebastian.

'He will not care for it, it is true, but if he tries to put a stop to it I will warn him off. He will not go against my wishes, whatever the provocation,' he added, with a significant glance at Sebastian.

'Well, just so long as he is out of the way at the crucial juncture.'

'I give you my assurance that he will not interfere. Come along then, Denver,' said Lord Bevan, rising from his chair and draining his glass again in one economical movement, 'let us see if Abby is still awake and acquaint her with your suggestion. Obviously, the final decision with regard to this plan will be hers alone to make.'

* * *

Abby breathed a sigh of relief when she was finally able to convince the ladies surrounding her that she was feeling, with the exception of a swollen ankle, perfectly well. They really should return to the drawing-room, since the dinner hour must be almost upon them, and she would easily be able to manage where she was if a light supper could be sent up to her. Shaking their heads and clucking with sympathy the ladies eventually filed from the room, leaving her with just Sally for company.

Abby enjoyed the ensuing silence and was reluctant to break it. Sally's mother had been Abby's own mother's maid and Sally, just a few years older than Abby herself, had been a great comfort to her when her parents were killed. She had moved to Castleray with her and remained the one constant link to her past. Abby did not doubt Sally's love for her, or her abiding loyalty, and had not hesitated to seek her assistance when she first hatched the scheme to approach Sebastian.

'It was fortunate that Lord Denver was able to come to your aid so quickly when you fell, my lady,' remarked Sally with an impish smile, removing the tray from the small table she had placed at Abby's side. 'I must say I think him rather dashing.'

Abby humphed. 'He is rather too full of himself for my taste. But what have you to tell me regarding your own behaviour, Sally?'

'What do you mean?' she asked evasively.

'I know they are not true, of course, but think it only right to warn you about what is being said. I am sorry if this offends you, Sally, but some would have it that you have behaved in an inappropriate manner with Lord Denver's man.'

Sally flushed scarlet. 'Not inappropriately exactly, my lady,' she said, unable to stop herself from giggling.

'So it is true: I cannot believe it! Sally, how could you? I defended you when Lord Denver dared to make the suggestion. I know how much you disapprove of loose behaviour.'

'Well, you *did* ask me to deliver that food to him,' responded Sally, making it sound as though it was all her fault, 'and Mr Hodges begged me to stay and talk to him whilst he consumed it.'

'Whilst he was in his bed?' said Abby, shocked.

'Where else could he be? He was, after all, feigning illness, and as we were the only two who knew it, it was pleasant to be able to speak of it. And besides, Mr Hodges is charming, and very virile,' she added with a sigh. 'He has seen and done so many things and knows just how to treat a girl.'

'I dare say!' remarked Abby, her sarcasm completely wasted on her besotted maid. 'But have a care, Sally, you would not wish to end up in an unfortunate condition.'

'Oh, there is no need to concern yourself on that score, my lady,' boasted Sally, suddenly full of worldly wisdom, 'he took the greatest care and withdrew — '

'Yes, thank you, Sally, spare me the details, if you please,' said Abby, who was actually bursting with curiosity: but even with a friendship as close as theirs, there were still some boundaries that ought not to be crossed.

'Sorry,' said Sally, giggling and blushing once again, seemingly unrepentant.

Abby lapsed into silence, wondering if she could devise a means of extracting further particulars from Sally about her scandalous liaison with Hodges, without raising her maid's suspicions about her reasons for wishing to know. Perhaps it would be her maid who would be able to satisfy her curiosity about so many things. But it would not do to pry. If Sally felt comfortable offering Hodges her favours, then what right did she have to censure her? Especially after the way she had . . . but no. Colour flooded her cheeks as she recalled the shameless way in which she had begged Sebastian to kiss her: about the way in which she had literally flung herself at him. How could she have been so brazen? No wonder he had looked upon her with disdain after the event.

Full of self-recriminations, she turned her mind to this latest attempt on her life. Renewed fear cascaded through her, banishing her salacious thoughts in respect of Sebastian most effectively. But she had spent so many hours already contemplating the matter from every conceivable angle, without reaching any firm conclusions as to the identity of the culprit that she could see little profit in continuing to dwell upon it. She could only trust that Sebastian had been more successful. She rather suspected that he had but was unwilling to share his thoughts with her. She straightened her spine, wincing as pain jolted through her ankle. In spite of her incapacity she did not intend to permit him to arbitrarily decide upon the best course of action. Just like everyone else who had anything to do with her life, he was far too ready to take matters into his own hands in a misguided effort to protect her, arrogantly assuming that he knew what was best for her.

Dash it all, why did she have to think about his hands? It conjured up an image of those capable fingers, gentling probing and caressing — and she was not referring to his examination of her ankle, either — seductive though even that innocent event had seemed to her in her current emotional state.

But it would not do! Furious with herself, and with him, she determined anew to consider his amorous advances, if she had to think about them at all, in the same casual manner he appeared to adopt. He was a man unaccustomed to being idle: a man who now had time on his hands. Hands again, it always seemed to come back to his wretched hands! She just would *not* think about them.

She bolstered her flailing self-esteem by relishing anew the expression on his face as he observed her descending the stairs — an expression which presented her with a very useful means of revenge. He might well proclaim indifference towards her but no one could feign the incandescent desire she had detected in his eyes, not even a man as experienced in such matters as he. His features had softened and she detected a wealth of emotional investment in his expression, and an encouraging amount of admiration, too. But most of all, just for one unguarded second, she thought she had detected raw, unadulterated passion in the depth of his eyes.

It had been an empowering moment. She had directed a collusive smile somewhere over his head, letting him know that *she* understood now just what influence she could wield over him, if she took the trouble to do so. She had exploited the moment to its full, surprised she was aware of how to go about it, but knowing she had got it right as she observed the fluctuating expressions dancing across his features.

And then she had ruined it all by falling!

Blast the man, where was he? Why had he not called to see how she fared and offered her his explanation for this latest attack? That he would not have reasoned it through by now did not occur to her. She might have cause to be out of character with him but that did not alter her faith in his ability.

Exhausted, Abby settled against her pillows and closed her eyes. She felt sleepy and would doze for half an hour. But when her strength was restored to her she would send Sally in search of Sebastian; protocol be damned!

A light tap on the door roused Abby from her slumber. She opened her eyes just as Sally bobbed a curtsey and stood back to admit her uncle. Sebastian followed him into the room. Abby was furious with her heart for appearing to beat faster at the sight of him and disciplined her features into a neutral expression. He smiled that wretchedly disconcerting smile of his as he took her hand in his — the one which made the rest of the world appear not to exist. Upbraiding herself for almost responding, Abby conjured up a warm smile for her uncle's benefit: one that completely excluded Sebastian.

'My dear, I trust we are not disturbing you? How do you feel?'

'Entirely comfortable, I thank you, Uncle.'

Uncle Bertram took a seat and her hand in his, simultaneously. 'My dear, after the dreadful occurrence this evening Lord Denver, very properly in my view, took it upon himself to enlighten me as to your difficulties.'

She glared at him, furious at this latest

example of his arbitrary attitude. 'You troubled my uncle without first consulting me? You had no right to do that,' she told him acerbically. 'I trusted you,' she added, in a lower voice, laced with bitter disappointment.

'Do not blame Lord Denver, my dear. He has extensive experience of these matters and did what he thought was right.' She made to protest but he silenced her with a gesture. 'You should have told me yourself, Abby,' he said gently.

'Oh, Uncle Bertram!' she cried impulsively, hating to see such deep concern in eyes that regarded her so lovingly. 'I wanted to, really I did. But I was not entirely sure and I did not know — '

'It is all right, Abby, pray to not overset yourself. I know now and that is what matters. I do not know how you contrived to make contact with Lord Denver in the first place, and perhaps it is better if I remain ignorant on that score. His lordship, however, has given me his word as a gentleman that nothing of an inappropriate nature took place and with that I shall force myself to be content.'

'What happened to cause my fall?' asked Abby, directing her remark to Sebastian.

He explained how her heel had been loosened. 'Did you not notice anything amiss when you put the shoe on?'

Abby wrinkled her brow as she considered the matter. 'Yes, actually it did feel a little strange, now that you mention it. But I had been delayed by little Ellen and, fearful of being late and earning your displeasure, Uncle, I simply imagined that I must be at fault for dashing about and did not spare it another thought.'

Sebastian and Lord Bevan exchanged a significant glance.

'Abby, Lord Denver feels that your antagonists will not stop until they achieve their objective and, from what he has told me, I tend to agree with him. He has come up with a somewhat unconventional plan to draw them out which, in the circumstances, I feel I have no option but to sanction.' Uncle Bertram looked grim and Abby felt a moment's concern on his behalf. He was no longer a young man and she was placing yet more strain upon him. 'He will outline it to you now and if you are brave enough to agree we will put it into place without delay.'

'Oh, Uncle, I must be a dreadful trial to you.'

'Abby,' he responded, patting her hand and wiping away a tear which had escaped from beneath her thick lashes, 'you are one of the few things in my life that gives me true pleasure. I am inordinately proud of your courage and want only, eventually, to see you happily established, with a family of your own, on the Penrith estate.'

Abby turned her tear-stained face in Sebastian's direction, unaware that her uncharacteristic display of emotion made him want to pull her into his arms and kiss away her devastation. In a gruff voice he conveyed his idea to her.

'Let me see if I understand you a'right,' said Abby, sitting up abruptly, disregarding the pain in her ankle in favour of allowing her indignation full rein. 'You wish me to suggest that you are remaining here, even though the snow is thawing rapidly and the roads should be passable again tomorrow, at my specific request? We are to spend all of our time together and pretend that a tendre exists between us,' she said, biting off the words as though they had stung her. 'And that after a day or so Hodges should casually mention in the senior servants' hall that you are taking me for a clandestine luncheon in the folly on the furthest edge of the estate. What good do you suppose that will achieve?'

Sebastian grinned at her indignation, fuelling her anger with his disgusting charm and a confidence which bordered on conceit, even as she reluctantly admired his coercive powers in persuading her uncle even to consider such a scandalous suggestion.

'You appear to have grasped the gist of my plan,' he told her, with a meltingly gentle smile. 'Whoever is behind these attacks will hear of my intentions from his man. You know as well as I how servants' gossip always finds its way upstairs. They are desperate and will not be able to resist such an opportunity to eliminate us both, if they think you have developed feelings for me, and I make it my business to ensure they have reason to believe those feelings are reciprocated.' His smile was almost wolfish now, making it abundantly clear that he relished the idea and intended to play his part to the full.

Just the thought of him holding her in his arms again — even if it was only being done to mislead her attackers — had the most disconcerting affect upon her and caused her to answer him with greater asperity than had been her intention. He was, after all, only suggesting the scheme in order to help her out of her difficulties but he seemed far too enthusiastic for the idea and deserved to be taken down a peg or two.

'Humph! It is the most ridiculous plan I have ever heard of. It will never work.'

'I believe that it will, Abby,' put in Uncle

Bertram gently, introducing the first sensible words into what was rapidly developing into a battle of wills between Abby and Sebastian. 'But it will require courage on your part and if you do not feel equal to it after your fall then no one will think the less of you. We will find another way.'

Sebastian was careful to keep his lips straight. Bevan had just — unwittingly? — said the only words that were likely to make Abby agree to the scheme. Even to suggest that her courage was in any way wanting was, he instinctively understood, all that it would take to bring her round.

'Very well,' she said with a reluctant nod, 'but you should know, Uncle, that I am only doing this because you deem it wise, and I do not like it above half. I think the whole scheme is ridiculous and cannot persuade myself that it has the remotest possibility of success.'

'Oh, it has a fair chance of exposing the villains,' Sebastian assured her, offering her a smouldering grin that softened his eyes and lit up his rugged features so compellingly that she was forced to avert her eyes, 'but only if we put on a convincing performance. I will allow you to rest this evening but first thing tomorrow you must start looking upon me with love in your eyes.'

Chuckling at her outraged expression he bent to kiss her hand and left the room in her uncle's wake.

14

Clear skies and a rise in the temperature lifted everyone's spirits the following morning. The snow in the garden was reduced to a watery slush and the girls' snowman had almost melted completely away. At breakfast the gentlemen were cheered to learn that a neighbouring hunt would be going ahead with its meet that day.

'Shame you can't stay and join us, Denver,' said Lord Wilsden, addressing Sebastian affably, presumably because he assumed he was about to see the last of him.

'Yes, doubtless you are anxious to be on your way now that the roads are passable,' added Evans rudely.

'Sorry to disappoint you, Evans,' responded Sebastian evenly, 'but I have decided to accept Lady Abigail's invitation and extend my stay.'

'What!' Evans choked on his coffee, spilling it over his coat.

The rest of the gentlemen also expressed surprise and the tense atmosphere which had been lacking for the first time that morning again made its presence felt. Sebastian showed no sign of being aware of it. Perfectly at his ease, he scrutinized each of the gentlemen, gauging their reactions to his announcement, but only Evans openly demonstrated his displeasure.

'I expect Lady Abigail was merely being polite,' remarked Sir Michael to Evans in what was probably supposed to be a supportive aside.

'Perhaps you will take the opportunity to put Warrior through his paces on the hunting field, then?' suggested Charlie who, intriguingly, appeared to be the least discomposed of them all by Sebastian's decision to prolong his stay.

'Now that would hardly be gentlemanly,' drawled Sebastian. 'The lady has particularly requested that I remain and, since she is incapacitated, the very least I can do is my humble best to entertain her. Don't suppose the task will be too arduous,' he added in a velvety smooth voice, designed to infer anything other than honourable intentions on his part and drawing a brief bark of laughter from Charlie.

Evans looked as though he might explode with anger and as soon as Lord Bevan rose from the table, declaring that he too would refrain from hunting today, Evans followed his host into the library. Sebastian could well imagine the nature of their discourse, the warnings from Evans as to the inadvisability of Sebastian being permitted into Abby's company; his choice remarks in respect of his reputation and the need for Lady Bevan to ensure he did not hone his seductive skills on Abby. Raised voices could be heard emanating from the library but that Evans was unsuccessful in pressing home his point became evident when he emerged ten minutes later, his countenance puce with rage.

Waving the huntsmen off and wishing them a good day's sport, Sebastian sauntered off in search of Hodges. He discovered him energetically polishing his master's boots.

'Any luck with Miss Frobisher?'

'Of course!' Hodges appeared affronted that Sebastian could have doubted it. 'She's just like all the others deep down, a few words of flattery, commiseration when she complained about how badly behaved her charges are, and she would have told me anything I wanted to know.' Hodges's smug expression gave way to a grimace. 'But don't ask me to go near her again, m'lord, 'cos I won't do it, not even for Lady Abigail's sake. And, what's more, Sally's overset 'cos she saw me making up to the old witch and so I've queered my pitch with her an' all.'

'No doubt you discovered enough to make the sacrifice worthwhile,' prompted Sebastian, grinning at his plight.

'That I did! It was Mary Bevan who told her that Abby wanted to see Ellen, all right. Miss Frobisher was all for saying no but said her mistress was in one of her uncompromising moods and that when she's like that there's no arguing with her.'

'I can imagine. Well done, Hodges!'

'Yeah, well . . . '

Sebastian's theory had just been proved beyond doubt, at least as far as Mary Bevan was concerned. It was too great a stretch of the imagination to suppose that it could have been coincidence; that someone else had loosened the heel and Mary had just happened to send her youngest daughter to see her aunt, causing Abby's arrival in the drawing-room to be delayed.

'Right,' he said to Hodges, his expression uncompromising. 'We now know for certain the identity of one of Abby's antagonists and can ensure that she, at least, has no opportunity to get too close.'

'But what of the other?'

'What indeed? All of the evidence still points to Charlie but . . . oh, I don't know why, but somehow it just doesn't sit comfortably with me.'

Sebastian cursed his inability to fathom what he suspected would prove to be blindingly obvious logic behind the attacks against Abby. Perhaps he was permitting his admiration for her courage to cloud his judgement, preventing him from thinking things through with his usual detached lucidity; hardly the best way to be of service to her. He had already permitted a near-fatal attack to be perpetrated against her, right under his very nose, and was damned if he would be found wanting a second time.

'Well, I must away and entertain Lady Abigail,' he said to Hodges, moving towards the door. 'Keep me informed of events below stairs.'

'How come you get all the best jobs?' demanded Hodges with a twisted grin. 'You get Lady Abigail and I get the Frobisher woman. It don't seem fair to me.'

Sebastian was still laughing when he knocked at Abby's door.

★　★　★

He was admitted by a blushing but subdued Sally, who appeared to have been crying. Sebastian paused to whisper something in her ear, which made her blush even more deeply. But she also brightened visibly. Abby was

253

fully dressed and reclining upon the settee in her anteroom: the same one that Sebastian had carried her to the previous day and which afforded her a fine view of the garden. Her injured leg was again supported by an abundance of cushions; her gown pulled down to respectably cover the affected area. Her dogs were sprawled on the rug before her, eyes only occasionally leaving their mistress to rest covetously upon the plate of sweetmeats at her side. Sally picked up the sewing which had been occupying her before Sebastian's arrival and, with another brief curtsey and beaming smile, moved to another chair a discreet distance away.

'Good morning,' said Sebastian, bowing to her and then tickling the dogs' ears in response to their tail-thumping greeting, 'and how fares your ankle this morning?'

'It is a little better, I believe,' she said, her tone cautiously formal. 'But tell me,' she added, lowering her voice and glancing round to ensure that Sally was out of earshot, a little of her former spirit sparkling from her eyes, 'what did you say to Sally just now to cheer her so? She has been miserable the whole morning but would not confide in me as to the cause of her distress.'

'I merely informed her that Hodges had been making himself agreeable to Miss

Frobisher on my specific orders.'

'Ah, I see.' She offered Sebastian a captivating smile, temporarily forgetting that she was vexed with him. 'But of course,' she added, belatedly straightening her lips and endeavouring to appear severe, 'I do not at all approve of the salacious nature of their relationship. It is altogether too shocking. I believe,' she added, wagging a judgemental figure in his direction, 'that your coachman has taken deliberate advantage of poor Sally, and no good can come from it, you just mark my words.' When Sebastian merely smiled and made no comment, Abby's indignation rose. 'He seduced her!' she declared hotly.

'I dare say he did,' agreed Sebastian smoothly. 'But have you stopped to consider the possibility that she may have wished to be seduced, or that she might even have enjoyed the experience?' Abby blushed furiously: this was too close a description for her comfort of what could so easily have happened in the garden between them yesterday — well, she was almost sure that was what could have happened if Sebastian had not been the one to show restraint. 'Who knows,' continued Sebastian in a speculative tone, 'but she must have enjoyed it, if her Friday face just now at the thought of his defection is anything to go by.'

'That is just ridiculous! Only a man could form such an opinion.'

'Perhaps, but Hodges does not force his attentions where they are not welcome.'

'Ha, so you admit it, then? That he makes a habit of this sort of thing only adds to his culpability.' She threw him a disapproving look. 'Like master, like servant, no doubt.'

'Very possibly,' he agreed smoothly. Unbeknown to Abby he was only prepared to enter into a discourse of this nature since her anger had conveniently made her forget to enquire whether it was indeed Mary who had sent Miss Frobisher and Ellen to her.

'But now it is your turn,' he continued, taking her hand and running his fingers slowly down the length of hers.

His almost casual, feather-like touch sent spangles of pleasure cascading through her, with devastating consequences for her equilibrium. She had spent most of the night disciplining herself to remain indifferent to whatever lascivious practices he might decide to employ, on the pretext of duping the rest of their party into believing that an amatory interest had sprung up between them, and failing so spectacularly at the first hurdle was most discouraging. Determined not to permit him to see just how easily he could arouse her passions, Abby snatched her hand away but Sebastian recaptured it, holding it too firmly for her to break free a second time.

'You seem to have forgotten that we are supposed to be on the brink of becoming lovers,' he whispered softly, his lips almost brushing her ear as he bent to issue this unnecessary reminder.

'We are merely putting on a show,' she countered, treating him to a quelling glance.

'Indeed we are.'

His eyes, mere inches away from hers, sent out an unmistakable message which registered somewhere in the most sensitive part of her core. His eyes were telling her that there was something he desired. And he was not, Abby instinctively understood, referring to the pantomime they had agreed upon to convince the rest of the guests that the tenor of their relationship had changed. In a blinding flash she understood that he had turned upon her the previous day because his passions had been at least as aroused as her own. His grin chose that moment to become broad and infectious, as if to prove a point that required no further collaboration.

'But we must put on a convincing show, must we not?' he asked her with a languorous smile. 'Whatever I do, I choose to do it well,' he warned her. He lifted a long curl from her shoulder and ran it through his fingers. She snatched it away from him, discomposed by his annoyingly coercive charm, against which she appeared to have few defences.

'We are not in public now and there is no one here to benefit from our performance.'

'Maybe not, but do you not think this an excellent opportunity to practise?' he enquired, supremely confident as he reached out a hand and traced the outline of her cheek.

Abby could not move. Her voice, too, appeared to have deserted her as the stimulant of his skilled fingers, delicately skimming across her features, caused her insides to turn somersaults. Oblivious to the presence of Sally, who had looked up from her work and was regarding them with eyes agog, he progressed to her lips, brushing his fingers against them in a sensuous glance, before moving on to her neck, exploring its length at his leisure with a touch that threatened to scorch. His fingers barely made contact with her flesh, swirling in lazy circles before continuing upon their tantalizing quest, but Abby felt as though she was on fire. Bewildered, she looked at him through eyes muddy with passion, wondering how the nascent pleasure he was giving her could possibly be created merely by the trace of his fingertips.

The surging tide of emotion cascading through her made her wish that he would never stop, but she knew that she must make him do so — immediately. She had little doubt that her reaction to his attentions, which surely must be transparent to a man of his experience, was quite shocking. But still she could not move: a circumstance which Sebastian could only interpret as permission to continue with this particular brand of torture. Her eyes widened, glowing and limpid, as his fingers moved to a new location. His touch, even lighter than before, traced the outline of her breast through the fabric of her gown, circling it with lazy disregard for the murmur of disapproval she managed to cobble together. His eyes were locked upon hers, smouldering with challenge. Never in her life before had she imagined that feelings of such exquisite sensitivity existed. She had convinced herself that what he had made her feel in the garden yesterday had been an accident, occasioned by her own curiosity and the sensuality of the moment. But it was impossible to continue with that lie now. With each touch of his fingers scintillating thrills surged through her with a searing intensity that took her breath away. If such ambiguous ecstasy went by the name of passion then perhaps the poets had got it right after all. But now was not the time to dwell upon such nebulous concerns; she had more pressing matters to consider. She must somehow find the strength to end Sebastian's attempts to consolidate his power over her and force him to tell her all he suspected about the people who intended her harm.

But desire overwhelmed reason and in spite of her best endeavours, she could not find her voice. Her arms appeared to have slipped around his neck, quite without her having noticed, and she found herself wondering who could have put them there. Her fingers were buried in the thickness of the curls spilling over his collar and, as he paused with his endeavours to meet her gaze, she found herself spellbound by the close proximity of his lips. What was happening to her? All those years of training appeared to have flown out of the window and Abby was uncomfortably aware that were it not for Sally's presence there could be no telling where this might all end, since ending it had clearly never been within her power.

So much pleasure from just the simple contact of his fingers, rioting with the guilt she felt at permitting him to overstep the bounds, eventually brought her to her senses. As if emerging from a daze she blinked twice and found the courage to look into his face. She did not altogether recognize what she saw there. His gaze was locked upon her features, his expression earnest and quite without artifice, which only caused the conflicting emotions within her to intensify. Drawing a ragged breath she somehow managed to find her voice.

'Sebastian, we must not — '

'Why not?' He whispered the words in her ear, his swirling tongue targeting the skin just below it, causing a fresh wave of pleasure to lance through her. 'You rather enjoy it.'

'You are taking shameful advantage of my indisposition,' she said accusingly, her voice a little firmer this time.

'Yes, I am.' His smile was gentle, and entirely unrepentant.

'Sebastian!' She tried to sound disapproving but, judging from his responding chuckle, made poor work of it. 'You told me yesterday that I should not — '

'Yes, but this is different. Besides, I am providing you with an opportunity to become acquainted with your passionate nature before you settle down and marry Evans.'

'I am not . . . ' She cleared her throat and

tried again. 'I have not agreed to marry Lord Evans.'

'Perhaps not, but I cannot see — '

There was a perfunctory tap on the door, which caused Sebastian to move with smooth fluidity and sit back in his chair, his expression perfectly innocent; a respectable six feet of daylight now separating him from Abby. Apart from the high flush on her cheeks and an expression of mild regret in her eyes, no one could have guessed what had been occurring between them a few seconds before Aunt Constance opened the door and walked towards them, beaming as always.

She greeted Sebastian warmly as he rose to his feet, not appearing to think it was at all strange for him to be virtually alone with Abby.

'How are you today, darling?' she asked Abby. 'How does your poor ankle feel?'

'A little better, thank you, Aunt,' she responded, wondering how her voice could sound so even so soon after Sebastian had reduced her to a hopelessly confused mixture of frustration and guilt, and leaned forward to accept her aunt's kiss. 'Mrs Burton's herbs have worked their usual magic and I already feel much more comfortable.'

'Is there anything you lack that I might arrange for you?'

'Nothing, thank you, Aunt.' Except the removal of an unconscionable rogue, who makes my pulse race and causes me to forget who I am supposed to be, she silently added. 'I have everything I need.'

The door opened again to admit Beatrice. Abby was, perversely, now unsure whether she was glad of the reinforcements, or regretted not having the opportunity to submit to just a little more of Sebastian's tutelage. Aunt Constance, satisfied that Abby was in want of nothing, went about her business, but Beatrice appeared intent upon remaining with them. A pack of cards was produced and when Mary Bevan put her sour face round the door an hour later, she was greeted with howls of laughter and the information that Sebastian was teaching the girls how to cheat at piquet. Abby was rather proud, given the distractions caused by Sebastian's questing fingers, with the speed at which she had mastered the art of dealing from the bottom of the pack.

Mary, not being invited to join in the game, made her children an excuse to leave them. Abby could see that Sebastian was observing her closely, whilst not appearing to take more than the mildest interest in her presence, and remembered she had not thought to ask him what discoveries Mr Hodges had made about

Miss Frobisher's unexpected visit to her the evening before. Left with the feeling that she had somehow been duped in that regard she returned her attention to the game, determined to have the matter out with Sebastian as soon as they were once again alone.

But, for the time being, it was not to be. Frustrated at his growing assertiveness she strove to speak up for herself when he refused to allow her to remain in her chamber, insisting she should take her luncheon in the dining-room with the rest of the company.

'Why must I go down?' she hissed, watching Beatrice as she exchanged a few words with Sally before leaving the room.

'To keep up the façade,' he responded. 'The gentlemen are all on the hunting field, it is true, but none of the ladies has chosen to accompany them today and so they will receive a full account of our behaviour when they return which is, of course, the point of it all. But it will only be possible for them to hear of our growing regard for one another if we are actually seen by all of them.'

Annoyingly she could find no fault with this logic and conceded the point with a reluctant nod. 'Very well,' she grumbled. 'I believe, if you give me your arm, I might be able to walk — '

She did not get to finish her sentence since

she no longer had sufficient breath in her body to do so. She felt it draining out of her as she was quite literally swept off her settee by a strong pair of arms.

'I can walk!'

'No, better for me to carry you,' he remarked, with an irksome grin. 'I have deliberately ensured that we will make a late entry in order that all of the ladies will witness me carrying you into the dining-room, holding you far closer against my person than is strictly necessary, of course.'

'There is no *of course* about it!'

'Oh, but there is. We need to be convincing. Do you think you will be able to endure the experience?' he enquired, his eyes brimming with laughter.

'Humph! You, my lord, are overdue for a good setting down.'

Sebastian chortled, a deep throaty sound which she could feel vibrating through his chest. 'Tighten your arms around my neck, sweetheart,' he said in a mocking tone, surely designed to try her patience to its limits. Her moue of distaste only seemed to amuse him further, his chuckle turning into a rumbling laugh. 'And, let me see, what else? You appear far too pale. You should be looking animated, your eyes should have additional sparkle and you skin should be glowing — all as a direct result of my attentions, naturally.' Seeming not to notice the most unladylike snort which escaped her at that moment, Sebastian continued to regard her with mock solemnity. 'Now, how can we put that right?'

Abby could feel herself blushing scarlet. 'You are enjoying this!'

'All in a day's work,' he assured her with a wink, offering her a smile that could have melted stone. She lost the battle to prevent it from affecting her and contented herself with a glare of lofty scorn. 'And, I must say, that maidenly blush is most becoming: very convincing. But there is still something amiss.'

'What now?' she grumbled.

'It is your lips. They need to look as though they have been thoroughly kissed.'

Understanding his intentions she struggled frantically, genuinely distressed. But no means of salvation presented itself. 'Sebastian, no: don't do this! You cannot possibly, you would not dare: not here!'

But, of course, he could. And he did. Ignoring her very real distress he paused at the head of the stairs, angled his head and captured her lips with all the assuredness of a man who fully expected his overture to be welcomed. She struggled against him, this really was too much! But he was so much stronger than she was, the expression in his eyes so persuasively compelling, that her struggle ceased almost before it had begun. Besides, just the feel of his lips upon hers had been enough to send a vortex of desire spiralling through her all over again, leaving her quivering with anticipation and ill-equipped to resist his demands. Her eyes fluttered to a close, the heavy sweep of lashes curling sweetly against her flushed cheeks. As his tongue probed, asking for and receiving her complete capitulation, Abby no longer cared that she was engaged in a most unseemly embrace with a rake of the first order, in a public place where anyone might come upon them at any time. In fact, she no longer cared about anything at all, other than the fact that Sebastian should continue to kiss her.

He could not do so: it had to end and he broke the kiss before they both got completely carried away. Abby was mortified when a tiny moan of protest escaped her mouth.

'Sorry, sweetheart,' he breathed quietly, as he commenced their journey down the stairs, 'but I promise to make it up to you later.'

'Do not delude yourself into supposing that I enjoyed that,' she hissed. 'I am merely following your instructions and playing a part.'

'Of course you are!' Holding her closely to him, he examined her face. 'That is better! No one will have any doubts about how we have been occupying our time. Now then, a gesture from you as I carry you into the dining-room, I think,' he continued, clearly enjoying himself enormously. 'Perhaps you should tangle your fingers in my hair, just as you did earlier.' He tilted his handsome head to one side, as though considering the matter. 'Yes, that would be just the right touch: very convincing. Ouch! Tangle, I said, Abby, not tug.'

'Oh sorry,' she muttered with a specious smile, 'I must have misheard you.'

He tightened his grip upon her and frowned. 'Look into my face and try to pretend that you enjoy what you see.'

'That might be asking a little too much,' she responded, enjoying herself almost as much as he was now. 'I have never been good at cutting a sham.'

'You, my lady, have all the makings of a jade!'

In view of the fact that she had just, shamelessly, allowed him to kiss her witless in public, she had to concede that he had a point. She was not about to admit it though.

'Coming from one with experience as extensive as yours that can only be construed as praise.' She paused, nibbling at her lower lip as she savoured her moment of revenge; aware that she had at last managed to rattle him.

'Act!' he hissed into her ear, as he carried her into the dining-parlour and made an inordinate amount of fuss about placing her gently in her usual chair, calling to a footman to bring a stool upon which to rest her ankle, and to another for a cushion to support the small of her back.

'Are you quite comfortable, m'dear?' he asked, with all the solicitation of a man gripped by the fiercest of passions, aware of but completely ignoring the intense interest being directed their way by all of the ladies seated at the table.

'Perfectly so, my lord, I thank you, although how I should have managed without your strong arms to support me I can scarce imagine.'

She batted her lashes at him and smiled into his eyes in a gesture that somehow managed to combine both innocence and bald provocation, wondering what he was making of her performance; aware that she was overacting to a ridiculous degree, but enjoying the revenge she was exacting too much to care. She wondered whether it would be going too far if she attempted to simper but, suspecting from Sebastian's warning frown that he would not be above kicking her bad ankle as a means of making her behave, she decided against it.

★　★　★

Sebastian watched her carefully as he continued to fuss over her. It was obvious that she was having the time of her life, even if she was an appalling actress. He reminded himself that she had never before done anything that might be considered the tiniest bit scandalous but today had calmly permitted a rakehell of the first order not only to carry her, far from innocently, into a room full of her friends and relations, but to kiss her in public, too. She had also discovered a little more about her passionate nature. The fact that she could survive both experiences, as well as a further attempt on her life, and find the strength of character to respond to him with such spirit had stirred his blood. He grinned a warning into her eyes, momentarily forgetting that they had a spellbound audience, eyes agog with interest as they attempted to interpret his every nuance.

Sebastian's brief annoyance at her terrible

acting quickly turned to respect. He took the seat beside her and, barely sparing a word for the rest of the diners, devoted himself to ensuring that she ate her luncheon. He speared delicacies with his own fork, placing it between her lips in what could only be construed by his mesmerized audience as a provocative gesture, insisting that she take just a little taste. Warming to her role she now played her part superbly, running her tongue slowly over her bruised lips, asking silent questions he would infinitely prefer not to answer, as she captured his gaze and held it. If this was her idea of revenge she could have no notion how well she was succeeding. Sebastian grimaced and shifted awkwardly in his seat.

Abby, genuinely fatigued by the rigours of the morning, rested for most of the afternoon: Sally inside the room with her, Hodges patrolling the corridor outside. None of the ladies attempted to intrude upon her repose and it was a refreshed Abby whom Sebastian carried into the drawing-room that evening, sending Sally down first to peep round the door and ensure that everyone was assembled before he staged his entrance.

The returned sportsmen made straight for Abby, Evans being hotly pursued by Sir

Michael and Simon Graves. Ignoring Sebastian, who had stationed himself beside her chair, his hand proprietarily resting on its back, Evans actually knelt in front of her. His eyes softening, he kissed her hand and gently enquired how she was feeling.

'Lord Denver has taken prodigious good care of me today, my lord, and kept me royally entertained.' She darted a saucy look in Sebastian's direction, her eyes sparkling, before returning her attention to Lord Evans. 'And my ankle feels much easier this evening, I thank you.'

'I am very glad to hear it,' said Evans, bestowing a glance loaded with pure venom upon Sebastian.

'How was your day's sport, my lord? I did try to persuade Lord Denver to catch up with the field but he would not hear of it.'

'What pleasure could compete with the privilege of being admitted to your company for an entire day?' responded Sebastian with conviction.

Throughout dinner Sebastian and Abby kept up their performance, which caused everyone to focus their attention upon them. Sebastian detected varying degrees of surprise, amusement, envy and disapproval in the faces of their audience but, significantly, nothing more telling than the merest flicker of interest in Charlie's demeanour. Sebastian was obliged to concede that the man had hidden depths: not once did he allow his true feelings to become apparent. All the same, he could not have failed to notice the turn events had taken between Abby and himself and by the time he made a flamboyant display of carrying her back to her chamber he was convinced that they had done all they could into frightening Charles and Mary into showing their hand.

15

None of the local hunts were meeting the following day and so the gentlemen occupied their time by escorting the ladies on a morning's excursion on horseback. Only Harold, at Lord Bevan's private request, remained behind. Before agreeing to Sebastian's plan he had imposed the condition that his son be made aware of their suspicions in respect of his wife's involvement. He might even be able to shed some light on the perplexing question of why Mary would choose to become embroiled with such an evil scheme.

Harold followed Lord Bevan and Sebastian into the library and listened in astonishment as his father revealed details of the attempts on Abby's life, and Sebastian's true purpose for being amongst them. Harold was as horrified as his father had been upon first learning of the plot.

'It is enough to test one's faith in the Almighty,' he opined morosely. 'Who would wish to do such a terrible thing to an innocent girl: one who has already suffered so much but is refreshingly unspoiled by the

274

attention she receives?'

'That is a question which Denver has been wrestling with these past couple of weeks.'

'Have you reached any conclusions, Denver?'

'I fear that I have.' And in a measured tone he outlined the case against Charlie.

'It is possible, I suppose,' conceded Harold with evident reluctance, 'but, like Abby, I find it difficult to accept that anyone of our close acquaintance could be culpable, however pressing his circumstances.' He paused, digesting all he had heard, his expression harsh and unyielding. 'You have suggested that there could be more than one perpetrator, Denver. But who could have been persuaded to go along with such an iniquitous plan? And how could Charlie even approach anyone, without running the risk of them rejecting his proposal and revealing it to you, sir?'

'How he managed it I cannot say, but I am of the opinion that he has recruited a woman,' said Sebastian, pathos in his tone. 'She would much more easily be able to gain access to Abby in her private quarters and initiate attempts upon her life, such as the one that happened here two nights ago, without creating suspicion.'

'Indeed, yes,' agreed Harold. 'But I ask you again, Denver, whom do you suspect?'

'I am very much afraid that all of the evidence we have collected points to your wife,' said Sebastian, his tone firm yet compassionate.

A gasp of astonished denial was Harold's first reaction. The ineffable silence which followed it was loaded and uncomfortable and Sebastian forced himself not to break it.

'Impossible!' snapped Harold eventually, his tone glacial. 'And I take extreme exception to your even suggesting it. And you, sir,' he continued, turning to his father, his expression beyond emotion, 'that you could for one moment countenance such a suggestion grieves me beyond words. My family and I shall leave here immediately and I cannot see that we will have anything further to say to one another.'

Harold turned towards the door, but his father's voice stayed him as he was about to turn the handle. 'Do you know me so little as to imagine that I have entertained Denver's suggestion lightly?' he asked in a sombre tone. 'I know just how enamoured you are of your wife, how happy you are as a family.'

'Then why? I do not understand.'

'Denver's evidence is fairly compelling.'

'Then I had better hear it,' said Harold, sounding weary all of a sudden, and seating himself in the nearest chair. 'And then, when she is proved to be innocent, I will have the pleasure of receiving your full apology.'

'I pray that it will prove necessary for me to offer it,' said Sebastian, who then proceeded to lay out all the evidence he had thus far accumulated.

Harold listened to Sebastian condemning the woman he loved without once interrupting. He scowled when he learned how Mary had sent Miss Frobisher and Ellen to Abby on the night of her most recent accident.

'Mary would, of course, have known that Abby's attire for that evening would be laid out during tea, since Sally performs the same task for Mary. My wife could also have tampered with that shoe without anyone being the wiser,' conceded Harold. 'But,' he continued, his voice rising to fill the room as effortlessly as it must fill his church from the pulpit when he got into his stride with a passionate sermon, 'the same could be said of all the other ladies in residence, too.'

'True, but — '

'And,' continued Harold, his anger appearing to give way to relief as he played his trump card, 'what possible reason could she have to wish Abby harm? They are friends. Besides, what would she have to gain from Abby's demise?'

'Her motivation is the one thing we have

yet to establish,' conceded Sebastian. 'We wondered if you might be able to shed any light on it,' he added hopefully.

'To condemn my own wife, do you mean? Well, I am sorry to disappoint you, Denver, but I cannot think of any reason in this world for Mary to wish harm upon one of her closest friends. And furthermore, unless and until you have definitive proof as to my wife's involvement I would thank you to refrain from bandying about such wild allegations and sullying her good name.'

'We plan to expose the villains today,' said Lord Bevan quietly. 'That is why I insisted that you be told in advance of our plans.'

Harold snapped his head in his father's direction, his expression now one of melancholic regret. But his tone, when he addressed him, remained glacial. 'So that I may be called to stand in judgement upon my own wife, do you mean?'

'If, as I sincerely hope, she is innocent no one will be more relieved than me,' said Lord Bevan in a manner that left little doubt as to his sincerity.

'How do you intend to draw them out?'

'My man is even now in the servants' hall, arranging a hamper so that I might drive Abby for a clandestine luncheon in the folly. Hodges will make a great play of grumbling about how his life is going to change for the worse, since far from pursuing Abby with my usual disreputable intentions, he is convinced that I am truly enamoured with her and intend to propose marriage. He will speculate as to whether that is my intention in driving her to the folly today. He will even hint that I am thinking of persuading her to forego her season and elope with me straightaway.'

Lord Bevan took up the story. 'We already know that the perpetrators are becoming desperate and if Abby's fortune is indeed their goal they cannot risk her entering into a speedy marriage and will be compelled to act immediately to prevent it happening. What better opportunity than if they suppose Abby and Denver to be alone in the folly? They have seen for themselves how much she appears to admire him and will not doubt his ability to talk her into the elopement. Any sort of accident might be contrived in that far region of the estate, conveniently resulting in the demise of them both.'

'But, of course, we will not be alone. My man and your father's will be armed and concealed outside the folly.'

'And I, and you too if you wish it, Harold, will hide ourselves inside the folly, ready to bear witness to events and intercede to protect Abby should Denver be overcome.'

'Of course I wish to be there,' responded Harold hotly, 'how could you doubt it?'

'That is what I knew you would say.' Lord Bevan offered up a taut smile. 'It is also why I contrived to get rid of the rest of the party this morning. Evans is on the verge of doing something ridiculous to deter Abby from spending so much of her time with Denver and I do not need his jealous possessiveness impinging upon our plan.'

A knock at the door preceded Hodges entering the room.

'It is all set in motion, m'lord,' he said grimly. 'I found Lord Wilsden's man, and Mr Charles Wilsden's, together and spoke in front of them both. Several other ears were flapping at such a juicy scrap of gossip and you may be sure that it will spread above stairs as soon as the riding party returns.'

'Well done, Hodges. Now do you have your pistol to hand?'

'Yes, m'lord, loaded and ready to be used in your defence.'

'Indeed, I am depending upon it. But now, gentlemen, I think I should collect Abby and head for the folly. Is her curricle at the side door, Hodges?'

'Yes, m'lord, and the hamper is in the trunk, along with your sidearm.'

'God speed, Denver,' said Harold, rising to

shake his hand. 'I know you are putting your life at risk for Abby's sake and I can only commend your courage. I bear you no ill-will for suspecting my wife since having recovered from my surprise I can see that to an impartial observer the evidence must point to her involvement. I am only grateful that, if your plan works, by this evening she will be absolved from all blame.'

★　★　★

Entering Abby's chamber, Sebastian found her warmly clothed and Sally in the process of wrapping a heavy velvet cloak around her shoulders.

'Here, allow me,' he offered, taking the garment from Sally's fingers and fastening it securely in place. 'Now do you have everything you require?'

'I think so, yes.'

'Then you are ready?'

'As ready as I ever will be.'

'Oh, my lord, do take good care of her.' Sally let out a little sob. 'I fear for her something awful.'

'She will be perfectly safe in my care, Sally. If you wish to be of assistance to your mistress, though, you must play your part convincingly. If any of the ladies call, wishing to see Lady Abigail, you must tell them that she is sleeping, does not wish to be disturbed, and turn them away. Keep the door locked at all times in case they try to enter without first knocking.'

'You may depend upon me, my lord.'

Sebastian carried Abby down the back stairs and lifted her into her curricle without, as far as he could ascertain, being observed by anyone. He drove at a brisk trot and reached the folly without mishap. Helping her down and carrying her into the draughty building he returned to the curricle, leading the horse into the lee of nearby trees. Unloading the hamper he returned to find Abby just where he had left her, sitting upon an old bench and shivering uncontrollably.

'Courage, sweetheart,' he cajoled, taking her gloved hand between both of his own. 'It will soon all be played out.' He turned her hand over and kissed the bare skin on the inside of her wrist.

'I should not have involved you,' she said, causing his heart to jolt when, looking into her luminous eyes, he realized her fear was not for her own welfare but rather more for his. 'You could be hurt, or even killed, and what would that achieve?'

Sebastian was tempted to inform her that more than one disgruntled husband would be delighted by the news but, deciding from the sombre nature of her expression that such an admission would hardly be likely to reassure her, he wisely remained silent on the point.

'I am not an easy person to do away with,' he told her with a somnolent smile. 'It has been attempted on more than one occasion and I am still very much of this world.'

'No doubt you did something to place yourself in peril on those occasions and only had yourself to blame,' she said, with a flash of spirit.

Sebastian considered those affronted husbands again and could not prevent his lips from quirking. 'You are in the right of it.'

'But this situation is an entirely different matter,' she continued, apparently determined to chastise herself and oblivious to the fact that her morose mood was in direct variance to the light-heartedness which had chosen to take him over at such an inappropriate juncture. 'I can see now that it was not at all fitting that I should have asked you, someone with no connection with me or my affairs, to take such risks.'

He brushed her furrowed brow with his lips. 'I would not have missed it for the world,' he assured her softly. 'And I would have you know that it is I who should be grateful to you. Gentlemen of leisure thrive upon a little danger to spice up their dreary existences, in case you did not know it. We rather depend upon a little excitement to relieve the tedium, in fact.'

'Stop it!' The words came out as a strangled cry. 'Stop making so light of it. I appreciate your concern for my feelings, but I can deal with the unpleasant realities of this situation. In fact I would feel better knowing the whole truth; which you appear intent upon withholding from me. I do not need to be treated as though I were made of porcelain, you know.'

'If I did not know better,' he responded, his tone as smooth as velvet, the expression in his eyes deliberately mocking, 'I might imagine that you did not have any faith in my abilities to act as your protector.'

'Oh no, pray do not imagine for one moment that I doubt you.'

Her disingenuous response was refreshingly honest, acting as a useful distraction from the explanations she required but which he would prefer not to make. 'Then leave the worrying to me and concentrate upon mustering your reserves of courage. And talking of courage, I think I have something that might be of assistance in that respect.' He delved into the hamper and produced a bottle of champagne, expertly popping the cork and filling two glasses. He bullied her into draining hers quickly and spread out the food, ordering her to eat and feeding her himself when she was slow to respond.

Hodges entered the room on silent feet, just as they had finished their repast and drunk the last of the champagne. 'The riding party have all returned to the house, m'lord, and no one attempted to go off alone. Bridges and I are now in place outside.'

'All right, Hodges, show Lord Bevan and his son in as soon as they appear.'

'Yes, m'lord,' he said, leaving them as quietly as he had arrived.

'Now then,' said Sebastian, pulling a pale-faced, shivering Abby into his arms. 'It will be some time before we can expect company and you appear to be falling victim to the cold. Let me see if I can do something about that.'

His kiss was not the gentle, reassuring affair she might have been expecting, but firm and demanding. It was a less than subtle means of diverting her fears until she could think of nothing but the exquisite pressure of his lips upon hers. He deemed himself successful when he eventually broke the kiss and, with a grunt of protest, she tangled her fingers in his hair and jerked his head downwards again.

'Warmer now?' he enquired, breaking the kiss and settling her head upon his shoulder.

'A little. How much longer must we wait?'

'The riding party should have returned by now and your uncle will have informed them that as you are fatigued you have chosen to take luncheon in your chamber. They will also learn that Hodges has driven me over to visit my friend Lord Falmington in Brigdon. You may be sure that everyone will have heard the rumours about us lunching here alone, but no one, not even Evans, will dare to voice them in front of your uncle.' He flashed her a deliberately challenging smile that was pure predatory male and held her gaze for a protracted period before speaking again. 'And so, we have some time to wait. Now, how would you suggest that we pass it?'

'Lord Evans is in the right of it: you are an unconscionable rogue!' She put up her chin and removed her head from his shoulder.

'A thousand pities,' he responded laconically, chuckling at her efforts to remain aloof.

'Of all the arrogant, ungentlemanly, self-opinionated scapegraces it has ever been my misfortune to . . . arrgh!'

Sebastian cut off her harangue by settling her bodily on his lap. Grinning at her scandalized expression, black hair falling across eyes that glowed with wicked intent, he lowered his head towards hers. 'That was not always your opinion of me, was it now?'

'No, I mean yes, I do not think it at all proper to — '

But Sebastian no longer cared about her notions of propriety. She was in urgent need of a distraction from her current situation, whilst he . . . well, he deserved a reward for saving her from those who would see her dead. He would leave here tomorrow, and would not allow himself to be alone with her again once they left the folly. He brushed the curls away from her face with a featherlike touch that caused her to gasp with astonishment, all protestations apparently forgotten. Her lips parted in a wordless invitation but Sebastian intended to savour the moment, the last occasion upon which he would ever permit himself to excite her passions, and continued to observe the gamut of emotions filtering across her lovely face, refusing to be rushed.

His kiss, when it eventually came, was searingly passionate but, judging by the strangled protest which escaped Abby's lips when he broke it prematurely, too short for her liking. Mindful of the dangers they were about to face in the shape of her aggressors Sebastian had merely sought to distract her, not intending to lead her into greater peril by arousing her passion. The sound of his name, whispered by her with such deep intensity, helped him come to his senses. He released her abruptly, causing her eyes to fly open as she fixed him with an accusatory glare.

'You are doing it again,' she complained.

'This is not a game, Abby.'

'Then why did you do it? Or is it your intention to lay the blame at my door again?' she enquired scathingly. 'You say one thing, attempting to claim the moral high ground, and then revert to your former means of carrying on. I do not at all understand you.'

'You have my apology, Abby, I never should have — '

'No, you should not. But since you did, it will not end here.'

'But it must!'

'No, I wish to know more.'

'That is impossible.'

'You are being unfair!' she cried, supremely confident as she lifted a hand to frame his face.

Sebastian could not recall ever having experienced such a deep feeling of exquisite agony before: not once in all his years. Damn it, she was destroying him! Fire lanced through his veins. He sought out her lips once again, convinced that he would never be able to sate the inexorable need he felt for her. She responded with an enthusiasm that drove his needs to unparalleled heights. Realizing it, he released her and lifted her from his lap.

'More,' she said with a sultry smile, her breath shaking.

Sebastian knew it was a dangerously bad idea, but when she looked at him with such incandescent desire shining from her eyes he was beyond denying her anything. Before he could decide what further action to take though, Hodges materialized from nowhere, coughing loudly to give Sebastian advance notice of his close proximity, Lord Bevan and Harold at his heels. They greeted Sebastian and Abby with grim smiles and lost no time in concealing themselves in the small chamber behind the main room. They knew they did not have much time to spare. Charlie and Mary would presumably come together and would likely do so by means of a curricle, since they did not know of the shortcut across the grounds which Lord Bevan and his son had taken advantage of on foot.

Almost immediately the sound of a conveyance being driven at speed reached their ears. A stark birdcall, made by Hodges, confirmed the fact that they had company. Looking towards the door Sebastian was grieved, but not surprised, when Mary Bevan entered. He was, however, astonished when not Charlie, but his father, Lord Wilsden, followed close on her heels.

It was then, in a blinding flash, that it all made sense to him. Everything was so ridiculously obvious that he could scarce believe he had been bone-headed enough not to have made the connection before now.

'Ah hello there,' said Sebastian calmly, offering them a sardonic smile. 'You are here at last. We had almost given up on you. Do come in.'

16

Mary Bevan's eyes rolled back in her head, darting nervously from face to face before coming to rest on Lord Wilsden. Her partner, by contrast, appeared to be perfectly at ease and demonstrated not one iota of concern upon discovering that their arrival had been anticipated.

'I told you this was a trap!' she hissed. 'You should have heeded my warning.'

With a placatory wave of his hand Wilsden strode into the centre of the room. He looked down at Sebastian and Abby and offered them a polite smile that would not be out of place in the most fashionable salon.

'Calm yourself, Mrs Bevan. They might think they have outwitted us but have clearly not taken into account the fact that they are here alone and completely at our mercy.'

'Why?' asked Abby, her expression one of wounded bewilderment as her eyes swivelled between the two of them in genuine consternation. 'What have I ever done to either of you that you should bear me such murderous ill will?'

'Oh, do not take offence, my dear, it is nothing personal,' Wilsden assured her affably. 'It is merely that you are in the unfortunate position of standing between me and something that I have long looked upon as mine.'

'That something being the Duchy of Penrith,' concluded Sebastian for him.

Wilsden inclined his head. 'Exactly so!'

'But, if I die the title becomes extinct,' said Abby, whose head was pounding as she struggled to come to terms with the defection of two people whom she greatly esteemed; simultaneously attempting to understand their motives and make excuses for them.

'Indeed, which means the Crown will once more have the gift of the duchy within its power. The prince cannot risk leaving our corner of the West Country without a duke to keep the populace in order indefinitely. He will require someone whose loyalty is beyond question; someone whom he can depend upon to keep control of affairs in that part of his realm; someone who has been successfully keeping the duchy profitable, and the local populace in order, since the demise of your dear father.'

'In other words,' interposed Sebastian

smoothly, 'who better than his most faithful of subjects Lord Wilsden, who is already respectably established in the area and has demonstrated the extent of his loyalty on several occasions by making substantial loans to the prince? Loans,' continued Sebastian, with a knowing glance at Abby, 'which, by the way, he has himself borrowed from your estate.'

Wilsden's languid smile faltered very slightly. 'You appear to have made a thorough study of my affairs, Denver.'

'I will confess that you had me confused for a while,' conceded Sebastian affably, sensing Abby's growing distress and squeezing her waist with the arm that still surrounded it. 'For some time I held the opinion that it was Charlie behind the attempts on Abby's life but, of course, that is what you intended me to think, is it not?'

Wilsden let forth with a derisive snort. 'That Johnny raw does not have the backbone for such rum capers!'

'You wanted us to believe that it was your dearest wish to see him married to Abby. But you also made sure that it was easy for anyone of a curious disposition to discover that his affections were already engaged elsewhere, leading to the obvious conclusion that Abby was standing between him and his heart's desire.'

'I was well aware that she would never seriously consider him as a husband, especially if Bevan did not endorse his candidature, but it suited my purpose for people to suppose otherwise; especially when our rather inventive methods for doing away with her failed. We knew it would become obvious eventually, even to one as trusting as she, that not all of her recent accidents could be ascribed to misfortune. It was always going to be simply a matter of time before she realized she was in danger. When that happened we had no idea whom she might turn to, but must confess we did not expect her to look outside the family for a confidante.'

'And you could not afford to keep failing, now that she is being pursued by so many gentlemen,' mused Sebastian, filling in the gaps as he voiced his thoughts aloud. 'She could marry at any time and your efforts to procure the wealth of the duchy for your own ends would then have been for naught. Her new husband would assume the title of second creation duke and, doubtless, sire a nursery full of heirs to make the succession secure. More to the point, though, the management of all the duchy's affairs would then fall to his lot and your lucrative stewardship would come to an end.'

'Quite so,' agreed Wilsden, pacing the room with agitated strides, appearing like one of the caged tigers Abby had seen in Vauxhall Gardens and for whom she felt such sympathy.

'I had come too far to risk the possibility that she would disobey her uncle and marry before the end of her season. Even girls as obedient as Abby are wont to act with spontaneity when they persuade themselves that they are in love. And so we had to do something to prevent her now.' He slammed his clenched fist into the palm of his other hand. 'The duchy should have been in my family from the very first but we were sufficiently misguided to back the wrong horse. In '66 my father was for the Duke of Grafton, whereas Carstairs backed Rockingham and it was Rockingham who was made Head of the Treasury that year. He persuaded the king that a dukedom should be created in Penrith and bestowed upon a deserving subject. Someone of integrity needed to be appointed to quell the dissatisfaction being openly expressed by the tin miners. And so, using his influence, Rockingham ensured that it was conferred upon his ally, Carstairs. My father was devastated, never quite got over his disappointment, and never forgave Carstairs for fulfilling the role that should have been his.'

'And never forgot, either?' suggested Sebastian.

'Precisely! Abby's great-grandmother was a formidable political hostess, who was as beautiful as she was ruthless. She wielded considerable power behind the scenes, and no one is precisely sure what lengths she was prepared to go to with Rockingham in order to further her husband's ambitions. It is a subject to which I have devoted many hours of conjecture, as you can imagine, and the answer must be as obvious to a man of your ilk, Denver, as it was to me. The whore!' he roared, colour invading an expression that was both pained and furious. 'Suffice it to say that we had no similar weapon with which to fight back. Matters were made worse by the fact that Rockingham only lasted two years at the Treasury before being replaced with our man, Grafton.' Wilsden's booming laugh bore no traces of humour. 'How was that for poor timing?'

'Rather than besmirching the good name of Abby's great-grandmother, Wilsden,' drawled Sebastian, 'has it not occurred to you that Carstairs was considered the better man for the job for reasons of greater gravitas?'

'What bag of moonshine are you implying now?'

Sebastian shrugged. 'I am merely reminding myself of the facts. It is common knowledge that the ingression of water into the shafts of the tin mines was the worst problem the miners faced in Cornwall at the time. Steam engine driven pumps were proving to be the answer, but they were expensive and their introduction was slow to come about. Carstairs was something of an authority on the subject, doing much to educate the mine owners as to their benefits, easing their introduction and avoiding further unnecessary loss of life.'

Abby raised her head and looked at Sebastian through eyes rendered luminous with surprise. There was no artifice in an expression that was full of gratitude, and a touching degree of trust, too. Her aesthetic beauty, delicate and susceptible within the shady light of the folly, sent Sebastian's mind on a journey of regret about what might have been.

'How did you know?' Abby asked him quietly. 'About my great-grandfather's knowledge, I mean? I had no idea; have never been told.'

Sebastian winked at her. 'I made it my business to find out.'

'Anyone could have gained the knowledge he supposedly possessed,' said Wilsden, sneering.

'Perhaps, but Carstairs understood its importance, and not simply because he wished to be rewarded by the Crown.' Sebastian stretched his long legs in front of him and affected a bored expression. 'But we digress. Do continue with your story, Wilsden. You were keeping Abby and I royally entertained.' He grinned. 'No pun intended, of course.'

Wilsden looked at Sebastian with dislike but could not resist the opportunity for further boasting. 'My father, on his deathbed, made me promise to one day see the duchy conferred upon our family: where it should have been in the first place.'

'And you are willing to resort to murder in order to achieve your end?'

'It is necessary,' responded Wilsden, with an indifferent shrug. 'One cannot fight a war without incurring casualties, Denver: as a war veteran yourself you ought to be the first to appreciate that fact. My father was adamant that we should remain on congenial terms with the Carstairs family, much as we privately disliked them. It was by paying heed to that advice that I became Abby's godfather and finally got my hands on the duchy's wealth when her parents departed this world.'

Abby visibly paled. 'Do not tell me that you had anything to do with — '

'Their accident? No, my dear, I regret to say that I can make no such claim, although when it happened I confess to being sorry that I had not previously thought of the idea myself. Their accident occurred by complete chance, but I knew when it happened that it was a sign that my moment had at last arrived.'

'You waited for a long time to put your plan into action,' remarked Sebastian, appearing totally unmoved by the tale of evil, spilling with vitriolic spite, from Wilsden's lips.

'As I told you before, we have learned as a family to understand the importance of patience. I knew that another accident so soon after the demise of Abby's parents would attract unwanted attention. And so I was prepared to wait, secure in the knowledge that I would eventually be successful.'

'But you tried very hard to have Abby live under your roof.'

'Yes, and had I been successful it would

have settled matters most conveniently, and no one need have died. Abby would have been thrown constantly into Charlie's company when at her most vulnerable. I would have ensured that she damn well relied upon him for everything and, if I'd had my way, they would have been married long before now. Charlie would have been the new duke, but in name only. He would never have been able to run the duchy efficiently, he is far too lazy to make the effort, and I would have had ultimate control.' He slapped his palm against his thigh in frustration, the noise unnaturally loud in the otherwise quiet room, causing Abby to start violently.

'But even then I thought I would have my way. It did not matter that Abby was not living under my roof, since I already had the prince's ear. He was not Regent at the time but everyone knew that his father was acting more bizarrely by the day and it would only be a matter of time. But Bevan, damn him, was determined to secure the succession through Abby and spoke to the king's advisers about it far sooner than I could have anticipated, leaving me no opportunity to counter his measures. I knew that if I tried to influence the decision by asking the prince to intervene it would immediately go against me, since the king and his son were not on good terms and His Majesty would be more likely to act against the prince's advice. And so, once again, my timing was appalling, especially,' he added with a twisted laugh, 'as the prince assumed the regency almost immediately thereafter. But by then it was too late and I could not attempt to overturn Parliament's decision in respect of the succession without arousing Bevan's suspicions.'

'You enjoy manipulating people, Wilsden, and I concede that it took me a while to realize what you were about.'

'How did you find me out?'

'It was something Bevan said, something about Abby's personal fortune not being entailed, that first alerted me. I blame myself for not thinking of it sooner, of course. Abby told me when we first met that her great-grandmother had ensured the entail through the female line, but of course that only referred to the Carstairs fortune and not, as she had supposed, the duchy. It would not have been possible to make advance arrangements in that respect. Only a Royal Decree, and Act of Parliament, could make that provision when circumstances dictated; which of course they did when her parents died.'

'You appear to have thought it all through,'

conceded Wilsden grudgingly.

'I believe I have. Knowing from your stewardship of the duchy, and willingness to borrow from its coffers whenever the mood took you, that you all but considered it to be your personal fiefdom, I could not imagine you taking kindly to handing the reins over to Abby's eventual husband.'

'The thought was intolerable.'

'Carstairs was not discouraged by the fact that his wife had only produced one child, a girl,' continued Sebastian, touching Abby's hand gently, 'or that his other children had not survived their infancy. They were still young and surely an heir must follow soon? Indeed, at the time of their demise the duchess was in an advanced condition once again. This time she was bound to produce a healthy son, who would survive infancy and inherit the dukedom, which includes the Penrith estate, with its vast income and extensive lands. But Carstairs's personal fortune, his other estates and town house, which are independent of the duchy, would be divided between his other sons, with substantial portions being set aside for Abby, and any other daughters', dowries.

'But, as it turned out, there was no time for them to produce more children: they never would have another healthy son.' Abby, with tears spilling down her lovely face, gulped with surprise but remained otherwise silent. 'I say another healthy son, because Carstairs had already sired one. Abby's brother did not die of natural causes, did he, Wilsden, and that was the missing part of the puzzle that had so eluded me, but which fell into place as soon as I saw you walk in here today?'

'Exactly so,' conceded Wilsden politely.

'You!' Abby gasped in astonishment, her voice shaking with emotion. 'You killed my brother? But he died of natural causes; as did my sister.'

'Your sister did,' explained Sebastian gently, covering her hand with his, 'which supplied Wilsden with the inspiration to do away with your brother, whom he could not permit to flourish. It is not uncommon for siblings to perish from the same malady and no one suspected him for a moment.'

She buried her head on his shoulder, overwhelmed with grief, and sobbed quietly.

'Your determination to be a leading force in the Carlton House set was all part of the plan, of course,' continued Sebastian, finding it increasingly difficult to conceal his growing anger at the evil machinations devised by the brute he was confronting.

'My loyalty to His Royal Highness has never been in question,' stated Wilsden pompously. 'But it did not hurt to be seen by him, to be in his company and take every opportunity to remind him that I was making a good job of my stewardship.'

'You clearly esteem the prince but was gaining your objective really worth committing murder for?'

'Unquestionably! Thank you for reminding me. Have you ever noticed,' he asked, turning to address Mary in a conversational manner, 'how often accidents of a similar nature occur within the same family? It is really quite remarkable. What consternation will reign when Abby and Denver have the misfortune to overturn their curricle in this unpredictable weather, perishing in the process. You know how ignorant and superstitious people can be; they will consider the Carstairs family to be truly cursed.'

'You really are out of your senses, Wilsden. Only an utter clunch would suppose that we'd willingly enter a conveyance, knowing you have tampered with it in some way, and calmly drive ourselves to our graves?'

'You are being very insensitive, my lord,' scolded Abby, whose tears had been replaced by the capricious expression Sebastian was starting to recognize. 'My godfather has clearly gone to considerable trouble to devise a fitting end for us both and all you can do is mock.' Despite her grief at recent revelations she managed an expression of mild derision and Sebastian understood then that she was attempting to place doubt in her godfather's mind by appearing to go along with his plans for her own death! Sebastian had never admired her courage more. 'Shame on you, sir!' she finished, shaking a finger at him.

'I accept your rebuke, m'dear, but my opinion remains unchanged. Your godfather has not thought it through properly.'

'It will work well enough,' said Wilsden, sounding a little less sure of himself.

'We shall do our best to oblige you,' Sebastian assured him graciously.

Wilsden glared at him, clearly shaken by his sudden mood of cooperation. 'Well, of course you will: what alternative do you imagine you have?' He rummaged in the folds of his cloak and withdrew a pistol.

Sebastian laughed in his face. 'You can hardly hope to shoot us both and expect to get away with it.'

'Why not? A lover's tryst gone wrong. It is all over the house that you intended to bring Abby here today with the purpose of persuading her to elope with you and, I don't mind telling you, everyone was most disapproving. Shouldn't be a bit surprised if Evans turns up any minute now and saves me the trouble of finishing you off by doing the job himself. However, let us see what the obvious conclusions would be when your bodies are found.' He stopped his pacing directly in front of them, his glowering features twisted with bitterness. 'When Abby remembered her duty and declined to be a party to your infamous elopement you decided you would prefer to see her dead rather than lose her to another man. Of course, once you saw your lady love perish at your own hand you were overcome with remorse and decided you no longer wished to live, and so took your own life. Yes,' he continued thoughtfully, 'that might work better than the uncertainties of a carriage accident, much as I preferred the poetic justice of my first scheme.'

'You surely cannot imagine that you would get away with such cold-blooded murder?' questioned Abby, turning a scornful glance upon her godfather. Her demeanour was now as full of denigration and unruffled calm as Sebastian's own. He knew just how badly her godfather's revelations had affected her but already she was calling upon her reserves of strength, refusing to be easily intimidated, or reduced to begging to his better nature either, since it was now obvious that he did not possess one. Sebastian had cause, for the second time in five minutes, to admire her courage and tightened his grip upon her waist in a gesture of encouragement. She ought to be swooning or fainting in his arms, for goodness sake! Instead she was fighting back, showing this amoral creature, who had taken to strutting before her in a manner designed to emphasize the power he supposedly wielded over them, that she was made of sterner stuff than he might have imagined.

'Why not? You were foolish enough to come here, fully expecting us to follow you, but did not think to bring any means of protection. I just knew your arrogance would lead you to suppose you could overcome us without assistance, Denver, and I was obviously in the right of it since if you had a weapon about you, you would have drawn it as soon as we approached. And we examined the place carefully before entering, in case you are thinking to persuade us that others witnessed our arrival and will come to your rescue. There was no conveyance in evidence, other than your own, and no fresh hoof tracks. Anyone leaving the house to follow you must have taken the same path as us, and we passed no one,' he added, confirming he was unaware of the route across the lawn and through the woods that had been taken by Bevan and his son and which could be achieved in less than half the time that the more circuitous route by road necessitated.

'You seem to have the better of us,' agreed Sebastian, so formidably smooth as to give Wilsden pause. He shared a questioning glance with Mary Bevan, who had seated herself but not uttered one word by way of contribution to their conversation.

'You do not care to be bested, do you, Denver? No matter, everyone must meet his match at some time. If, by some means, you have managed to call for reinforcements and there is anyone concealed outside they are not close enough to be of service to you. Besides, you would not have risked sharing your suspicions with anyone else, just in case you were wrong about Charlie being behind it all and inadvertently tipped off the real culprits.' Wilsden rocked on his heels, clearly well pleased with his reasoning.

'Since we appear to be doomed,' responded Sebastian, who sounded quite off-handedly casual at the prospect of meeting his Maker, 'perhaps you would be good enough to satisfy our curiosity, Mrs Bevan. We suspected your involvement from the first but have been unable to come up with an explanation as to what you might hope to gain from it.'

'Yes,' said Harold, his features contorted with suppressed fury as he stepped with his father out of the adjoining-room and confronted his wife, 'that is an explanation that I would very much like to hear, too.'

17

Mary, rooted to the spot in dazed shock, blinked several times as though to dispel the image of her husband standing before her with blistering anger radiating from eyes that usually reflected no emotion stronger than compassion and understanding. She reached out to touch his coat and a strange wail escaped her lips when her fingers made contact with the solidity of his person. She clutched at her throat with a claw-like hand, eyes rolling wildly from side to side, shaking her head in violent denial.

'I told you!' she yelled at Wilsden, sounding almost demented. 'You are the one who does not want for arrogance. I warned you we were being duped but you could not bear to think that someone might outsmart you, anymore than you could resist this all too convenient opportunity to confront Abby and Denver. You must be a simpleton indeed to fall for such an obvious trap.' Spittle dribbled in an ugly stream from the corner of her mouth and her arms thrashed in helpless frustration against her skinny frame. 'We are done for now, and no mistake.'

Wilsden looked over his shoulder, assessing the likelihood of his being able to escape, but the solidly reassuring figure of Hodges blocked the doorway, with Bevan's man behind in close support. Hodges held his pistol in a hand that did not waver, keeping it trained directly in the centre of Wilsden's chest.

'Give me the slightest excuse,' invited Hodges in an emotionless voice, 'and it will be my pleasure to fire.' His coldly detached manner left no one in any doubt that he would carry out his threat without a moment's regret.

Sebastian watched as Hodges disarmed Wilsden, before returning his attention to Mary Bevan, more anxious than ever to hear her explanation. When she appeared to be in no mood to oblige them Sebastian prompted her.

'You were dissatisfied with the hand life had dealt you, I think, and ambition dictated that you should improve yourself by whatever means presented themselves. You attracted the love of a decent man who offered you the opportunity to make a most advantageous marriage, but that was not enough for you.' Mary snorted her derision but did not deny Sebastian's supposition. 'I have observed for myself the manner in which your resentment of Abby is eating away at you, fuelling your dissatisfaction.'

Mary was shocked into showing a reaction, albeit simply a raised brow and contemptuous sneer. 'You think you have all the answers but you know nothing.'

'Really! I would wager that I know more than you give me credit for,' responded Sebastian calmly. 'To someone who knows what to look for, you give yourself away at unguarded moments: that is how I first learned that you viewed Abby with envy, which in turn alerted my suspicions. I also detected genuine longing in your voice when I was describing my tour of Italy to you.'

'You are quite the student of human nature,' she said sarcastically.

'Thank you.' Sebastian inclined his head in graceful acknowledgement of what he knew had not been intended as a compliment. 'But I dare say I am not alone. Wilsden obviously noticed your dissatisfaction as well, which is what made him approach you in the first place. He must have been aware that a female accomplice, one whom Abby trusted completely, would have unlimited access to her and, consequently, more opportunities to contrive her downfall. But what I still do not understand is — '

'No, I am sure you do not!' shouted Mary,

her face puce with rage at Sebastian's laconic tone, which finally drove her to explain herself. 'No one can understand what I have been forced, what all of us have been forced to endure, since she came amongst us.' She glared at Abby with unconcealed hatred.

'Then do us the honour of explaining yourself,' invited Harold, his tone glacial, as he placed himself four-square in front of his wife. 'Explain, if you can, how you could even contemplate taking the life of an innocent young girl, who has already suffered so much but has never shown you anything but kindness and consideration. Make me understand, if you are able, what wickedness could have encroached upon your soul.' He examined his wife's defiant expression with sadness in his eyes, softening his tone before he spoke again. 'Are you unwell, Mary? Have you contracted some ailment that has caused you to take leave of your senses?' Harold sounded almost hopeful that he had hit upon an excuse to exonerate his wife's behaviour. Sebastian felt for him excessively.

Mary's response was to flare up as she moved towards her husband, her sharp features screwed into an ugly mask, until mere inches separated them. 'You would never understand! You who are so good and pure of mind: always willing to put others before yourself. You could not see what chaos and disruption her arrival caused within the family,' she raved, pointing an accusing finger at Abby.

'But I did not mean to — '

Sebastian stayed Abby with a warning touch, permitting Mary to further condemn herself with her own words.

'Nothing could be done any more without first considering the impact upon Abby's safety. Even the smallest excursion became a major undertaking, with everyone else's needs taking second place to hers. Did you not feel the neglect?'

'No,' said Harold shortly, 'and you were not unduly inconvenienced by the necessary precautions we took to protect Abby, either.'

'Huh, not inconvenienced — how can you say such a thing? Nothing was ever the same again. The whole family must arrange their affairs to fall into line with hers, always putting our own concerns to one side in order to comply with whatever your father thought best for her. We were not masters of our own households any more because nothing was more important than the wretched duchy.' She pulled at her hair, pins tumbling to the floor like a flurry of autumn leaves. 'It became insupportable!'

'That is completely untrue,' said Lord

Bevan, speaking for the first time. 'You were welcomed into this family, Mary, and made to feel a part of it from the first day upon which Harold made the introduction. That your background was not all that I would have wished his wife's to be was never once mentioned, not when I saw how highly he regarded you. Your unspeakable lack of gratitude for the affection we have lavished upon you is nothing short of scandalous.'

'I wondered how long it would be before my origins were mentioned,' countered Mary scathingly. 'Oh, it is true, no concerns have ever been voiced in my hearing, but one does not have to hear the words in order to sense the overwhelming disappointment you felt when your second son did not make a better match.'

'Enough of this!' cried Harold. 'You still have not explained what you expected to gain from your villainous association with Wilsden, or why you should have taken so fiercely against Abby. She is not to blame for her situation and I do not see why you should bear her such animosity. What does she have that you so desire?'

'Money, of course!'

'Money? Wilsden offered you money?' Harold seemed totally bemused. 'We already have plenty of money of our own.'

'Hah, not for much longer, what with the way you give it so readily to needy causes. You seem to forget that you have three daughters to launch. I am determined that they will do well for themselves on the marriage mart, and that costs money. But, by the time they reach that age, there is unlikely to be much of our own fortune left. Charity should begin at home, Harold, and we should not have to go cap in hand to your father or her, just because you put the welfare of others before that of your own family.'

'How much did he offer you?' asked Harold, barely able to conceal his disgust.

'Nothing! But her personal fortune,' she said, once again pointing at Abby, 'the monies her father had before he became a duke, would be inherited by your father in the event of her death. I want nothing for myself but would have appealed to him to set up trust funds for our daughters, since you appear incapable of taking responsibility for their futures. He would have done it, too. He does not need her money and, freed from his responsibility for Abby, he would have turned his attention to where it should have been all along: to the welfare of his own grandchildren.' Mary crossed her arms over her scrawny breasts, appearing in her madness to consider her argument irrefutably logical, and flashed a defiant expression at her husband.

'You are wicked,' said Harold, cutting across her remarks to his father in a gentle tone that was somehow far more sinister than if he had railed against her. 'Wicked and completely evil. I thought I knew you, Mary,' he said, shaking his head with a mixture of sadness and repulsion, 'and would have given you the earth, had it been in my power to do so. I thought, too, that we were of one mind, that you shared my determination to improve the lot of those less fortunate than ourselves. I felt empowered with you beside me.' He shook his head again. 'How cruelly deceived I have been!'

'Well, it is not too late, but perhaps now you will put your own children before the needs of your flock,' she said in a brisk voice far more like her own.

Amazingly, Mary appeared to consider that things could go on just as they had before and that she would again be able to twist the trusting Harold around her little finger. She had just admitted to entering into a murderous conspiracy but did not appear to think it signified and that Harold would take her back as though nothing untoward had happened. Sebastian suspected that she had grossly underestimated him.

'Perhaps we should return to the house?'

she suggested, making to take his arm.

Harold brushed her hand harshly away. 'I hardly think so, madam.'

For the first time Mary looked unsure of herself. Perhaps it was the steely glint of determination in her kindly husband's eye which gave her pause? But she soon recovered her poise and touched him for a second time, speaking with brisk authority and complete confidence in her ability to bring him round.

'Come, Harold, I can see now that perhaps I should not have got carried away in Lord Wilsden's scheme and, what is more, I do accept that Abby is not to blame for being thrust into the bosom of our family. But you must see that this scheme was not of my making. Wilsden convinced me that it was necessary and once I became involved with him he permitted me no opportunity to renege. But no real harm has been done and we can scarce make public what has happened or the family will become embroiled in scandal. Best leave things as they are, my dear. I will beg Abby's pardon and, if she can find it in her heart to forgive me, we can carry on as we were before.'

'If that is your belief then you have indeed taken leave of your senses. You, madam, will be escorted back to the house immediately.'

He motioned to his father's man, who stepped forward and took her arm. She demonstrated a surprising strength by shaking him off like an irritating fly.

'Whatever do you mean?'

'Take her back to the house and lock her in her room,' Harold instructed, ignoring his wife's stricken expression. 'If you will grant me leave to keep her at the lodge until the morning, Abby, I will relieve you of her loathsome company at first light.'

'Of course, Harold, whatever you consider best.'

'What do you mean?' Mary had fallen to her knees in front of her husband, realizing too late that she had underestimated both him, and the power she had supposed she wielded over him. 'Come, Harold, perhaps you have reason to be vexed with me, I really do see that now, but it will soon be forgotten. You cannot mean to lock me in my room and treat me with disrespect. After all, my children will — '

'You will never see your children again!'

It was clearly at that point Mary finally understood he really did mean what he said, yet she still appeared unable to comprehend the enormity of what she had done, much less accept responsibility for her actions. Coming to terms with the fact that she was her husband's chattel, and that her punishment lay entirely in his hands, was equally beyond her capabilities. Sebastian recognized the exact moment when the stark truth hit her and she comprehended that she was to be hidden away from society altogether, and denied access to her children for the rest of her days. She clawed at the hem of her husband's coat, keening with anguish, howling out her inner pain: a terrible sound that added more tension to an atmosphere that was already taut, embarrassing them all.

A commotion behind Hodges heralded the arrival of Evans and Charlie Wilsden; a circumstance which did not entirely surprise Sebastian.

'We heard rumours at the house of inappropriate trysts,' said Charlie with his usual cheerful disregard for convention. 'Sounded too exciting to miss and so we thought we would see what was a-foot. But I see that others have already prevented you from making away with our lovely hostess, Denver,' he added, winking at Abby and not appearing especially distressed at the prospect of her abduction.

'Not quite.'

There was nothing for it but to reveal the true nature of this strange gathering; a gathering which was taking place in an even stranger location. Evans was not slow to comprehend the full implication and, more specifically, Sebastian's true purpose for being at the hunting lodge. He looked at Abby, still held protectively at Sebastian's side, and visibly paled.

'That you have been in such danger for so long and did not confide in any of us, preferring to place your trust in a stranger. I cannot bear to think what agonies you must have endured.' He looked as though he wanted to take over as her main source of solace but when Sebastian made no move to cede his position he took to moving about the room in a distracted manner whilst Charlie stared at his father in open-mouthed disbelief.

'I thought, at first, that you were the culprit,' Sebastian told him with a rueful grin. 'Sorry about that, but I am glad to discover that I was wrong.'

'Apology accepted,' mumbled Charlie, his eyes still burning into his father's face. 'I knew he wanted me to marry you, Abby, but you know me too well to imagine that we would have suited. No offence, my dear.'

'None taken,' said Abby, managing a weak smile for his benefit.

'Besides,' continued Charlie, 'I am not cut out for the role of a duke. It was no good the pater constantly ringing a peal over me on the matter, since he ought to have known that it wouldn't serve. None of us can be what we are not. All that money and responsibility, I would have made a complete mull of it.'

Charlie shuddered at the thought, lightening the tension in the room with the return of his irreverent attitude. From what he had observed over the course of the past few days, Sebastian rightly surmised that Charlie had little respect or liking for his father, which would account for the speed with which he had absorbed the truth about his iniquities.

'Of course,' he added, 'I had to play my part and when he was watching me, do my best to convince Father that I was making myself agreeable to Abby.'

'That was why we were suddenly so awkward together in public,' reasoned Abby, 'but fell back into our more comfortable ways when unobserved.'

'Got it in one!' grinned Charlie. 'I knew that you would take immediately you were let loose on the *ton*, m'dear, and that you would be bound to accept an offer by the end of your season. I could then assure Father that I had done my best and he would have to consent to my marrying Lady Isabel.'

'Yes, I can quite see how difficult it must have been for you,' said Abby sympathetically.

'Especially when your heart was not really in it and all you wanted was to be in another lady's company.'

'Yes indeed, you have no idea! Lady Isabel, now there's a woman!' Charlie's expression reflected his unbridled admiration and he appeared unaware that his words could be interpreted as an insult to Abby. 'She shares my passion for horse flesh and is a first rate whip, as well as being deuced attractive. I am sure we will rumble along together splendidly and there is nothing to prevent me from approaching her father now. Although . . .'

His words trailed off as he turned and faced his own parent, roused to something close to anger as he belatedly realized what scandal his father's actions would bring to bear upon the Wilsden name. Lady Isabel would never be permitted to marry into such a family. Defeated and beyond despair he slumped beside Sebastian, who clasped his shoulder and turned towards Lord Bevan's man.

'Take her away,' he said, indicating the still prostrate Mary Bevan, whose fingers had to be literally prized away from her husband's leg. She wailed her supplication, expressed her remorse and begged forgiveness: all of which went completely unheeded by a stony-faced Harold.

Nodding in the direction of Wilsden's pistol, Sebastian had Hodges place it a short distance away from its owner. Helping Abby to her feet he swept her into his arms, pausing to speak to Wilsden in a barely audible undertone as he carried her to the door.

'You have one chance to take the honourable way out,' he said, 'and save the rest of your family from sharing in your disgrace.'

With Abby beside him, and Hodges standing guard outside the folly in case Wilsden attempted to escape, Sebastian had driven the curricle halfway back to the lodge when a shot rent the air. Abby, still suffering from the combined affects of sadness, disappointment and delayed shock, was too subdued to ask what it implied.

But Sebastian knew and his jaw tightened with grim satisfaction. Wilsden had saved both families from censure by putting a bullet through his own head.

18

The rest of the day passed in a frenzy of activity. Sebastian's first priority was to deliver Abby into Sally's care. He and Lord Bevan then dealt with the local magistrate. Using their combined influence they were able to have Wilsden's death recorded as misadventure: an accident which had occurred whilst cleaning his gun, thereby sparing Wilsden's family from having their lives tainted by the stigma of suicide.

'Do you suppose Wilsden would have succeeded in assuming the dukedom?' asked Lord Bevan, regarding Sebastian contemplatively from a chair in front of his library fire.

'It is difficult for me to offer an opinion since I cannot recall another situation quite like this one. In the event of Abby's demise no one would have a solid claim, perhaps with the exception of your son, Tobias.'

'He would never dream of — '

'I am aware of that and so, I suspect, was Wilsden, which he would have seen as an encouraging sign. But even if Tobias did claim to be the closest male relative to the late duke, it could take years of legal wrangling before the matter was resolved.'

'But if the title became extinct do you not consider that the prince would be far more likely to leave it so, keeping the spoils for himself?'

Sebastian offered up a sardonic smile. 'We all know that Prinny is permanently in deep and it would be temptation indeed for him to absorb such a rich prize as Penrith into his own meagre coffers, but Wilsden was right to suggest that a permanent presence would be necessary to keep that area of the West Country under control. Wilsden had certainly placed himself in the position of being the obvious claimant, both through his unquestionable loyalty to the prince, and by establishing himself as a figure of authority in the eyes of the locals.'

'Hm, and I made it easy for him by agreeing that he should take over the running of the Penrith estate. What a fool he played me for!'

'Do not distress yourself. You were not the only one taken in by him. He even managed to fool his own son, who is not quite the numbskull he makes himself out to be.'

The door opened to admit a subdued but determined-looking Harold.

'Ho, Harold!' Lord Bevan stood and clasped his son's shoulder.

Sebastian excused himself, leaving father and son to discuss Harold's problems in private. Aware that Harold was still determined his wife would never see her children again but would live in seclusion, with only the dour Miss Frobisher for company, he supposed there must be a great many arrangements to be made.

Dinner that evening was a subdued affair, given the demise of Lord Wilsden and the absence of Mary, and all that it implied. Desultory conversation did little to disguise the fact that the guests were full of curiosity and brimming over with questions, most of which they were too well bred to voice openly. Abby was absent from dinner, too. Sebastian knew from Hodges — who had naturally obtained his information from Sally — that she had partaken of a light supper and was now sleeping, thanks to a draught of laudanum supplied by the redoubtable Mrs Burton.

Sebastian, gripped by a fit of the blue devils, took little part in the conversation that swirled in fits and starts around his place at the table. His mind dwelt instead upon Abby; more especially on the havoc she had wreaked in his well-ordered life. He had done what he came here to do and tomorrow, as soon as he had attended to his remaining business with the magistrate, there was no reason why he and Hodges should not be on their way.

It was the only sensible thing to do. To put as much distance between himself and Abby as possible was now his highest priority. He could then look forward to the resumption of his former ways and forget all about compelling silver eyes, which had the uncanny knack of intruding upon his consciousness when he least expected it, regarding him with unqualified trust: when they were not mocking him, that is, or dancing with delight as their owner shed her inhibitions and wheedled her way into his arms.

It was unthinkable that a man of his age should have fallen in love at last. Love? Sebastian sat a little straighter, shocked by the turn his thoughts had taken. Was that the name of the affliction that had beset him? He had never believed in its existence before but a mere slip of a girl appeared to have put him right on that score without even having the decency to apologize for the turmoil she was creating.

Resuming his seat as the last of the ladies left the dining-room, Sebastian filled his port glass to the brim; draining it in one. And then he filled it again. He would not see Abby before he left, he vowed with determination.

In spite of her temporary fit of rebellion, Sebastian knew she was a dutiful girl who would be disinclined to do anything to overset her uncle. Sebastian managed a mirthless smile as he imagined what Lord Bevan would have to say if he declared himself to Abby and she, out of some sense of misplaced loyalty, informed her uncle that she had settled upon a dissipate such as he, who was old enough — well, almost — to be her father. Better that she should never know the true nature of his feelings. Then she could enjoy her season and marry the much approved of Evans at the end of it all. The jealousy that invaded Sebastian's body at the very thought caused him to reach for the decanter for a third time.

But he must stand firm. Obviously this was merely a temporary obsession, brought about by the singularity of the situation, and from which he would recover as soon as he distanced himself from her. He thought of Lady Redford and was surprised that the bolt of desire which he was accustomed to experience did not shoot through him when he contemplated her delightful body. No matter: other diversions beckoned. Maybe a reckless game of cards for high stakes would be the thing to bring him round? But he found little to attract him in that prospect, either.

Enough of this self-pity! Sebastian pushed his chair back with unnecessary force and accepted Charlie's challenge to a game of billiards.

★ ★ ★

Abby refused all of Mrs Burton's potions the following morning. She felt rested and much of her former strength had been restored to her. She even discovered that she could place some weight on her injured ankle. Cheered by this progress she insisted upon dressing but did not put in an appearance at the breakfast-table. She was not up to facing the collective concern of the company. Doubtless the ladies would call upon her individually and she felt better equipped to receive them in smaller numbers.

Aunt Constance was the first to bear her company, crying with relief when she observed her restored to health. Beatrice expressed grave concerns at her disinclination to confide in them, but otherwise was more interested to learn how she had contrived to make contact with Lord Denver in the first place. Abby was compelled to indulge in a hum, crossing her fingers behind her back and implying that she had written to him to beg his assistance.

Harold brought his daughters in to see her and to say his own goodbyes. The girls lightened the mood considerably with their chatter. They had no notion what had occurred, made no mention that their mother had not been seen by them that morning and were more enamoured with the fact that they were to remain here, without the hated Miss Frobisher to keep them in order. Abby kissed Harold fondly and hugged each of the girls in turn.

The door opened as the last of the ladies had left her, causing Abby's head to swivel in eager expectation for at least the tenth time that morning. Surely it would be him this time? He must come to her soon: they had unfinished business between them.

But it was Lord Evans and Abby had to struggle to hide her disappointment.

'I rejoice to see you looking so much more like yourself,' he told her, raising her hand to his lips.

'I am fully restored to health, I thank you,' she said, indicating the chair next to hers.

'You are being too hasty, as always, and not paying proper heed to your health.'

'Not at all! I am even able to place some weight upon my ankle again,' she said, standing to prove her point and almost toppling over. Lord Evans jumped up to steady her and helped her back to her seat. 'Perhaps I should ask Sally to procure a stick for me,' she admitted, biting her lip in frustration.

'It might be wiser to resist standing altogether until you have recovered properly.'

'Nonsense!'

An uncomfortable silence ensured, which Lord Evans eventually broke. 'I have lost you,' he said bleakly.

'Lord Evans, I do not think — '

He took her hand and held it tightly. 'I know this is not a suitable time, but I think it best that we discuss this now, for we will never have another opportunity. You would have settled for me, had it not been for this unfortunate business, and I would have devoted my life to making you happy. I think we would have done well together. But I know now that you will not have me. I observed, you see, the way you looked at Denver, with such complete faith brimming from your eyes, even when you had just received such dreadful tidings about those close to you whom you trusted.'

He dropped her hand and walked about the room, too emotionally charged to remain in one place. Turning to face her he spoke again. 'If I had but once observed that expression on your countenance when addressing me I would never give up on you.' He smiled briefly. 'In fact, I would sacrifice ten years of my life if I could but see it now. But I know I never will and I care for you too much to see you unhappy, my dear, and so I am giving up any claims upon your affections that I might dare lay claim to.'

Abby was quite overcome and it was some moments before she could find her voice. 'Sir, I do not know quite what to say to you, other than that you have quite mistaken the nature of the relationship between myself and the gentleman we are discussing.'

Lord Evans halted her flow of words with a wave of his hand. 'Even if I had not seen the proof with my own eyes, it would have been apparent anyway in that you went to a stranger with your concerns, rather than trusting them to me, when you must have known that I could not have been responsible for the attacks. I would never harm a hair on your head and would have done everything in my power to save you from danger.' He smiled at her, preventing her from interrupting. 'Best to say nothing, m'dear. I merely came to say goodbye and wish you well. I shall be gone within the hour.' He kissed her hand again and moved towards the door. 'Oh, and one more thing, in case you were not aware, Denver also plans to depart this morning.'

Abby stared at the closing door, too dumbfounded to speak. Her respect for Lord Evans, and the sacrifice he had made when he clearly felt deeply for her, struck her to the core. But, to her shame, that was not what occupied her thoughts. She had spent most of the night, when her watchers had supposed her to be enjoying a drug-induced sleep, wondering how to handle her next interview with Sebastian. She had spent most of this morning jumping every time the door opened, in case it was him. It had never once occurred to her that he would leave without saying goodbye.

'Sally!'

Her maid scampered to her side. 'Yes, my lady?'

'Please present my compliments to Lord Denver at once,' she said with determination, 'and ask him to have the goodness to wait upon me at his convenience.'

Abby was so angry with Sebastian for thinking to sneak away without even bidding her farewell that she wanted to scream with frustration as the wait for him to respond to her summons appeared to drag on interminably. Attempting to arrange her disjointed thoughts into some semblance of order, she decided that it was all very simple really. Having a season and being fêted by the denizens of the *haute ton* suddenly seemed like a pointless and disagreeable method of marking time. She no longer had any need to present herself for the inspection of suitable husbands because she now knew, with a blinding certainty that left not the slightest room for doubt, that she had already met the only man who was *ever* likely to excite her passions. She had met the man whom she would readily entrust with the precious gift of the Penrith estate; the only man worthy of siring the next Duke of Penrith.

Paradoxically though the gentleman in question appeared to have not the slightest interest in fulfilling that role.

'We will soon see about that!' she declared to her dogs, who flapped their tails with encouragement before resuming their mid-morning dozes in front of the fire.

An agonizing half an hour later a knock sounded at the door. He was here at last! With a calmness of expression that belied her agitated emotions Abby waited for Sally to show him in. And then he stood before her, resplendent in a superfine coat of dark blue, unsmiling and somehow rather forbidding. His severe expression was at complete variance to her expectations and for a brief moment her confidence wavered. She had managed to convince herself that he must be in love with her as well, and that was why he was seeking to avoid her, but suddenly the idea appeared ridiculous.

He was dressed for the road and, had she not asked to see him — a request which he could not in all politeness decline — he really would have left without seeing her again: something she had managed to convince herself could not possibly be the case. This realization bolstered her failing courage and, straightening her shoulders, she addressed her maid in a tone that conveyed a confidence she did not altogether feel.

'Thank you, Sally, you may leave us.'

Sally's eyebrows shot skywards and, simultaneously, a beatific smile graced her lips.

'Very good, my lady. I will be in the next room should you have need of me,' she said, bobbing a curtsey and ensuring that she closed the door firmly behind herself.

'I am rejoiced to see you looking recovered,' said Sebastian, swishing the tails of his coat aside and seating himself beside her without making any attempt to touch her. He did not even take her proffered hand, appearing not to notice it as he arranged his coat tails with far greater attention to detail than this tiny ritual usually warranted.

'You are leaving?'

'Indeed,' he responded, not meeting her eye. 'My work is done here. I was waiting only to assist your uncle with the magistrate's enquiries before setting out.'

'I see,' she said. And she did; far too clearly for her liking. 'Are you so anxious to resume your other activities that you could not spare the time to take your leave of me?'

'I understood you were still resting and did not wish to intrude upon your privacy.'

Abby knew he was shamming it. His eyes were restlessly searching the walls with single-minded determination not to meet her gaze. Perversely this display of indifference offered her a glimmer of hope. Perhaps he did harbour feelings for her: feelings that he was seeking to deny. Abby decided to put her theory to the test.

'Really! I did not take you for a coward, Lord Denver.'

That got his attention. No one, not even a lady, was likely to brand the Marquess of Broadstairs a coward and get away with it. Sure enough, for the first time since entering the room his gaze collided with hers. And held it.

'I wonder why you would make such a suggestion.'

She pretended surprise. 'Why, surely you have not forgotten? We made a bargain, you and I, and you have yet to collect your final payment for the service you rendered me.'

Sebastian appeared confused, but she was watching him closely and was able to gauge the exact moment when her meaning registered with him. He was ruffled out of his complacent attitude and, shifting uncomfortably in his chair, appeared to find something to fascinate his interest in the picture on the wall above Abby's head.

'Nothing to say in your own defence?' she enquired sweetly.

'I have already taken more advantage from the peculiarity of our situation that is seemly, Lady Abigail,' he muttered, his gaze still avoiding hers. 'Your debt is more than paid and you owe me nothing.'

'Oh, but I beg leave to disagree!' she told him, her sensuous smile reflecting her growing confidence in her ability to unsettle him. 'A bargain is a bargain, Sebastian, and I always pay my debts.'

He stood so abruptly that he almost overset his chair. 'Abby, I do not know what it is that you are hoping to achieve, but this is a dangerous game you appear intent upon playing. I think I should leave now.' He made a slight bow and turned towards the door.

'No!' She staggered to her feet, using the back of her chair as a support. 'Not before you tell me what you intend to do about this situation.'

'About what situation?' he responded, making no move to offer her his support when her ankle appeared in danger of giving way. She could not know the extent of the turmoil that had beset him since receiving her summons to wait upon her; how he had almost ignored it and left her house anyway: that if so much as their hands touched what resolve he had managed to muster would be lost beyond recall. As would he.

'It is all your fault that I am now awake on every suit and, that being the case, it is your responsibility to mend the situation.' She looked straight into his eyes. 'Obviously you cannot leave me in such a farrago and I wish to know what you intend to do about it?'

'Abby, I do not have the pleasure of understanding you.' He shot her a beseeching look. She had never before seen him so discomposed and almost felt sorry for him: almost. 'Why not resume your seat and endeavour to tell me what it is that now bothers you,' he invited, sounding irascible and therefore much more like his old self again.

'I am well able to stand,' she informed him

imperiously. 'But I repeat, my lord, you are a coward. You deliberately stimulated my passions, made me understand that there could be so much more in a relationship between a man and a woman who are mutually attracted to one another than I had ever thought to be possible, offering me tantalizing glimpses and then withdrawing, holding me to blame for my wantonness. Well, if I am such a lost cause, what harm can there be in my learning a little more?'

'Abby, I — '

'I was perfectly content with the arrangements that had been made for my future: until you can along and spoiled it all. Arrangements, I might add,' she continued, talking across his interruption, 'which I had no occasion to question. But now you are not even prepared to accept the kiss I owe you. How can it be that you will face down a man who is pointing a gun at you, and who is sufficiently unbalanced to discharge that weapon without warning, but would prefer to creep away from my house like a thief in the night rather than wish me a civil farewell? What are you afraid of, Sebastian?' she taunted.

'Abby,' he said, raking his hand through his hair but only succeeding in agitating the smooth locks briefly before they obediently fell back into place again. 'I have already told you, my work for you is done here and I have no reason to remain in your house.'

'Then kiss me farewell,' she invited, astonishing herself with her own boldness, 'and prove to us both that you have nothing to fear from contact with me.'

He offered her a raffish grin. 'Abby, sweetheart, that would not be wise. If I were to kiss you now, if I were to so much as touch your hand, I would want more: far, far more, and that I can never have.'

A fizz of excitement spiralled through Abby as he all but admitted how badly he wanted her. She tilted her head to one side, scarcely able to conceal her satisfaction. 'Now we are getting somewhere! That is precisely what I require from you, do you not see? I wish to learn more.'

'Oh no: I don't think so! I am leaving now and you will soon forget all about me. You will have your season, marry Evans at the end of it all and be perfectly content.'

'No, I will not. You have sabotaged any possibility I might have had to be happy with such an existence. I admire Lord Evans, but I do not desire him, don't you see? And desire is the key factor: you taught me at least that much. But one cannot make it exist where it has no place. But it has a place between us, does it not, Sebastian? That is what we feel for one another.' She paused, looking him square in the eye, and he eventually conceded the point with a reluctant nod. Feeling victory invade every corner of her being, Abby spoke again. 'Besides, Lord Evans has left for ever.'

'What?'

'He no longer admires me.'

'I cannot believe that.'

'It is true.'

'Even if it is, there will be many others anxious to take his place. You are a courageous and beautiful woman, Abby: few men would be able to resist.'

'Except you, apparently?' she suggested, her expression rife with suppressed amusement, making it clear that she did not believe a word of it. 'I am aware that many gentlemen wish to appear agreeable to me and can hardly claim ignorance as to their motives, either.'

'Well, there you are then.'

Sebastian appeared to deliberately misinterpret her meaning and turned away, on the verge of leaving her. But he did not move towards the door. It was as though his head and heart were in conflict and he could not summon the resolve to do what he thought was right. She gloried in this further demonstration of the power she wielded over his emotional condition. Never before had she seen him acting in anything other than the most decisive of manners.

'Why is it that any of the gentlemen you mention would likely be delighted to accept the invitation I am offering you, once they got over the shock of my being so forward, that is, but you appear intent upon pretending a lack of interest which does not exist?'

'You are playing a dangerous game, Abby,' he said, his eyes giving him away as she discerned brief glimpses of a burning passion in their depths.

'It is a game which you started, Sebastian, if you recall, and I wish to know how it finishes. You awoke my passions, when I was more than content to allow them to remain dormant. Do you not think that at the very least you now owe me the opportunity to discover what comes next?'

'Abby, stop it! That is not possible and well you know it.'

'I know nothing, Sebastian; that is precisely my point. But I very much wish to learn more and you are going to teach me.' She sounded supremely confident and took one wobbly step in his direction.

'No!' He almost screamed the word at her, parrying her step towards him by taking a longer one backwards. He sighed and flapped his arms helplessly at his side. 'You occupy too important a position to indulge in such pursuits. Abby, you know very well that only your future husband can indoctrinate you into the delights you seek.'

'Precisely!'

Sebastian's jaw dropped open: Abby had never before seen him so discomposed. 'Are you proposing to me?' he uttered in complete astonishment.

'How slow you are on the uptake, my lord,' she responded with an impish grin. 'And what is more, if you were even half the gentleman you make yourself out to be, then you would not leave me in the embarrassing position of having to do the proposing and would attend to the matter yourself.' She placed her hands on her hips and gave him the benefit of her best assault glare, spoiling the effect because she was unable to keep the desire she felt for him from invading her expression.

'Abby, I am honoured and flattered,' he stuttered, regaining a modicum of composure. 'How could I not be? But I cannot marry you.'

'Why not? You must marry at some time, surely?'

'Indeed, but you and I would hardly suit, sweetheart. I am too old for you.'

'Nonsense! You will have to do better than that if you expect me to accept your rejection. Heavens, you are a mere twelve years my senior. Many successful marriages have transcended a far greater age gap.'

'Maybe so, but it is of no consequence in our case since your uncle would be vehemently opposed to such a match. I am hardly a man with a spotless reputation,' he added gently.

'My uncle would be more than agreeable to the scheme, if he knew it was what I wanted. You saved my life and my aunt has spent half the morning telling me that Uncle Bertram holds you in the greatest esteem. Besides, even if he did not, he has always made it clear that the eventual choice of a husband would be mine alone to make. He wishes to see me happy and, for some reason completely beyond my comprehension, you are the only gentleman in a position to make me so.' She managed another step in his direction and smiled vaingloriously. 'You, Sebastian Denver, are my only choice and I have not the slightest intention of permitting you to escape me.'

Sebastian, for once in his life, was speechless. In an effort to gain a respite he paced the room, his mind in turmoil as he attempted to think of more compelling objections; objections which would only serve to deny him that which he wanted more than life itself. His mind refused to co-operate, though, and he could think of none.

'Why is it, do you suppose,' enquired Abby, her voice intruding upon his thoughts, 'that you appear impervious to my supposed charms?' She lowered her lashes, overcome by modesty, and hobbled a little closer to his position. 'It is not at all flattering for a lady to be thus rejected, you know, and I am quite distraught at your shocking want of manners. Am I so repellent to you?'

'Abby,' he sighed, disrupting his silken locks with his hand again and shaking the resulting disarray out of his eyes, 'you are enough to try the patience of a saint! Are you always so determined when there is something that you want?'

'I cannot say since I have never wanted something before as much as I want you,' she admitted with brutal honesty. 'I do intend to have my way and so it is useless you putting up objections.' Her saucy smile gave way to a serious expression. 'I love you, Sebastian. There will never be another for me. If you reject me then my godfather will get his way in a manner he could not have predicted, even if he is no longer in a position to benefit from it, since I will not marry another and the title will become extinct.'

'That is nonsense, m'dear, and it is also blackmail,' he told her sternly, sighing as he conceded that he was dangerously close to capitulation.

She smiled, a gurgle of laughter escaping her lips as she regarded him with her heart reflected in her eyes. 'So it is,' she agreed.

Sebastian turned away from her, frustrated for more than one reason. Trying to dissuade a determined woman from her purpose, especially when his heart was not really in it, was proving to be one of the hardest endeavours he had ever undertaken.

'You cannot be serious when you declare your love for me, Abby. After all, you hardly know me. What you feel is most likely nothing more than gratitude.'

'Do not tell me what it is that I feel, sir. I know my own heart, even if you are not yet prepared to admit what is in yours.'

'You cannot know, sweetheart. You are, after all, only eighteen.'

'Eighteen and a half,' she reminded him.

Sebastian's lips quirked. 'Ah yes, forgive me, I had not taken into account the extra half-year. That would account for everything.'

'Sebastian!' She stamped her good foot in exasperation, almost toppling over. He noticed, for the first time, tears slipping slowly from the corners of her eyes. 'You are treating me like a child. Surely, after all that has passed between us, I am at least worthy of your respect.'

'I have seldom respected anyone's courage more,' he admitted quietly.

And it was then, as he watched the trickle of tears turn into a flood, that he stopped trying to put up objections. She had hardly cried at all, even when her life had been in the gravest danger and she had discovered the full extent of her godfather's evil, but he had managed to reduce her to a watering-pot with a few flippant words. It would not do! He could scarce dredge up reasons for repulsing her any more and abruptly gave up the attempt. She was everything he had always wanted in a wife: he had known that almost from the first, much as he had tried to deny it to himself. She was right too, the little minx, to say that the passion which simmered between them was totally unique. He certainly had never known its like before.

He retraced his backward steps, closing the gap between them, turning the key in the lock as he passed the door and pocketing it. He continued to advance upon her, his gaze locked steadily upon hers, acutely aware of the tension that fuelled the air between them.

'Come here!'

He pulled her into his arms, her body colliding against his with a soft thud, the feel of her filling his head as he lowered his lips towards hers.

'Does this mean you are accepting my proposal?' she whispered, halting him just as their lips were about to meet.

'You talk too much,' he complained.

'Possibly,' she conceded, 'but you yourself said that only my future husband could indoctrinate me into the art of lovemaking.' Her breath caught as he did something entirely pleasurable with the hand that had wandered lower than her waist. A piquant thrill ripped through her body, she was floating on a wave of unimaginable pleasure which she hoped would never end as she abandoned herself completely to his control. 'Oh! Um, that is rather nice!'

'Be quiet!' he ordered, wiping the remnants of salty tears from her face with the tip of his tongue.

'But I need to know, Sebastian,' she reasoned sweetly, her eyes wide open, reflecting an innocence which was at complete variance with their current situation, 'are you accepting my proposal?'

'It would appear so,' he murmured.

'Oh, but then I need to know — '

Sighing, Sebastian cut off her seemingly

endless flow of words in the only manner he could think of that was guaranteed to succeed.

With his lips.

THE END

We do hope that you have enjoyed reading this large print book.

Did you know that all of our titles are available for purchase?

We publish a wide range of high quality large print books including:
Romances, Mysteries, Classics General Fiction Non Fiction and Westerns

Special interest titles available in large print are:
The Little Oxford Dictionary Music Book Song Book Hymn Book Service Book

Also available from us courtesy of Oxford University Press:
Young Readers' Dictionary (large print edition) Young Readers' Thesaurus (large print edition)

For further information or a free brochure, please contact us at:
Ulverscroft Large Print Books Ltd., The Green, Bradgate Road, Anstey, Leicester, LE7 7FU, England. Tel: (00 44) **0116 236 4325 Fax:** (00 44) **0116 234 0205**

THE SOCIAL OUTCAST

Wendy Soliman

Eloise Hamilton, the illegitimate daughter of a wealthy banker, knows that society will never open its doors to the likes of her. So when Lord Richard Craven, heir to the dukedom, singles her out, she harbours no false illusions about the outcome. Her neighbour, the formidable rakehell Harry Benson-Smythe, is not only suspicious of her high-born admirer but inexplicably jealous too. It is only as Eloise and Harry work together to solve the mysterious abductions of local girls that Richard's true purpose becomes apparent. As do Harry's feelings for Eloise, which go beyond the merely neighbourly . . .